To her surprise the man who entered was neither Ned nor Adrian but the Marquis, from whom she had departed so recently on equivocal terms.

"Good afternoon, Miss Wynstan. You do turn up in the most unusual places. I suppose you will think it churlish of me to suggest this is not the proper setting for you."

Feeling both foolish and chagrined, Nicola was also annoyed to find herself blushing.

"Not that I owe you an explanation, my lord, but I was escorted here by my brother. He has gone to find an acquaintance." She managed a saucy smile while repressing an inclination to ask him what business it was of his how she conducted herself.

"I am glad to see you have some vestiges of propriety."

"Oh, yes, my lord. I have been very well brought up." Her expression was demure and she lowered her eyes. It would never do to let him glimpse her real feelings.

"Perhaps I have misjudged you, Miss Wynstan." The Marquis sat down across from her.

"Oh, I don't think so. I suspect you have a very cynical view of females."

"Not at all. I find them fascinating, maddening and expensive."

"Yes, no doubt a man in your position and with your proclivities probably has had quite a stable of Cyprians under his protection. Alas, respectable females cannot compete with those charmers." Nicola hoped to shock him by speaking so bluntly, but she misjudged him.

"Quite astute of you, my girl. I find respectable females a dead bore."

"Just as well. From what I hear you would not be acceptable to them either."

BOOK YOUR PLACE ON OUR WEBSITE AND MAKE THE READING CONNECTION!

We've created a customized website just for our very special readers, where you can get the inside scoop on everything that's going on with Zebra, Pinnacle and Kensington books.

When you come online, you'll have the exciting opportunity to:

- View covers of upcoming books
- Read sample chapters
- Learn about our future publishing schedule (listed by publication month *and author*)
- Find out when your favorite authors will be visiting a city near you
- Search for and order backlist books from our online catalog
- Check out author bios and background information
- Send e-mail to your favorite authors
- Meet the Kensington staff online
- Join us in weekly chats with authors, readers and other guests
- Get writing guidelines
- AND MUCH MORE!

**Visit our website at
http://www.zebrabooks.com**

THE DARK STRANGER

Isabelle Patrick

Zebra Books
Kensington Publishing Corp.
http://www.zebrabooks.com

ZEBRA BOOKS are published by

Kensington Publishing Corp.
850 Third Avenue
New York, NY 10022

First Printing: March, 1999
10 9 8 7 6 5 4 3 2 1

Printed in the United States of America

One

"Surely, Father, you are for progress," Nicola challenged, acting the innocent, although she knew quite well her father was no such thing.

General Charles Pelham Wynstan looked at his daughter with suspicion. He had a great deal of experience with his daughter's teasing. The General had always insisted that his family report for breakfast promptly at eight o'clock. He had no patience with females lounging in bed over their chocolate, since it led to lazy minds and bodies. But if he was forced to listen to such nonsense it might be better if Nicola did not come down. She did quite put him off his food.

Across the table from Nicola her brother Edward winked at her, amused at her efforts to win over their hidebound father. Edward, a junior officer in the Scots Guards, had learned one lesson in his military career. Never attack an enemy head on unless your forces were superior. If Nicola expected him to support her in this harebrained scheme she would be disappointed. He knew when to retreat if she did not, but he intended to enjoy the skirmish.

"Building the tunnel across the channel is not progress, my dear. It's a tactic for disaster. We have just spent more than twenty years keeping the Frenchies at bay. Why would we want to bring them ashore at Dover?" the General asked in what he thought was a reasonable tone, but he could not disguise his contempt for such foolishness. So typical of females.

They had no grasp of politics or military reality. But then why should they?

"We have defeated the French and now we can be friends," Nicola said.

The General snorted. Having spent the major part of his career fighting Napoleon he had no illusions about his former enemies. He disliked quarreling with his spirited daughter. How could he stay angry with the girl? She was the pride of his heart. This morning she looked especially lovely, her chestnut curls caught back with a ribbon matching her simple blue muslin gown, her cheeks flushed with emotion, her hazel eyes sparkling in defiance. A frown darkened the General's ruddy face. He knew whom to blame for this insurrection in his domestic circle.

"It's that damned jackanapes, Pettifer, filling your head with these nonsensical notions."

"Adrian is a very clever young man, and his plans for the tunnel have been taken seriously by respected engineers and statesmen. Some years ago Charles Fox thought it a fine idea."

"Charles Fox was a drunkard and a gambler, besides holding what I consider treasonable views during the late struggle with the colonies. Pettifer is a fool if he thinks Parliament would vote money for such a plan." He was annoyed at his daughter's interest in this unacceptable suitor, a Detrimental if ever there was one. Why couldn't she favor one of Edward's fellow officers, stout fellows. They seemed eager enough.

Edward, watching the battle with some amusement, raised his eyebrows at his sister and entered the discussion. "You just want easier access to the Paris shops and salons, Nicky. I suspect your motives." Edward was an engaging young man, with his sister's bright hazel eyes and chestnut hair, but where she could easily be aroused to passion, he cultivated a languid air, and preferred to take life easily.

"Oh, Ned, don't be so cynical. It's unbecoming in an officer in His Majesty's forces."

"Your brother is absolutely correct and I want no more talk

of tunnels. It's putting me off my kidneys." The General laid down the law, ignoring the fact that he had managed to eat his way steadily through two hearty slices of Yorkshire ham, coddled eggs and the kidneys, without any sign of distress.

"I think, Nicola, you should leave these matters to the gentlemen," her mother reproved. Mrs. Wynstan had spent her married life soothing her often irascible husband. She could never understand why their daughter insisted on stirring up her father whenever she had the chance. Her chief aim in the past two years had been to see Nicola safely married to an eligible man. Lately she had even been prepared to accept Adrian Pettifer for it did not appear that Nicola would take anyone more attractive. Two seasons in London had not resulted in any success in the marriage stakes and Pettifer might be her last chance. She interceded in his behalf.

"Charles, Adrian Pettifer might be deluded with this tunnel scheme, but he is a perfectly worthy young man, and comes from a decent Shropshire family with a respectable income."

"Don't be ridiculous, Prudence. The fellow's a lightweight and his plan for the tunnel will be the ruination of him. The Duke has already expressed his opinion. He thinks it not only unworkable but dangerous." The Duke of Wellington, under whom the General had served, was his best weapon, his heaviest gun. Where the Duke disapproved no right-thinking person would persevere.

"Oh, Father, the Duke is a reactionary," Nicola scoffed.

"That's enough, my girl. I will entertain no criticism of the Duke and no more of this radical claptrap. I am off to the stables. Are you coming, Ned?"

"Of course, Father." Passing his sister's chair, Edward patted her shoulder. "Better give it up, Nicky, and Pettifer, too, I think." He followed his father from the dining room, leaving his sister flushed and angry.

"Really, Nicola, I don't understand why you delight in upsetting your father, especially at breakfast. It puts him in a temper for the rest of the day." Mrs. Wynstan looked at her daughter unhappily.

"He needs to be upset. He's as hidebound as his precious Duke." Nicola was reluctant to abandon her defense of Adrian and the tunnel, but she took pity on her mother. Mrs. Wynstan shrank from any argument, being a timorous soul, and wanting only peace in her domestic circle. In her youth she had been a gentle, acquiescent girl, schooled in the belief that gentlemen were to be deferred to and honored. The wispy beauty that had attracted the General had faded with the years but her belief in the infallibility of men had never been questioned.

Nicola decided to attack from another front. "Adrian wants to come down here. Will you write and invite him?"

"I find him a delightful young man, so courteous and mannerly, except for this temporary obsession with the tunnel. I think he is very acceptable. But I don't think it wise to have him here now when your father has taken him in dislike."

"Oh, he'll get over it. I can talk him around. Still, it might be best to wait a few weeks," Nicola conceded, understanding her mother very well. Mrs. Wynstan wanted her daughter married, and if Adrian was Nicola's choice she would do her best to encourage the match. However, tact and diplomacy were needed, not outright defiance.

"Do you want Adrian as a serious suitor, Nicola?"

Nicola smiled. Her mother was not about to mention love. That was not a consideration in Mrs. Wynstan's mind, only suitability. Nicola was not about to confide in her mother about her feelings for Adrian. Actually, she was not at all sure of how she felt toward the young man aside from her enthusiasm for the tunnel. She liked pricking her father's pomposity at times, not that she didn't love and respect him, but she was not about to marry just to spite him.

"Perhaps later, dear, we might invite him for a visit. Now, what are your plans for today?" Mrs. Wynstan was only too willing to drop any further discussion of Adrian and the tunnel.

"I am going to visit Nanny. She hasn't been well, you know." Nicola was referring to her old nurse, now retired and living in the village.

"How kind. That will cheer her up. I will ask cook to give you a few meat pies for her." Having thus discharged her obligations and satisfied herself that her daughter was usefully employed for the next few hours, Mrs. Wynstan went off to interview the cook.

Nicola sat at the table brooding over her parents' antiquated attitudes. Her mother thought only of marriage and her father lived in the dark ages. Even Edward was not cooperative.

Really, it was so disheartening. She wanted to be involved in this exciting venture of Adrian's, not languishing in the country visiting the sick, doing her tapestry, arranging flowers. Now that Napoleon was incarcerated at St. Helena's a new age was opening in England. The possibilities were dramatic. And Adrian was so different from the beaux who had courted her in London, most of them more concerned with the cut of their cravats or the vintage of their claret than any of the real issues of life. He had vision, could see stagecoaches rushing through the projected tunnel bringing England into the modern world. Why, the tunnel would help farmers, merchants, workers of all types who were suffering now from lack of employment after the war. The tunnel was a marvelous idea, and Adrian's talent would make it all possible if only he could get the backing. She sighed.

Perhaps she would go to London, visit her Aunt Chloe whose salon attracted all the most powerful men in the government. Nicola saw herself as a moving force in bringing the tunnel into being. Then she laughed at herself. How naïve. Females had no roles in such affairs, especially unmarried females with no position at all in society. Oh well, enough of this dreaming. She had best be about her humble duties. She went off to see Nanny.

A few minutes later, dressed in a becoming pelisse and matching bonnet in a fetching shade of her favorite blue she met her mother crossing the hall.

"All ready, Nicola. Are you taking the pony cart?"

"Yes, I planned to. I have Nanny's pies in this basket. I would have ridden but it's too difficult with the pies."

"Give Nanny my love. Oh, I forgot to tell you, Nicola, don't go wandering on to Cranbourne land. I hear the new Marquis is down and very averse to trespassers. Mr. Arnold says he caught some picnickers the other day and was very severe."

Her mother's warning surprised Nicola. Mr. Arnold was their agent and not a man to rise easily.

"I didn't know the heir had appeared. I miss the old Marquis. He was a dear, always welcomed me when I wandered into his land riding or blackberrying. What's the new man like aside from resenting trespassers?"

"He's not a man you should have anything to do with, very unsavory reputation," Mrs. Wynstan said rather unwisely for that description only whetted Nicola's interest. She would have liked to learn more, but her mother sensing this, made her excuses and hurried off to her domestic duties.

Nicola looked with affection on the old pony and cart that young George had brought round to the stable yard. She remembered many youthful rides on Daisy's back when her legs could barely reach the stirrups. Now Daisy had retired to a well-deserved old age, content to browse in the meadow and only reluctantly allowed herself to be harnessed and driven. Nicola gave her part of an apple and mounted the cart, taking the reins capably and nodding to George.

"Sure you don't want me to drive you, Miss Nicola?" he asked, eager to leave his duties for a trip to the village and escape from McGregor, the head groom who kept him mucking out stalls and polishing tack.

Nicola, who got on well with all the stable hands and had helped George in the past to evade his duties, smiled but refused.

"Not this time, George. I'm off to visit Nanny, and McGregor would be most annoyed if I kept you hanging about the village waiting for me."

"That old McGregor is a slave driver. Never lets a lad have a pint or have a bit of fun," Georgie complained, but gave Nicola a cheeky smile and accepted his defeat.

Flicking the reins, Nicola started down the long drive from the Queen Anne manor house. The grey clouds that had threatened earlier in the morning had given way to patches of blue and along the drive the avenue of lime trees was in bud. Despite her yearning to get involved with Adrian's tunnel scheme, Nicola did not really want to return to London. She loved her home and the surrounding Sussex countryside. Wynstans had owned these acres for three hundred years and she knew that her father, for all his regret at the ending of his military life, had been happy to retire to his ancestral home. London, even with its luxury, salons, balls and shops, was often a depressing, dirty and lawless city. She had enjoyed her two seasons but had no wish for another. Not that the General would offer the funds for another. She had her chance and now must settle to the role of dutiful, unwed daughter at home, not that she was as dutiful as her father wished, she admitted.

She turned out of the drive and proceeded at Daisy's leisured pace toward the village, a few miles to the south. Daisy plodded along and it was no use chivvying her to go faster. As they passed the outlying cottages and turned into the main street, a phaeton came up rapidly behind them, driven at a breakneck speed by a dark man. Nicola just had a brief glimpse of a tanned face and a caped shoulder as he careened down the road, making no effort to slow for her pony cart and disappeared in a whirl of dust. Daisy snorted and tossed her head in annoyance for the phaeton had almost grazed the cart.

"Quite right, Daisy. Appalling behavior," Nicola agreed

and soothed the pony. Who could it be, racketing down the street in that headlong manner? As she reined Daisy to a stop before Nanny's cottage she noticed the phaeton pull up before the Crown and Anchor, the village pub, at the end of the street, and the driver leap down. Shaking her head at such discourteous and arrogant indifference to others, Nicola alighted, tied Daisy to the hitching post, patted her, and gave her the rest of the apple.

"Now, stay here quietly and recover, Daisy. I will be a while with Nanny."

Taking her basket of pies, Nicola walked up a short path to the cottage door admiring the neatly bedded out daffodils and primroses in the small garden. Before she could knock, the door opened and she was greeted warmly by Nanny, a round short woman, her white hair tightly enclosed in a bun and her button brown eyes sparkling with welcome.

"Ah, there you are, Miss Nicola, come to cheer old Nanny." She hugged Nicola who planted a warm kiss on the smooth cheek. Nanny was rising eighty but looked as healthy and spry as a woman much younger.

Passing into the neat cottage and placing her basket on the scrubbed pine table, Nicola looked at her old nurse with affection.

"You're an old fraud. I heard you were ailing and you look bright as a new penny."

"It's Master Ned. He came by, good lad that he is, as soon as he got home, to see his old Nanny, and he thought I looked poorly. Not that I haven't had a touch of the rheumatism, but the warmer weather has cured me a treat. Now sit down and have some of my rock cakes and a glass of milk and tell me all your news." Nanny bustled about, setting out her offering and Nicola knew she could not refuse.

Nicola was well aware that Ned was her favorite nursling, and she herself came a poor second, but held no rancor for Nanny's partiality. She obliged with what family news she had, and indicated the basket.

"Mother sent you some of cook's meat pies, to keep your strength up."

"I thank your mother. That Mrs. Cummings has a light hand with pastry but her syllabus is not a patch on what Mrs. Downs used to make." Nanny, nostalgic for the days when she enjoyed the company of the servants at Wynstan manor, would never admit the new cook had her old friend's talents.

"Now, Nanny, you know all the village gossip. On my way here I was almost run down in the pony cart by a dark stranger in a spanking phaeton. Who could it be?"

"That's probably the new Marquis. He's a devil of a rider and takes no heed of anyone. He's just come down after inheriting, been in foreign parts since he was no more than a lad. The poor old one had no sons so this one, his brother's, gets the title and the estate. I'm not surprised your parents haven't told you. From what I hear the man has a fearsome reputation, not acceptable in a respectable drawing room. Your mother won't call, I suspect, as there is no lady in residence."

"He's not married then?"

"No, and any female at the Hall would not be one you should meet, I wager."

"Oh, Nanny, how exciting, a rake and a reprobate. He must be stirring the dovecotes." Nicola had no interest in the scandalous stranger, but she could see that the villagers were all agog, natural since the Marquis owned the village and if he failed to act with the generosity and charity of the old Marquis hard words would be bruited about.

"Don't act so daft, Miss Nicola. He's a bad one, that Jocelyn Sturbridge, and no fit person for you to meet. Why didn't you accept one of those proper beaux you met in London? You had plenty of chances, I hear."

"Too boring, Nanny. Not my style. I'll just have to settle down to spinsterhood and be a doting aunt to Ned's children when he gets them."

"Is Mr. Ned thinking of entering the parson's trap?" Nanny was all excited at the prospect.

"Not that I know of. He's much too lazy to go courting."

"Nanny doesn't like to hear any criticism of Mr. Ned. He's a fine lad and a brave one. He'll turn out to be a good officer and gentleman like his father."

"Ned's all right. But tell me more of the new Marquis," Nicola insisted, her curiosity aroused by the stranger in their midst. A newcomer in their small community was always the subject of interest and this latest arrival promised to be the subject of much conjecture despite his reputation, or perhaps because of it.

Nicola had, as usual, a difficult time getting away from Nanny's cottage. The old nurse was lonely and missed the camaraderie of the servant's hall. She chattered away and Nicola listened patiently for she really loved and admired her Nanny despite their former tussles in the nursery. At last she was able to make her farewells with a promise of returning before too long.

As she untied Daisy and mounted the pony cart she looked toward the Crown and Anchor. The phaeton had disappeared from the pub. No doubt its driver had rushed away in the same reckless fashion she had noticed on his earlier journey. Well, he was no concern of hers. No doubt he would not stay long in the country. With his new title and estates he would be a prime catch on the marriage mart and London hostesses would be vying for his company. London was the proper milieu for rakes and he would join that set of idle wealthy young men to drink and gamble his life away before some clever matron caught him for her daughter. She just hoped he would continue the old Marquis's care of his acres and the village, but she doubted it.

Two

Jocelyn Sturbridge, the Marquis of Cranbourne, who had not noticed his near brush with the pony cart on his ride to the Crown and Anchor, had completed his errand and ridden back to the Hall at his usual breakneck pace. Inactivity was foreign to him. He had spent his adult life adventuring in distant continents, never dreaming he would be called upon to take up this lord of the manor role. The old Marquis, his uncle, was his father's elder brother. There had been three brothers. The old Marquis had lost his son in a boating accident, his next brother's only son had fallen at Waterloo, so Jocelyn was the only remaining son of the line. If he had refused, the title Cranbourne would have gone to a distant Canadian cousin.

Standing now at the window of the library and looking down the long drive and across the beginning of his acres, he was surprised how willing he had been to take on this burden, for that was what it was. He was well aware that the villagers viewed him suspiciously, for they had lived comfortably for many years under the benign rule of his predecessor. There was little that was benign in Jocelyn Sturbridge's appearance or character. He neither suffered fools nor paid any heed to his reputation, which he admitted to himself was well deserved. He had been an unruly boy, brooking no restraint, consorting with stable hands and poachers. Sent down from Oxford for drunken and rebellious behavior shocking even to the masters of the university, who were accustomed to the sons of aristocrats misbehaving, he had immediately plunged into the fleshpots of London. His father cut off his allowance but an old aunt had left him a competence which he increased at the gaming tables. He might have been excused his reckless conduct, not so unusual for his station, if he had not committed the final bêtise. He had run off with the wife of a nobleman, some ten years his senior, and the subsequent scandal could not be overlooked. Remembering the fair Clarice he could not understand why he had been so enamored. However, the lady had soon tired of his juvenile passion and put herself under the protection of an Austrian count, to everyone's satisfaction.

At twenty-one he had been thrown upon the world with little but his wit and a certain determination to make his way. He had lost and won a fortune at the tables in the less respectable gambling haunts of Europe and then made his way to the Far East where he had parlayed that fortune into a larger one through the spice trade. He had been enjoying himself in Ceylon when the lawyer's letter informing him of his changed status had finally reached him. His first instinct had been to ignore the summons to come back and take up his inheritance, but some atavistic sense of his heritage had impelled him to return. If he could not stomach the life, he decided, he would leave again, after having put his affairs in order.

The villagers of Cranbourne Hall, if not pleased with their new overlord, at least accepted his presence while waiting to see how he did. The gentry, on the other hand, would have nothing to do with him, for which he held them in no animus. No doubt they considered him a threat to their daughters and unacceptable in proper society. Well, he did not miss them. He had discovered his uncle's affairs in somewhat of a mess and suspected his agent had feathered his own nest to the old Marquis's detriment. A few more years and the estate would have been in a sorry state. Well, he had thrown out the villain and was now searching for a replacement. He had neither the time nor the inclination to worry about society. He must be feeling his age, thirty misspent years, he decided, and with a chuckle returned to his desk and the papers that awaited his perusal.

If the new Marquis of Cranbourne cared not a bit for his neighbor's opinion, this indifference was not returned. He was the object of much discussion in the neighborhood and as far away as Brighton and Chichester. Lady Mumford, a large lady of imposing form who had just returned from the former watering place, hurried to discuss the Marquis with Mrs. Wynstan, her bosom bow. Having reported on the Prince Regent's latest extravagances at his Pavilion and the iniquitous influence of Lady Hereford, she came to the real business of her visit.

"Have you called on the new Marquis yet, Prudence?"

"No, and I don't intend to. I understand he's a ramshackle libertine, not a fit companion for Edward and even less so for Nicola." Mrs. Wynstan sipped her tea, disapproval quite evident in the set of her mouth.

"Are you sure that is wise, my dear? After all, he's one of the largest landowners in the county and with a purse to match. He might do for Nicola. She didn't take in London, did she?" Lady Mumford had successfully launched three daughters on the marriage mart and felt quite smug at this impressive feat. All her daughters had married well and were now setting up their nurseries in Wiltshire, Somerset and distant Cumberland.

"He wouldn't do at all for Nicola. I don't understand the girl, Moira. She had every opportunity. Why Lord Ponsonby was most épris, but she wouldn't have him, and there was Eversham and Wittingly, too, all eligible." Mrs. Wynstan would not have her friend think her daughter had not attracted the best beaux. She thought Lady Mumford's pleasure at her own daughters' matches inappropriate. One of them had wed a widower with six children, another a weedy baron and the last a rough squire from the north, none of them exceptional, she thought. Nicola was in every way the Mumford girls' superior, she thought with a mother's fondness.

"Well, of course, Sturbridge had a frightful reputation, but I blame Clarice Ainsworth, ten years his senior and a really fast woman with designs on every attractive man that had the misfortune to swim into her orbit. What chance did the poor boy have once she set her sights on him? She led old Ainsworth a merry dance with her follies, her lovers and her debts. Young Sturbridge was but one of her victims and he was dazzled by her favors. He never married her, you know, after the divorce. Not gentlemanly but who could blame him? Perhaps he has reformed now that he has come into the estates and title. He will need to marry and set up his nursery. He's rich, too, and that will make him a target, for money overcomes scandal every time." Lady Mumford was a gossip, but a realist, and knew society far better than the General's lady.

"He's a loose screw and will not be received anywhere." Lady Wynstan clung obstinately to her principles.

"You just wait, my dear, and if I were you I would call before society takes him up."

Mrs. Wynstan turned the conversation, quite annoyed at Lady Mumford's cynicism but not swayed in her determination to ignore the new Marquis.

Her scruples were somewhat undermined that evening when the General informed his family at the dinner table that he had met Cranbourne that very day riding along the boundary of their estate which marched with his.

"Not a bad sort, Sturbridge. Has some very sound ideas on farming and he's a great admirer of the Duke."

"Really, Charles, the man is the veriest rake. I couldn't possibly receive him. It would be shocking to expose Nicola and Edward to such a man."

"Nonsense, Prudence. The man committed some youthful follies, but he's going to be a fine landlord, and probably the Lord Lieutenant of the County when Mumford resigns, as he has told us he will do after the next quarter sessions."

"So typical," Nicola intervened. "A man can create the worst sins and be forgiven but a woman always pays."

"You don't know what you're talking about, Nicola."

"Yes, I do, Father. But my curiosity is aroused. What heinous crime did he commit?"

"He ran away with another man's wife and then refused to marry her," Edward informed his sister, ignoring his mother's frown and pursed lips.

"Really, Edward, this scandalous affair is not fit for your sister's ears," Mrs. Wynstan admonished, reluctant as she was to criticize her son.

Edward laughed. "You'd be surprised, Mother, at what Nicola knows about the follies of the ton."

"That will do, Edward. Sturbridge may not be welcome in your drawing room, Prudence, but believe me he will make a mark in the county." The General spoke in a dismissive tone that warned his wife he wanted no more discussion of the Sturbridge affair at his dinner table. If he ordered his wife to receive the miscreant she would obey. The General did not brook disobedience in the mess, on the battlefield, or in his own home. Deciding he had settled the matter he turned to another matter.

"Young Forrest is arriving tomorrow." He was referring to the secretary he had hired to help him with his family history.

"Yes, I remember, Charles. He seemed a pleasant young man when he came for the interview."

"He'll do," the General agreed. He was used to aides and young officers eager to obey his orders and expected no trouble from this newest addition to his household.

Nicola, who had also met Roger Forrest when he interviewed, had no opinion of him. She was far more interested in the Sturbridge scandal. Not because she had a partiality for rakes, but because she enjoyed rebelling against her mother's outraged propriety. She was not a conformable girl.

Later that evening she quizzed her brother while besting him at piquet.

"Have you met the wicked Marquis, Ned?"

"Yes, I was with father this morning when we came upon him near the north forty acre. Seemed a decent chap." Edward brooded over his discard and answered his sister absentmindedly.

"But he isn't decent, mother insists. What do you know about the old scandal? Tell, tell."

"Really, Nicky, you are incorrigible." But he smiled. He found his sister refreshing, having large experience with vaporish misses of no conversation.

"I know, but what did the Marquis actually do?"

"He was kicked out of Oxford for some youthful misdemeanor and went on the town where he met the delectable Lady Ainsworth and fell victim to her charms. Whether she induced him to run away or he persuaded her to elope who knows. They ended on the Continent at Baden-Baden and she finally left him for a wealthy noble protector, well before the divorce. It was some time ago, ten years or so. He must be about thirty now, not much older. But the business left him with an arrogant, cynical attitude and I expect he cares damn all about the county's opinion now."

"Did you like him?"

"Well, he has a good seat on a horse, rather brusque manners, and lots of guineas. He would have made a good officer, I think. But as far as you are concerned he's a non-starter."

Nicola trusted her brother's judgment far more than her father's, or certainly her mother's. She was intrigued.

"Sounds more interesting than Roger Forrest, anyway. Aha." She laid down her hand with a flourish, a capot.

"Nicky, you must cheat or you couldn't beat me so easily." Edward threw down his cards in disgust.

"You owe me a florin."

"Moneygrubber." Edward threw a coin on the table, signifying his defeat. Theirs was an ongoing competition with no animosity on either side.

The next day Nicola was arranging some daffodils when

Paxton, the butler, announced that her mother requested her presence in the morning room.

Paxton's regal appearance and stern visage hid a real affection for his employer's daughter, and he had a good suspicion what awaited Miss Nicola in the morning room.

"You'd best be prepared, Miss Nicola. Mr. Moffett has called."

"Oh, dear, Paxton. You should have said I was out."

"Your mother knows you are doing the flowers and seemed very pleased to see the reverend gentleman."

"She would be. I greatly fear she sees him as a suitor for my hand. I do wish Mother would stop all this matchmaking." Nicola sighed. Really, her mother's efforts to settle her into marriage were becoming a distinct bore.

"Oh, I hope not, Miss Nicola, although it's not my place to say so."

"Of course it is, Paxton. You've known me since I was in leading strings and who I marry, if I marry, is certainly your business." She smiled and added, "And I would not want a husband who had not earned your approval."

"Really, Miss Nicola," the butler cautioned but still pleased at this sign of affection. Washing her hands neatly in a nearby bowl, she dried them, taking a long time about it, and then, accepting the inevitable, made her way to the morning room. Paxton watched her go with a grim look. It really was a shame the way madam chivvied the girl. There was plenty of time to put up the banns and the Reverend Moffett would not be his choice of a suitor.

Nicola, looking very charming in a jonquil morning dress, the squared modest neckline and puffed sleeves edged in ruching, entered the morning room. She schooled her face into an expression intended to hide her displeasure but not to show any undue signs of gratification. A great fan of Jane Austen's novels she found Mr. Moffett a perfect match for Mr. Collins in *Pride and Prejudice*.

Rising to greet her, he seemed at first glance to be far less revolting than that sycophantic vicar. He was tall, with a fine head of dark hair carefully combed into the Titus style, and a pale complexion. But his small dark eyes were beady and his narrow shoulders sloped under an inadequately padded coat of black superfine.

"Good morning, Mr. Moffett," Nicola greeted him politely, ducking into a small curtsey.

"Nicola, my dear, Mr. Moffett has a matter to discuss with you. I might say that he has received your father's permission to speak." And before Nicola could demur her mother had scurried from the room. She might hope that Nicola would see her duty and accept this respectable parti, but she knew in her heart that the possibility was remote. The General had told her she was a fool.

"If Nicky would not have any of those fine bucks in London or those fellow officers of Ned's she'll hardly look with favor on that mealy-mouth parson," the General said in his trenchant manner. "I told him he could speak because I know he will go off with a flea in his ear, but you could have prevented this embarrassment, Prudence. Use your head, woman," he concluded in disgust.

"But, Charles, she must marry. She's twenty and in danger of being on the shelf."

"Nonsense, the right man has not appeared, that's all." The General abandoned the fruitless discussion and hurried out to the stables where his importuning wife could not follow, feeling a bit uneasy at abandoning his daughter to the parson. The General was a staunch churchman, read the lessons on Sunday, and supported the state's religion as he did the monarchy no matter how much he disapproved of the incumbents in either position. But he would hate to welcome Reginald Moffett as a son-in-law.

Nicola, abandoned by her parents to the horrid fate she suspected awaited her, asked Mr. Moffett to sit down, and sat herself in an uncomfortable Louis XIV chair.

However, Mr. Moffett refused her invitation, and instead approached her, looming in unappetizing fashion over her.

"It cannot have escaped your attention, Miss Wynstan, that I hold you in high regard. Since your return from London I have watched you with much interest, and have decided that my life would be enhanced by joining it with yours. I am asking you to be my wife," he said with some dignity.

Nicola rose quickly to her feet. "I am honored by your proposal, sir, but feel we would not suit. I am not disposed to be a vicar's wife and do not return your feelings. I must decline." She stared him straight in the eye, repressing a repulsion she had ever felt in his presence, noticing the beads of perspiration on his forehead and the nervous clasping and unclasping of his hands. The thought of those hands, wet and clinging on hers made her shudder.

"Don't be hasty, Miss Wynstan. I realize most young females refuse the first offer from a gentleman as the proper mode of modest conduct. You must be overwhelmed by my offer."

"On the contrary, Mr. Moffett, I am only amazed and embarrassed by your temerity. I have never given you any indication that I returned your regard, and in fact, I do not, and can never envisage a situation when I would. I must ask you to leave."

Flushing with mortification, he reached over and grabbed one of her hands, dragging her to her feet. He might have ventured further indignities in his anger, if the door had not opened. Paxton stood respectfully at the entrance.

"I am sorry to disturb you, Miss Nicola, but Mr. Ned is asking for you. He was quite insistent."

"Thank you, Paxton." Nicola gave the butler a blinding smile then turned to the vicar with a moue of distaste.

"You will excuse me, Mr. Moffett. I see no need to continue this conversation now or ever. Good day."

Mr. Moffett, not so lost to propriety that he would create a scene in front of the butler, bowed, and watched in frustration as Nicola ran from the room. Paxton, in his turn, waited, intent on seeing this unwelcome visitor from the premises and Mr. Moffett had no recourse but to obey, vanquished on all fronts.

Three

Of a naturally resilient disposition, Nicola did not normally surrender to moods and megrims, but after her irritating interview with Mr. Moffett she felt she might just go into a temper tantrum, trying for the household and producing little satisfaction for her. The chief object of her resentment was her mother. She had not been unaware that her mother, with whom she usually enjoyed an affectionate relationship, although she had little opinion of her common sense, wanted desperately to marry her off. What annoyed Nicola the most was that her mother did not seem to care with whom she made this necessary alliance.

Nicola herself took a very dim view of the institution as well as the emotion, love, that appeared so consuming to many of her friends. She enjoyed the company of young men but she had met none that inspired a deeper feeling. Contemplating spinsterhood, she decided it was a superior situation to a marriage of convenience. She felt occasionally that if she had to endure much more of her mother's matchmaking she might elope with the most unsuitable parti she could find just to escape. But not Mr. Moffett. How could her parents have thought she would accept him? Her father, at least, had enough sense to know that he was a pompous windbag who had entered the church as a last resort. Nicola had little doubt that his spiritual conviction was weak and his regard for his own consequence, strong. She disliked him exceedingly.

If she met her mother now she would be in danger of losing

her temper and that would never do. Her best recourse was to ride off her dark humor. There was still plenty of time before luncheon to enjoy a good canter on her prized mare, Bluebelle. She lost no time in putting her decision into action. Hurriedly changing into her habit, she scurried out to the stables through the kitchen, avoiding her mother.

Only George was in the stables, lazily sweeping out an empty stall.

"Good morning, George. I am going out for a ride on Bluebelle. Don't bother saddling her up. I'll do it."

"You had better let me do it, Miss Nicola, and let me come with you. Your mother don't like you wandering about on your own." George much preferred riding to the numerous chores the head groom, Jacob, seemed to think were suited to his limited skills. George's dream was to run off to Newmarket and become a jockey riding winners at Epsom but so far he had not the bottom to put his dreams to the test.

"Well, if she complains to Jacob, tell him I would not have you. I'll deal with Jacob and my mother." Nicola was just in the mood to take on both these critics of her behavior.

"The General and Mr. Ned have ridden over to the Home Farm. You can meet up with them." George's cheeky grin implied that she would probably do no such thing, but if he was questioned he had a ready answer.

"You're a lazy good-for-nothing, George," Nicola replied cheered by the stable hand's efforts to protect himself. She liked George and did not want to get him into trouble, and his careless disdain for authority echoed her own impatience with the proprieties. He was a cocky boy, not out of his teens, an orphan with a shock of red hair, bright bold eyes, and a sangfroid she found enviable. But even George would intrude today. She wanted to be alone. Seeing that she was adamant, George turned back to his pitchfork. There was no arguing with Miss Nicola when she took one of her pets.

Bluebelle responded eagerly to her mistress's hands on the reins and cantered briskly out of the stable yard just as Millie, one of the under housemaids, arrived searching for Nicola at Mrs. Wynstan's order.

It was a grey damp morning, the sun hiding under a bank of ominous clouds that promised rain, but Nicola was impervious to the threat of a storm. In fact she would have welcomed one for her mood was also black. After a half an hour of hard riding her spirits improved somewhat and she was able to laugh at her bad temper. She could forgive her mother if not Mr. Moffett. The poor woman was only doing her duty, trying to get a rebellious daughter off her hands. Nicola was quite capable of thwarting her mother's maneuvers and she was a ninny to let them depress her. It was just as she expected, a good gallop had cleared away her mood.

She drew up in the wood that divided her father's land from the vast Cranbourne acres and gentled Bluebelle to a walk. She had always loved these woods, a dense mass of the famous Sussex oak which thrived on the chalky soil and the ubiquitous beech. The trees now were in bud and would soon provide a leafy refuge for the rider. Bluebelle's hoofs snapped the dead twigs, and the song of birds and the rustle of small animals broke the silence, soothing sounds.

Well into the woods she came upon a vast clump of yellow primroses and on an impulse jumped off her mare to gather them. Tying Bluebelle to a convenient sapling, she knelt to gather a bunch, delighted with this harbinger of spring. So intent was she on her task she did not hear the approach of another rider and looked up startled when Bluebelle whinnied, to see a black stallion ridden by a stranger, a dark man scowling down at her.

"What are you doing picking my primroses, girl?" he asked. His tone was brusque and unfriendly.

Nicola rose and looked at him in some distaste. Another arrogant male intruding on her privacy. "Oh, are they your primroses?"

"I'm Cranbourne and these are my woods. Who are you?" The dark stranger had no manners, Nicola decided. Obviously she was not a poacher, but a neighbor. He must be the new Marquis and with none of the charm or amiability of his late uncle. Refusing to be intimidated, she looked at him serenely and answered.

"I am Nicola Wynstan. My father's land lays just to the north of yours."

The Marquis stilled his restive horse. "Well, your father ought to keep you in better order, Miss Wynstan. I don't encourage visitors."

"So I've heard. I wonder why?"

"You are a pert chit. Now, be off with you. Interlopers are not welcome here." He rode his horse closer to where Nicola stood, attempting to frighten her, she thought. She put out a hand and stroked the stallion above his nose, an attention he seemed happy to suffer. Then, turning her back on the Marquis, she walked slowly to Bluebelle, clutching her bouquet of primroses and untied her mare. The Marquis watched silently, making no effort to help her mount. Really, the man was a rude creature, she decided, not worth a second thought. She mounted and turned her horse, riding up to him.

"Since you feel so deeply about the primroses, I present them to you." She laid the bunch on his saddle and without another word cantered away, deeper into the woods, wondering if he could accept her challenge. He looked after her, and down at the primroses with an odd expression. Then he followed, coming up alongside, and halted her horse with a strong pull on the reins.

"You're trespassing, Miss Wynstan. I could have you up before the beak."

"You could but you would look very foolish. And it's not the best way to insure a welcome here, you know. I wonder why you are so angry? I am doing no harm in your woods. Perhaps your breakfast did not agree with you."

Surprisingly he laughed. "I don't envy your inevitable husband having the schooling of you. I can see the General can't control you."

"That's no concern of yours, my lord. Now, if you will release me I will be on my way." Nicola looked him fully in the face daring him to do his worst. But her defiance appeared to amuse him now and he only nodded.

"I suppose my uncle allowed you to roam around here as you chose. Well, go ahead. But a word of advice, next time I might not be so amenable." And he turned and galloped away before she could reply.

The encounter both puzzled and pleased Nicola. She felt she had come out of it well, not allowing herself to be cowed by the imposing Marquis. She wondered why he was so unsociable, so determined to protect his privacy. Did he have something to hide? Well, he would earn little favor in the neighborhood if that was his attitude. She wondered what had caused his hostile unsociable stance. It was more than bad digestion, she warranted. Perhaps it was just females. He might be the victim of a blighted romance. She chortled, not likely. The man had little address and although not unprepossessing, had less charm. Well, she would not disturb his solitude. She had quite enough of men and was no threat to him.

Returning at a slow canter to the stables, she decided that the new Marquis of Cranbourne could be ignored. It was unlikely their paths would cross often or at all. Turning over Bluebelle to George, she made her way to the house to change for luncheon. Her mother greeted her in the upstairs hall and Nicola braced herself for an uncomfortable interview, but most of her anger over *l'affaire* Moffett had disappeared.

"Where have you been, Nicola? I have been asking for you."

"Riding, Mother. I thought I would find Ned and Father, but they must have gone to the village." She looked at her mother with innocent eyes, barely hiding her amusement. She knew her mother wanted a full report on the interview with Mr. Moffett. Most of her anger at being exposed to that fatuous gentleman had dissipated but she was not about to excuse her mother.

"You are a maddening and ungrateful girl, Nicola. What did you say to Mr. Moffett?"

"I was quite polite considering my first reaction was to box his ears for his pompous effrontery. I sent him about his business and told him not to return or he would regret it. Why in the world did you and Father give him permission to speak to me?" Nicola believed taking the offense with her mother was the best plan.

"Nicola, the vicar is a perfectly respectable man, and admires you greatly. I suppose you would make a poor wife for a man of the cloth, but then I fail to see any man who has won your approval. I know you believe I am being too assiduous in pressing marriage for you, but what other option does a gently bred girl have?" Mrs. Wynstan looked miserable. She knew that she had little influence over Nicola and had never persuaded her that her happiest future lay in marriage.

"I could run off like the ladies of Langowen," Nicola suggested, realizing that such a scandalous possibility would overset her mother. "Or perhaps become a bluestocking, take to spectacles and found a school for orphaned children."

"Nicola, you wouldn't. You are just funning me because you are annoyed about Mr. Moffett."

"Quite right, I am. Stop worrying, Mother. I suppose eventually I will meet my fate, but I promise you it won't be the vicar. Now, I must go change for luncheon." She placed a consoling kiss on her mother's forehead and ran into her room, shutting the door firmly, just not slamming it.

Mrs. Wynstan sighed, hesitated and then descended the stairs. Nicola was so impulsive, so rebellious. What had she done to deserve such a wayward daughter? But she soon forgot her recent contretemps with Nicola. Paxton approached her to inform her that Roger Forrest had arrived and he had settled him in the morning room.

"I have had Jasper take his luggage up to the Blue Room,

that Mary prepared for him. And I informed the young gentleman that the General will be in for luncheon and was expecting him."

"Thank you, Paxton. I will welcome him myself." Mrs. Wynstan hurried off to tender hospitality and hoped that Mr. Forrest would prove an easy addition to the household.

Changing for luncheon without ringing for her abigail, Nicola felt she had handled her mother quite well. She disliked causing her unhappiness, but she would not be forced into an alliance just to soothe her mother's sensibilities. Could her mother really feel that marriage, any marriage, was the only solution for a girl? Her own had not been without problems. Fond as Nicola was of her father, she conceded that the General had not been the most agreeable of husbands. He was obstinate, reactionary, domineering and demanding. And she suspected he had not been faithful. Her parents' union had meant enforced separations due to his military career, and she wondered if her mother had not welcomed these periods of peace. She preferred domestic tranquillity, and had not the character to stand up to her husband even when justice was on her side. And yet she must have loved him once, and perhaps still did. Her observation had convinced Nicola that love was a dangerous emotion, clouding the judgment and leading to unwise matches. Several of her schoolmates had made injudicious marriages and were now paying the price. She would not make their mistakes, even if she went to her grave a spinster. Laughing at her somewhat jaundiced view of the wedded state, she gave her hair a ruthless brush and looked at herself in the mirror. This eau de Nile mull gown was flattering, she decided, and fastening her pearls she decided she would do. She would have a word with her father after luncheon about Mr. Moffett. He could usually be persuaded to see her point of view, even if he were behaving badly about Adrian Pettifer. She wondered what Adrian was doing about his tunnel. She had expected to hear from him before now.

* * *

Coming into the morning room she was surprised to see her mother chatting with a young man. He rose politely when she entered and her mother introduced them.

"This is Mr. Forrest, Nicola. My daughter, Mr. Forrest. He has come to help your father with the history, you remember I told you," Mrs. Wynstan explained hurriedly, sensing that Nicola was in no mood for any more young men and only hoped she would behave herself.

"Of course, Mr. Forrest," she said acknowledging his bow. She saw a tall, thin, very young man, dressed soberly in correct but rather worn clothes. He had a diffident air and blushed easily, overcome by this lovely young woman. In his favor were a pair of honest brown eyes, a clear complexion and fair hair arranged rather carelessly.

Nicola joined her mother on a settee and looked expectantly at Mr. Forrest. He needed to be put at ease.

"Mr. Forrest has only recently come down from Oxford and was recommended to your father by General Spotswood. I am sure he will be of great assistance. And I hope you will be happy in our household." Mrs. Wynstan was trying her best but Roger Forrest looked overwhelmed.

"This is a great opportunity for me, ma'am. I hope I will suit," he offered with a slight stammer of nervousness.

"Where are you from, Mr. Forrest?" Nicola asked.

"Just recently from London, Miss Wynstan, where I have been tutoring young Viscount Woodbridge. But originally I am from Leicester where my father is a vicar in a small parish."

Nicola, who was not feeling kindly toward the church and its defenders, only hoped Mr. Forrest was not of a sanctimonious and pious persuasion. Still, in his favor, he had not chosen the church toward which she entertained some mixed emotions after her experience with Mr. Moffett. Really, there were too many men floating about on her horizon. But she doubted that Roger Forrest would give much trouble.

Before the conversation could continue, Paxton announced that luncheon was served and that the General and Mr. Ned were already in the dining room. Mr. Forrest leapt to his feet, his wary eagerness at meeting his employer apparent.

"Don't worry, Mr. Forrest. My father might bark a bit, his normal stance with subalterns, of which he will consider you one, but he's really harmless."

Mrs. Wynstan, outraged, reproved her daughter. "Really, Nicola, you must not frighten Mr. Forrest. The General is looking forward to your arrival and I know your services will be valued." Mrs. Wynstan reassured the young man who remained apprehensive.

"Ah, Forrest, you've arrived and met my wife and daughter, I see." The General greeted his new secretary kindly. "This is my son, Edward, a lieutenant in the Coldstream Guards, home on leave."

"Your servant, sir." Mr. Forrest bowed and directed to his seat stood courteously waiting for the ladies to be seated. Hurriedly he remembered his manners and rushed to settle Nicola while Edward did the same for his mother. The luncheon passed off agreeably with the General doing most of the talking, as usual.

"That rapscallion George told us you were out riding this morning, Nicky." Ned intervened when the General had finally exhausted his repertoire. "He told you we were at the Home Farm, but we must have missed you."

"I went into the woods and had a most fascinating encounter with our new neighbor."

"The Marquis?" the General barked, frowning. He did not like the idea of Nicola wandering off on her own and meeting Sturbridge, not a fit companion.

"He was not pleased to see me, and at first I thought he might ride me off, but in the end he just laughed and told me

I was incorrigible and that he did not envy you the schooling of me, Father."

"Impertinent fellow. How dare he?" bellowed the General, frightening Mr. Forrest, but only raising laughs in Ned and Nicola.

"Nicola, you should not ride alone. If you had taken a groom such an unfortunate meeting would never have happened. It creates such a bad impression. The Marquis must have thought your conduct unseemly." Mrs. Wynstan was appalled.

"Not at all. I think he was amused. He is certainly a strange man, so cross and unmannerly, not a nice neighbor."

"Let that be a lesson to you, Nicky. You cannot charm us all," Ned teased.

"Right now I don't want to charm any of you. And I want a word with you, Father, after luncheon."

"Yes, of course, my dear, in the morning room. Ned, you will show Forrest the library and I'll join you later."

Having disposed of his forces tidily, the General finished his meal. He was not completely successful in ignoring his suspicion that the coming interview with Nicola would be delicate. He was forced to agree with the Marquis's assessment. He could not always handle his daughter as easily as he did his troops. She often failed to obey orders, and even had the temerity to issue commands herself.

Four

The General knew what Nicola wanted to discuss with him. He had prepared a defense but doubted that she would accept it without an argument. Attempting to give the appearance of a man of affairs, he hurriedly gathered a mass of papers onto his desk so that he could seem to be busy with weighty matters.

When Nicola marched in she was not impressed. The General had used this ploy before. Sitting down in the chair opposite him she launched immediately into her complaint.

"Really, Father, what possessed you to allow Mr. Moffett to offer me that ridiculous proposal? You knew I would not accept, and you could have spared him embarrassment and me some annoyance."

"Now, Nicky, be fair. There is nothing really objectionable about the man. He's respectable, pious and has a small private income."

"You couldn't have thought for one moment that any of those assets would weigh with me. He's mealy-mouthed, toadying and boring beyond belief."

"Your mother thought . . ." The General's voice trailed off, and he realized he was not in a good strategic position.

"That's the problem, Father. Mother is determined to marry me off. I had no idea you were both so eager to get rid of me." She adopted a wistful air implying that her father and mother disliked her presence about the house.

"Now, now, Nicky. You know that's not true. Your mother

just thinks its her duty to try to get you married, and feels a failure, especially when she has to endure the boasts of Lady Mumford who has arranged matches for her three unexceptional girls. Have a little patience with your mother. I tried to warn her that you would send Moffett about his business. Frankly, I would not care for him as a son-in-law. I can barely endure him as a padre."

"Surely you can stand up to mother and tell her to stop badgering me. After all, you have faced stronger battalions."

The General was not about to admit that a monstrous regiment of women were far more intimidating than the French Imperial Guards.

"I'm entitled to a little peace in my home, and your mother keeps on about your unwed state until I am thoroughly overcome. At least Moffett is not as unacceptable as that tunnel man, Pettifer." The General was determined to justify himself before his adamant daughter.

"Adrian Pettifer is far more interesting and attractive than Mr. Moffett. At least he has worthwhile goals, and believes passionately in progress."

"Building that ridiculous tunnel. No, Nicky, I agree that Moffett will not do, but neither will Pettifer, and I wish you would stop championing him. Do you love him?" Suddenly the General had an appalling idea that his beloved daughter was embroiled with a jackanapes and he might eventually be forced to acknowledge the knave. On the other hand if she really cared for the man he would have to accept him. The General wanted his daughter to be happy.

"Father, if you would just talk to Adrian, listen to his scheme. After all, that would be only fair. I would not like to believe that my father is so prejudiced he cannot entertain a view opposing his own." She appealed, knowing quite well that her father had little tolerance for any opinion with which he disagreed.

"Of course not. I am not an unreasonable man."

Nicola raised her eyebrows but remained silent. She had

placed her father in an untenable position and intended him to remain there until he consented to her plan.

"I suppose you want to invite him down here." The General wondered how he had been forced into retreat.

"That would be lovely. I would be very grateful. You really are an old dear." Having attained her goal Nicky was prepared to be generous. She crossed to the desk and gave her father a resounding kiss and whisked out the door before he could change his mind.

She left behind a confused man who did not quite see how he had been maneuvered into allowing Pettifer, whom he had met once and disliked, into becoming a guest in his house. The girl was a minx and needed a strong hand on the reins. Unfortunately, he conceded, his did not seem to be the hand. He sighed. She was such a beguiling girl, and he admired her, even if he could not control her. Perhaps it was not a bad idea having Pettifer here. Close contact with him might dim her enthusiasm not only for the man himself, but for his stupid tunnel. Having persuaded himself that he had acted with some cleverness he strode to the bell and rang it. He would put the whole matter from his mind and initiate young Forrest into his duties.

Nicola danced into the morning room, looking for her mother to tell her she must write immediately to Adrian, inviting him down. As she crossed the hall Paxton intercepted her.

"This letter just arrived for you, Miss Nicola, delivered by hand. Young Jasper took it in and stupidly did not ask the boy if there was an answer."

"Thank you, Paxton. Don't be upset with poor Jaspar. He's very willing." She rather liked the young apprentice footman and thought Paxton was too hard on him.

"He has a lot to learn and spends too much time flirting with the maids." Paxton was not as easily cajoled as her father.

"It's spring and romance is in the air," Nicola gaily replied and went off up the stairs to read her letter. Paxton, like his employer, often sighed over his young mistress's antics but was not impervious to her charms.

Nicola, in her bedroom, tore open the missive, a short note from Adrian himself, telling her he was at the Crown and Anchor and eager to see her. Could he call?

A little surprised at Adrian's unexpected arrival, but pleased that her plan could so quickly be put into action, Nicola decided she would persuade Ned to escort her into the village and deliver her father's invitation to Adrian in person. But first she must find her mother and procure the formal message.

A half an hour later Edward and Nicola were on their way in Ned's phaeton. He was quite proud of this new acquisition and not at all averse to displaying it to admiring villagers. He was not so happy about their errand. Like his father he did not think much of Pettifer's schemes for the tunnel and he did not take to the young man, especially as a future brother-in-law. But unlike his father he was wise enough to keep his opinions to himself for the moment. No good could be achieved by irritating his sister with his disapproval. He would save his fire for a more opportune time.

Nicola and Ned had an excellent understanding. They had always enjoyed amicable relations and secretly Nicola was very proud of her brother and he returned that regard. He considered his sister not only lovely to look at but intelligent and full of enthusiasm, qualities only too rare in her contemporaries. Ned, like Nicola, had never been pierced by Cupid's dart. His chief interest was horses, and he had a fervent desire to acquit himself heroically on the battlefield, rather difficult now that the war had ended. Ned's ambition was to be posted to some far-flung outpost where he could win his martial spurs.

The two chatted easily as they rode toward the village.

"So you talked the old man around to inviting Pettifer for a visit?"

"Yes, but it took some clever conniving on my part. He's such a staid old dear, fearing any kind of new idea."

"Well, this tunnel business is pretty radical."

"But not impossible. All revolutions are despised by the entrenched forces. And the tunnel would revolutionize our world."

"It seems to me there are a host of problems in engineering, financing, and politics," Ned offered sensibly.

"Naturally. They must be overcome."

"And Pettifer is the man to do it."

"I hope so. Don't be so timid, Ned. You'll see when you talk to Adrian. You know, it just occurred to me that he might have come down here to try his chances with the new Marquis. The man is very plump in the pocket and might be persuaded to put up some of the money for the scheme."

Before Ned could shoot down this unlikely hope they arrived at the Crown and Anchor, an establishment of some reputation for elegance and refinement. Ned tossed the reins to a hostler and helped Nicola down from the phaeton.

"Now, behave yourself, Nicky. I will leave you in the private parlor and discover the whereabouts of Pettifer. Don't go wandering about and get into trouble. Respectable females are not appreciated in the public saloon."

"I promise, Ned." Nicola looked meek while decrying the necessity to be chaperoned. But she settled docilely into a chair by the fire in the empty parlor, while Ned went about the business of finding Adrian. She was all impatience but had enough respect for her brother to obey his strictures. She would not want to cause him embarrassment. She had been there only ten minutes when the door opened and she looked up with anticipation. To her surprise the man who entered was neither Ned nor Adrian but the Marquis, from whom she had departed so recently on equivocal terms.

"Good afternoon, Miss Wynstan. You do turn up in the most unusual places. I suppose you will think it churlish of me to suggest this is not the proper setting for you."

Feeling both foolish and chagrined, Nicola was also annoyed to find herself blushing.

"Not that I owe you an explanation, my lord, but I was escorted here by my brother. He has gone to find an acquaintance." She managed a saucy smile while repressing an inclination to ask him what business it was of his how she conducted herself.

"I am glad to see you have some vestiges of propriety." The Marquis looked at her expecting a furious reaction. She seemed a risible girl and it would be entertaining to send her into a pet.

But if Nicola felt like telling him to go to the devil, she suspected that was just what he wanted, a chance to score off her. Well, she would surprise him.

"Oh, yes, my lord. I have been very well brought up." Her expression was demure and she lowered her eyes. It would never do to let him glimpse her real feelings.

"Perhaps I have misjudged you, Miss Wynstan." The Marquis sat down across from her.

"Oh, I don't think so. I suspect you have a very cynical view of females."

"Not at all. I find them fascinating, maddening and expensive."

"Yes, no doubt a man in your position and with your proclivities probably has had quite a stable of Cyprians under his protection. Alas, respectable females cannot compete with those charmers." Nicola hoped to shock him by speaking so bluntly, but she misjudged him.

"Quite astute of you, my girl. I find respectable females a dead bore."

"Just as well. From what I hear you would not be acceptable to them either."

The Marquis bit back a sharp retort and raised his eyebrows. "And just what do you mean by that?"

"Well, you must realize that you are the object of some curiosity and gossip, my lord. In a small community such as ours, any newcomer, and one of such exalted rank, naturally creates a furor of speculation." Nicola, watching him closely, saw a flash of anger cross his dark face and wondered if she had gone too far.

"I think you are mistaken, my girl. Plump pockets excuse a multitude of sins. Whatever my past misdeeds I will be welcomed for my prestige, wealth and estates."

"Which were not earned by your own efforts, but inherited. I prefer a man who achieves success by hard work and talent."

"You are a romantic and a socialist, an incompatible combination." If the Marquis was offended by her frank appraisal he did not show it. "Do I take it that some fortunate young man has earned your approval with just these qualities?" He sounded bored, as if the conversation had no interest for him.

"That's hardly your business, my lord."

"I do wish you would stop my-lording me. I find it offputting. My name is Jocelyn."

"We are not on those terms, my lord."

"If you insist. But perhaps I would like to be."

Nicola felt matters had gone far enough. She ignored his last remark and studiously avoided his teasing glance. She wished Ned would interrupt with Adrian. Sparring with the Marquis might have some entertainment value, but the man raised her hackles. He was much too sure of himself, and she thought, viewed her as providing a suitable target for jest. He was laughing at her and she did not like being treated as of no consequence and an object of amusement. Fortunately, before she could forget herself and tell him what she really thought of him, the door opened and Ned and Adrian appeared. Adrian hurried to her side.

"How wonderful to see you, Nicky. You had my note?" If he was aware of her companion he ignored him. Ned, mindful of his manners, nodded to the Marquis.

"Good afternoon, Cranbourne. I see you have met my sister. And may I present Adrian Pettifer."

"Your servant, sir." Adrian bowed, his whole aspect changing. How fortuitous, the very man he wanted to meet.

"Pettifer." The Marquis gave him an indifferent nod. He saw a young man of average height, a pale complexion and rather bulging blue eyes. He wondered if the engaging Miss Wynstan found this puppy attractive.

Nicola wished the Marquis would leave them. She had a great deal to say to Adrian and had no intention of sharing that conversation with the haughty lord.

But Adrian had different ideas. This was just the opportunity he had been seeking, an introduction to Cranbourne, who might listen to his plans for the tunnel and possibly support them. "I am so pleased to meet you, my lord. I was hoping for such a chance for I have a matter of business to discuss with you."

"Really. I can't imagine what that might be." The Marquis's tone did not encourage such liberties.

"If I could make an appointment?" Adrian was impervious to snubs when it concerned his tunnel project.

Cranbourne raised his eyebrows and dismissed this encroaching fellow, "I don't think so. And now, Miss Wynstan, since your brother has rescued you I will make my adieux. Pettifer, Wynstan," he nodded to the two men and bowed. Before Adrian could pursue his objective the Marquis had left the room.

"Oh, dear, I must have done something to offend him." Adrian looked most unhappy. He had muffed his chance.

"Nonsense, Adrian, the man is an arrogant, cynical, abominable aristocrat, quite puffed up, and not worthy of any attention. Now, let me tell you our news." Nicola decided that she would be foolish to waste another thought on Cranbourne. And neither must Adrian. The man was impossible.

"I must protest, Nicky. Cranbourne is not such a bad fellow. What has he done to raise your hackles?" Ned asked rather delighted at his sister's dislike of their august neighbor. If she had been tilting at Cranbourne she had been rolled up, he suspected, and that would do her good. Most men fell for her charms instantly and she treated them very cavalierly. Several of his friends had been rebuffed by his sister and he thought she needed to be put down. She would be no match for Cranbourne.

"He's rude and insolent. But don't let us bother with him. Adrian, our parents have invited you to stay. I am hoping you can persuade my father of the possibilities of your tunnel."

"How kind. I accept with pleasure. I am afraid the General did not understand what is involved with this scheme, and I know he will be interested when I have explained it to him."

Ned felt a word of warning might be appropriate.

"I'm afraid, Pettifer, he is most opposed, and I would go carefully. If your object in coming down here was to see Nicky, I can understand that, but trying to get Father to see some sense in your tunnel will be a difficult job, I fear."

"Oh, don't be such a wet blanket, Ned. Once Father has a chance to hear Adrian out I am sure he will understand how important his ideas are. But let's get along home."

Always agreeable, Ned shepherded his party out to the phaeton. It would be a tight squeeze for the three of them, and he suggested that Adrian's luggage could be sent on by a drayman's cart later. Having settled his bill and made the appropriate arrangements, Adrian left for the manor with Ned and Nicola.

The Marquis, in the courtyard awaiting his own conveyance, watched them go. He found himself wondering if the fatuous Pettifer was courting Miss Wynstan. He hoped not. She needed a man with a great deal more bottom than that fellow could provide.

A most intriguing girl, he thought. He supposed she had not married because few men could stand up to her wayward spirit. She certainly could benefit from some managing. If he were in the market for a wife she might offer a temptation.

As they rode away he noticed her chattering away to Pettifer. He could not believe she found the man either attractive or charming. What was her interest in him? Perhaps he would allow the puppy to make an appointment and discover what his object was in coming to Sussex.

At first glance Pettifer seemed little more important than a clerk, but he must have some attributes or the beguiling Miss Wynstan would not welcome him. He shrugged. That was the trouble with the country. So few distractions. One became overly concerned with one's neighbors. As if he did not have enough problems of his own, what with bringing some kind of order to the estate, and now this latest occurrence, troubling indeed. Just then the hostler brought up Cranbourne's phaeton and he rode off in the opposite direction to the Wynstan party, on his way to Chichester.

Five

Nicola, constrained by Ned's presence, could not caution Adrian as she hoped about his approach to the General. She skirted about the subject, dismissing Adrian's gratitude for the invitation, as of no account. Ned, always amused at his sister's intricate plotting, finally could bear it no longer.

"Why not just come out with it, Nicky? If Pettifer here continues to argue the merits of his precious tunnel, Father will probably throw a fit and throw Pettifer out the door."

"Really, Ned, what fustian you talk. Father would never be so inhospitable. But I must urge, Adrian, that you approach the subject carefully, with tact."

"Dear me, you quite frighten me, Nicola. Is your father such an ogre?" Adrian pretended to be taken aback. He had angled for this invitation for reasons he was not prepared to confide in either Nicola or her brother and he would not be foolish enough to jeopardize his position by antagonizing the General.

"Of course not. He's really a dear, but he gets these fancies. He's not wedded to progress and he judges everything by what the Duke of Wellington endorses."

"The Duke is violently opposed to the tunnel," Adrian agreed with a sigh.

"He has a war mentality." Nicola admired the Duke as the victor of Waterloo but thought most of his ideas were antiquated.

"Well, he has no reason to want the Frenchies on our doorstep." Ned hoped to squash some of his sister's enthusiasm.

"The tunnel would be a harbinger of peace." Adrian really believed the tunnel would bring profit to all who invested in it, but had enough sense to appeal to Nicola's more idealist views.

"Quite, but I think you should heed Nicky's warnings, Pettifer, and tread gently." Ned wanted no fruitless arguments spoiling his leave.

"I will be circumspect," Adrian promised.

Nicola looked at their guest with barely concealed scorn. Really, Adrian should have more faith in his scheme. Sometimes she thought he lacked courage. But she was prepared to fight his battles for him.

"You could try a little diplomacy yourself, Nicky," Ned insisted with brotherly candor. And determined to get away from the consuming topic of the tunnel, changed the subject. "I suspect you were not a model of diplomacy with the Marquis."

"He may be the great man of the county but he has hateful manners. He was very rude."

"Immune to your wiles, I bet. I think he's an interesting chap."

"Ned, he has a fearful reputation as a libertine. Surely you would not want me to encourage a man like that. Mother refuses to call on him, says he is unacceptable." Nicola made this claim in dulcet tones although Ned suspected that their mother's disapproval had less influence than the Marquis's own reception of Nicola. He had put her in her place and she would not forgive that. Ned chuckled. Had his sister at last met a man who knew how to outmaneuver her?

"Nicola, the Marquis appears to be a forward thinking man, has traveled widely. He might support the tunnel." Adrian was not bold enough to challenge his champion, but he thought a gentle reproof might not be inexpedient.

Nicola bit back a scathing reply. She was not unreasonable.

If Adrian thought the Marquis might supply some funds for
Adrian's tunnel she would have to revise her opinion of the
haughty lord, but she would not flatter or cajole the man.

Before she could continue the discussion they had pulled
into the entrance of the manor. Adrian, she noticed, looked
about with awe. The grey Queen Anne house, built on the site
of a Tudor mansion, with its hipped roof, cornered eaves, dor-
mer windows and balustrades, was indeed an impressive residence, but to Nicola it was much more. It was her home and
she loved it.

For the first time she wondered about Adrian's own background. He was obviously well-educated with the manners
that assured him acceptance into polite society, but she realized she knew little of his parents or home. Not that such
matters were important in this modern age, but she suspected
her parents would find them so. She trusted Adrian could
satisfy them on all counts but a niggling doubt remained. That
he was ambitious and talented she conceded but neither of
these qualities would win over the parents. They would want
more practical assets, like his income and lineage. Adrian
always seemed to have a comfortable competence but Nicola
had no idea if this was inherited wealth or money he earned
at some undefined work. In a better regulated society all this
would not matter, but Nicola sadly confessed her parents
would think differently.

Mrs. Wynstan welcomed Adrian with every appearance of
delight and he responded with gratitude. Paxton was called
upon to deal with Adrian's luggage which was coming from
the Crown and Anchor, and the young man dispatched to his
room, a gracious apartment overlooking the gardens to the
rear of the house. Nicola, deciding that his introduction to the
General, who had met him once, but must be reminded to
behave suitably, could be deferred, went with relief to her own
bedroom. She had a lot to think about.

Mrs. Wynstan told Adrian they would meet for tea within
the hour, saw that he had comfortably settled in, and left him

to his own devices. She thought it a bit odd he was not accompanied by his valet but sent Joshua to be of service. She only hoped the young man would not stir up her husband who despite his agreement to entertain him did not approve of him. She wished yet again that Nicola would settle and they could be spared all these upheavals.

Left alone, Adrian sighed with satisfaction. The first hurdle was over. He was installed as a guest at Wynstan manor. He must tread warily, but it was obvious that Nicola liked him, perhaps more than liked him. Passionately as he cared about the tunnel, his own future would be assured if he could marry sensibly, a well-dowered wife, whose funds and position could assure his acceptance into the ton where he aspired to be. He had made some careful inquiries and learned that the General was well placed, with a conservative fortune. Certainly this home was far more imposing than he had expected. He had his foot on the first step of the ladder and intended to climb even higher.

Adrian refused to think of himself as a fortune hunter but he wanted desperately to rise above his station. He was the only child of a solicitor in a small Shropshire town, and his father had sacrificed to send him to an indifferent preparatory school and then to Cambridge. There he had ingratiated himself with young men far more affluent than himself and had been accepted. He had been introduced onto the fringes of London society when he came down from Cambridge and had met Nicola at the home of a striving hostess not of the first rank. Clever, courteous and ambitious, he had used the tunnel scheme as a way of making his mark. He was sincerely interested in the scheme but saw it mainly as a tool to force his way into high society. He knew his views were anathema to some members of the ton and he was very careful not to offend where it would earn him scorn. Money was a problem, but he now thought he had solved it temporarily and, if he won Nicola, broad options would be open to him. Not really a villain, he was a man with aspirations, prepared to do what he must to attain them.

He might not have been so optimistic if he could have read Nicola's thoughts. She had championed Adrian, not because she felt for him any but the most tepid feelings. She was entranced by the tunnel scheme, and admired the man who could present this revolutionary idea with such ability. That Adrian might see the tunnel as a vehicle to promote himself never occurred to her.

As she combed her hair, and freshened herself for tea, she found her mind returning to the Marquis and their duel in the parlor of the Crown and Anchor. She was accustomed to admiration and felt frustrated that the Marquis seemed impervious to her charm. Ned had been right there. Spoiled by adulation in London where she had attracted some very credible beaux, she had never met a man who roused such a welter of emotions in her. Certain that she disliked him, she was annoyed that her thoughts kept returning to their passages at arms. He was everything she hated about the aristocracy, arrogant, domineering, indifferent to others, and mannerless. She had known many like him, but perhaps not quite like him. She wondered about the woman with whom he had eloped. Obviously he had treated her shamefully. Of course, he had been young, but selfish and heedless.

She jerked the hairbrush and threw it down in disgust. She was a fool to be thinking of the man. What difference could he make to her? Determined to push all thoughts of him from her mind, she hurried from the room, eager to talk to Adrian again about what progress he had made in enlisting support for his tunnel. Perhaps even the despicable Marquis might be persuaded to endorse the plan. When her enthusiasm was engaged Nicola was prepared to make every endeavor and she must not let her antipathy to the Marquis dampen Adrian's chances.

The General did not appear for tea. Nicola suspected he would manage to have as little contact with Adrian as possible.

But if the General had decided to avoid his duties as a host for the moment, Mrs. Wynstan more than made up for her husband's transgressions.

"I do hope you enjoy your stay with us, Mr. Pettifer," she said, passing him his cup and a plate of cakes.

Adrian, looking about the cozy morning room, thought that would not be difficult. If not the lavish luxury he had seen in London houses, the Wynstans made themselves very comfortable, he decided. "I am sure I will, Mrs. Wynstan. You have a charming home, and Sussex is such a salubrious county. I understand the house has been in the family for many years."

"Yes, indeed. Of course, my husband's career necessitated much travel, but now that he has retired he is happy to be back again and overseeing the estate."

Adrian wanted to ask how large the estate was, but sensed that would not be politic. He devoted himself to flattering Mrs. Wynstan for her approval was most vital.

Unaccustomed to having her views attended with such interest she beamed at Adrian. Really, a most intelligent and affable young man, she concluded, solely on the basis of his cultivation of her opinions. She rarely received such respect from her family. The General paid little heed to her views. Her children often treated her with an affectionate contempt.

Nicola, sitting silently while Adrian beguiled her mother, was rather disillusioned. She applauded his attempt to win over her mother but scorned his methods. She wanted to talk about the tunnel and her mother insisted on discussing inanities.

"I so enjoy having guests. There is not a great deal of good company hereabouts," Mrs. Wynstan confided.

"There is the Marquis, mother." Nicola could not refrain from adding a little spice to the conversation.

"He is not a man I think suitable for inclusion in our circle." Mrs. Wynstan frowned at her wayward daughter.

"You do not approve of him, Mrs. Wynstan?" Adrian asked.

"Not at all. He is a Detrimental." Having given her most inflexible judgment on the Marquis she hurried to introduce a new topic.

"We will be a pleasant party." Turning to Nicola she informed her daughter, "I have invited your cousin, Julia Overton, for a visit, my dear. There are so few young women in the neighborhood for companionship. And Julia's mother thought she might benefit from a change."

Nicola, who had no opinion of her cousin, could not resist twitting her mother. "Poor Julia. Has she suffered another disappointment?"

"I believe so, dear, but we will not mention that when she arrives later this week." Turning to Adrian, she explained.

"Julia lives in Sidmouth with her widowed mother. There are so few opportunities for a girl there since most of the gentry are retired people, a rather staid social circle for a young girl."

Ned, who under pressure from Nicola, had joined the tea party, groaned. "Julia is a dead bore, Mother. Whatever induced you to invite her?"

"That's unkind, Ned. Julia is perhaps a bit over nice in her manner, but she is a lovely girl."

"Well, you can entertain her. Don't count on me to escort her about. She's a danger to any unattached male, Pettifer, so I am warning you."

"I am sure that Julia will be a great addition to our family group. You will welcome her, I am sure, Mr. Pettifer, and you, too, of course, Mr. Forrest."

The General's new secretary looked a bit frightened by this order, but only nodded and blushed. He found Mrs. Wynstan a comfortable woman, but did not quite know how to approach her daughter. He admired her exceedingly but she was so resolute, so outspoken, so foreign to his experience of females, with whom he had little contact as a rule, that he was not easy in her company.

"She's a menace, Forrest," Ned added his bit with a wicked grin.

"Really, Ned, you are giving Mr. Pettifer and Mr. Forrest the wrong impression. No one could be more conformable than Julia."

"True, that's what makes her such a bore. And I do think it's mean to foist her on us. She will spoil my leave." Ned wanted to make it clear to his mother that he had no interest in his cousin and would not be cajoled into developing one.

Ignoring her son, Mrs. Wynstan continued. "We will have a little party for her, I think. And she will arrive in time for the Mumfords' dance next week. You see, Mr. Pettifer, we can offer you some pleasing society."

Adrian, sensing that neither Edward nor Nicola were at all pleased with this addition to their company, only smiled his agreement. It was not his intention to vex his hostess nor her daughter. He would be careful with Miss Overton.

Finally Nicola managed to extricate Adrian from her mother's orbit and took him into the garden for a probing discussion of the latest advances with the tunnel. Mr. Forrest escaped to the library where he was trying to restore some order to the General's chaotic notes on his family, and Ned went off to the stables where he hoped to find his father.

The General, who had spent a satisfying day with his tenants and agent, appeared before dinner in the drawing room, pleased with life. He liked young Forrest who treated him with the respect his consequence demanded and was prepared to endure this young puppy that Nicola had foisted upon them. His reception of Adrian was restrained, considering he had no opinion of the young man and would have been angry if he thought he had serious intentions toward his daughter. This interest in the tunnel was just Nicola's latest whim.

"My wife has settled you in properly, Pettifer, I hope."

"Yes indeed, sir. You have a charming home and I am delighted to be here." Adrian was going to act with all circumspection. He considered the General an officious old soldier with little understanding of the world beyond the battlefield and the officer's mess. In this judgment he made his first mistake. The General might be orthodox in his views, and heavily influenced by tradition but he was a shrewd judge of men and far from stupid.

However the meal went off well. Adrian did not mention the tunnel and listened with respect to the General's views on the state of the country, Wellington, the Corn Laws and Catholic Emancipation, all of which he saw in a far more radical light than that of the General. Nicola gave him a smile of approval and he felt he had gained in her eyes. He did venture one daring thrust.

"I met the Marquis of Cranbourne at the Crown and Anchor today. I would be grateful for your opinion of him, sir."

"Seems a decent fellow. I have had several worthwhile chats with him. My wife won't receive him, not that he has attempted to further the acquaintance. He came into the title and the property sideways, so to speak. His father was the younger brother of the old Marquis, who was very highly regarded in the neighborhood. We will have to see how he does." The General believed he had said the last word on the Marquis and could not conceive that any of his family would dispute it.

"He appeared to be a sound man." Adrian ventured this view diffidently. He would need the General's cooperation if he were to meet the Marquis and win his support.

A melting syllabus having concluded the dinner, Mrs. Wynstan signaled to Nicola that they would withdraw and leave the gentlemen to their port. She was anxious to remove her daughter before Nicola launched on an impassioned plea for the tunnel. All had marched so well this evening, she was determined to keep that dangerous topic in abeyance as long as she could.

Ned rose and opened the door for his mother and sister, giving Nicola a wink as she passed through. He found her efforts to force the efficacy of the tunnel on her father an entertaining diversion in their staid household. He knew she could handle their father, and how she had persuaded him to accept Pettifer in their home was evidence. His own view of that young man was cautionary. For the most part Ned found little in common with men outside the army, but he was tolerant and could enjoy most society. He usually agreed with his father because he did not care enough about the topics that raised his parent to a passion. But he cared for his sister, and he would assess Pettifer with a discerning eye if he thought he might become his brother-in-law. Little danger of that, he decided. Nicola showed no signs of succumbing to the fellow's lures. Not his style, of course, but that did not mean the man had few qualities. There was a lot beneath the surface amiability, Ned decided. In that he was wiser than his sister.

Mrs. Wynstan settled herself in the drawing room and took up her tapestry. She beamed at her daughter, who was wandering about the room, a high-ceilinged gracious apartment furnished with Sheraton chairs, two mahogany bergeres with lyre shaped legs and a bowed front chiffonnier. Eau de Nile damask swagged draperies framed the large windows and the color was picked up in the striped silk of the settees. Mrs. Wynstan longed for a Chinese cupboard much favored by the Prince Regent in his Brighton Pavilion but the General would have none of these fripperies.

"Mr. Pettifer seems a nice gentleman, very courteous and attentive. Of course, I met him in London but really had no chance to further the acquaintance. I was a little worried because you met him at Mrs. Sharpless's at home as she is not of the first stare. He might have been a stock-jobber or some other low type but it is obvious he is well bred and well educated."

Nicola held her temper. She could hardly blame her mother for wanting her daughter to meet suitable young men, but her fatuous comments tried her patience.

"He's very clever. Did well at Cambridge." Nicola offered this sop.

"But what about his people? He's never mentioned them."

"I've never asked, Mother. Why don't you quiz him?"

"Oh, I would not be so rude. I do wish you would not rake me up, Nicola. A mother naturally is concerned about the various men her daughter meets. There are so many fortune hunters about. And you will have a comfortable settlement and competence you know."

"I understand you are only trying to protect me, Mother. But matters have not reached that stage with Adrian, so calm your fears."

Mrs. Wynstan pursed her lips but did not persevere. Really, Nicola was a trying girl. She failed to see the necessity for making a good marriage.

In the dining room the General was in no mood to linger over the port. When the decanter had gone around once he stood up and said abruptly, "Forrest and Pettifer can join the ladies. I want a few words with you, Ned."

Forrest scuttled to the door, afraid of incurring his employer's wrath, and Adrian followed in a leisurely fashion, annoyed at being dismissed so cavalierly but not wanting to make much of the General's treatment.

Ned turned to his father who had sat down again.

"That was rather abrupt, Father." Ned thought the General discourteous. No matter how much he disliked Pettifer he should not be so rude. Forrest was in such awe of his father he scuttled away as if he had created a gaffe.

"I don't want to discuss this matter in front of strangers." The General seldom took offense at Ned's criticisms. Secretly he was proud of his son and thought him a perfect officer and gentleman although sometimes he did not understand his son's wry humor.

"What's the trouble?"

"Arnold told me today that there is a highwayman active in the neighborhood. I don't like the sound of it. We've never had any trouble like that before. And Smithson, the constable, is no protection. If he can't catch poachers a highwayman has little to fear."

"Arnold is an old woman." Ned did not take the threat seriously.

"He's a damn fine agent. I want you to keep your eyes peeled. What would you say to talking to the Marquis about the matter? He can enlist the authorities and force them to take action. I think he would carry more weight. We should not be exposed to such villainy. The country is a hotbed of lawlessness."

"You are a justice of the peace, Father, with influence. Inform your fellow magistrates and demand that an effort be made to catch the fellow."

"I have to think of your mother and sister. Nicky is always roaming around on that mare of hers. She could be in danger."

"I pity the highwayman that encounters Nicky. She'd rout him in seconds." Ned laughed, picturing his stalwart sister dealing with the rogue.

"I'm serious, Ned."

"I promise to keep an eye on Nicky, not an easy task." If Ned thought his father was fussing he had enough respect for him not to show it.

"I knew I could rely on you, Ned. And I believe I will discuss the matter with the Marquis. He seems a sound man."

Ned realized that his father was really concerned and promised his cooperation although what he could do was a mystery. These highwaymen were a reoccurring threat, more numerous since the peace, when unemployment and poverty were rife. Eventually most of them were captured and deported to the Antipodes. If the rumors were true it added a bit of excitement. Ned was fond of his family and home but he found his leave a tame affair after London, where the Guards were posted. This affair might add some spice to his weeks in the Sussex countryside.

Six

Betsy, Nicola's abigail, stood back, and looked with admiration at her mistress. Done up a treat, she was. That apricot silk with the low cut square neckline edged in seed pearls flattered her complexion, and Betsy felt she had done a fine job with Miss Nicola's hair. Fit for a London ball, she was. Betsy missed London and the elegant soirees and routs Miss Nicola had attended during her two seasons. This Mumford dance was just a country affair, not worthy of her mistress, but better than no party at all. Most of the time Miss Nicola rushed about in a shabby old riding habit and never gave a thought to how she looked. Betsy mourned those officers and lords who had courted her mistress in London. Who was there in this dull village worthy of her? Betsy had little opinion of Adrian Pettifer and could not understand her mistress's interest in him. A paltry fellow, she thought. Miss Nicola could be a countess, even a duchess, if she wanted. Maybe this Marquis would do. Gossip in the servant's hall insisted he was no better than he should be for all his title and fine estates, but Betsy was prepared to dismiss the lord's scandalous past if he married Miss Nicola. Then she would move to the Hall where they had a large staff, twenty at least, instead of the half dozen the Wynstans kept. Betsy, true to her class, was a tremendous snob and identified with the family she served. She hoped that Miss Nicola would make a grand alliance which would increase her own prestige.

"You won't be asitting out any dances, Miss Nicola." Betsy

gave her approval and handed her mistress the pearls which Nicola clasped about her neck.

"Thank you, Betsy. I think you have worked wonders."

Not a vain girl, Nicola could not help but be aware that she usually outshone most of the females she met but she paid little attention to her appearance, and took no credit for it. Just an accident of nature, she thought, although she was grateful for it. But beauty could be a problem. Few gentlemen believed she had a brain and wanted to use it. That was why Adrian appealed to her. He understood her interest in the tunnel and appreciated it. She acquitted him of any baser emotions.

"Hand me that reticule, Betsy. Then I had better go down." Turning away from the cheval mirror, satisfied, she was about to leave when the door to her bedroom opened and Julia Overton poked her head in with a nervous giggle.

"Oh, Nicola, how lovely you look. Of course, you are not nervous having had two seasons in London where I hear you were all the rage."

Why such flattery should annoy Nicola, she could not fathom. Just that Julia herself irritated her whenever she uttered these inanities. She looked at her cousin, masking her dislike. Julia was so tentative, pale face, pale blue eyes, pale blond hair, and pale character, a thoroughly tedious girl.

"Don't be a ninny, Julia. And come along. Father hates to be kept waiting."

"Do I look all right? This is such a dowdy old dress."

Dowdy was not the word, Nicola thought. Fussy was a better description. The pink silk was the wrong color for Julia and the ruffled hem and bodice edging did little to enhance Julia's angular figure. Her chest was bony and she slumped. Nicola made an effort to be kind.

"You look charming. Shall we go?" That was the best she could do, and Nicola chided herself for lack of charity. Julia always raised her hackles and no matter how sternly she vowed to treat her cousin with sympathy she rarely managed more than an indifferent tolerance.

As the two girls walked down the staircase, Julia continued her lament.

"I suppose your dance card will be filled immediately. You won't have to sit out at all."

"I like sitting out sometimes. Then I can survey the company. Come, Julia, try for some optimism. I am sure you will have a fine time."

"Well, perhaps. But I never seem to attract really eligible men. You know I have just had a grievous disappointment. Frank Lawson, the squire's son, seemed most épris. Then all of a sudden he seemed to lose interest, and now he is engaged to Margaret Manners, quite a dull stupid girl. I was quite overset. That is why Mother thought a visit to Cousin Prudence would cheer me up."

"Let us hope it does." Nicola spoke more sharply than she intended. Feeling cross with her impatience, she tried to make amends. "Try to enjoy yourself this evening, Julia, and forget Frank Lawson."

"I'll try." Julia's tone was mournful. Really, Nicola was not sympathetic. She did not understand how lowering it was to be poor, and with neither intelligence nor beauty to mitigate this disaster.

Thankfully Nicola turned Julia over to her mother who made a fuss over her, flattering her as to her gown, and then taking her across the room to introduce her to Roger Forrest and Adrian Pettifer, who were talking idly with Ned by the fireplace in the drawing room.

The General was struggling manfully with Mr. Moffett, whom his wife had included in this small dinner which would precede the Mumford dance. Evidently the Rev. Mr. Moffett's self-esteem had suffered so little he was comfortable in confronting Nicola. He had brought his aunt, who ran the vicarage for him, a vinegary spinster of uncertain years, Julia's equal in moaning her lot. Sometimes her mother's generosity overcame her sensibility, Nicola thought, but she determined to do her duty.

"Good evening, Miss Moffett." She greeted the vicar's aunt pleasantly.

"What a lovely gown, Miss Wynstan. Not perhaps the best color for a young girl. I always believed that young females should wear white, but, of course, you are up on the latest London fashions." Miss Moffett herself wore a dull magenta gown, an old favorite, that drained color from her sallow complexion. She had small close-set dark eyes, and a permanent droop to her mouth, a symptom of her dissatisfaction with her lot.

Nicola wished her mother would not encourage the woman but suitable companions were rare in their country village, and Miss Moffett had to be endured. She only hoped that Mr. Moffett had not told her of his disdained proposal.

"Oh, I do think you are correct, Miss Moffett, but white is so dull. I hope this apricot is not too bold."

Her criticism deflected, Miss Moffett was about to embark on another complaint when Adrian came up and complimented Nicola.

"You look ravishing tonight, Nicola."

"Thank you, Adrian. You have met Miss Moffett."

"Yes, indeed. We have been talking about good works," he said slyly.

Miss Moffett, watching the pair avidly, restrained her disapproval. Of course, Miss Wynstan was just a tiny bit fast, and her London season had done nothing to restrain her free and easy ways. What kind of terms was she on with this dubious young man that he could hail her so informally? The young today were much too familiar, not at all the thing. She was about to put this notion into words when Paxton announced dinner and the General came across to escort her to the table, an honor she felt only her due. Since she was the only mature female among the guests he could hardly do otherwise, while silently cursing his generous wife. Berated for inviting Miss Moffett, Mrs. Wynstan had pleaded that she felt sorry for the poor woman, and after all, they had to remain on good terms with the Moffetts. The General thought that debatable, but he usually surrendered to his wife on these occasions. He had real affection for her and was prepared to make small concessions while remaining in command of all important family decisions.

Dinner was a leisurely meal for it would never do to arrive at the Mumfords too early. Turtle soup was followed by turbot, roast pigeon, lamb cutlets, salad, meringues à la crème and a macédoine of fruit. Nine was an awkward number at the table but at least Nicola was spared having Reginald Moffett as a dinner partner. He sat across from her on her mother's right and every time she looked up he gazed with reproach at her. Mrs. Wynstan had invited the Moffetts before the vicar's proposal and her hostess skills were taxed by avoiding the subject that Mr. Moffett was determined to pursue. Julia simpered at Roger Forrest who blushed and stammered, unaccustomed to dealing with encroaching females. He found Miss Overton's appearance and conversation unappealing but courtesy demanded he pay her some attention. She would have preferred to simper at Ned, on her other side, but he postponed that unenviable chore until the meringues appeared. An awkward meal that seemed to drag on forever, Nicola thought, but at last her mother signaled the ladies would retire. Leaving the men to walnuts and port, they withdrew to the drawing room.

Miss Moffett settled herself beside her hostess prepared to quiz her about the Marquis.

"I have heard the most shocking stories about Lord Cranbourne, Mrs. Wynstan. Surely, you are not planning to call upon him."

Mrs. Wynstan, who had made vehement objections to the new heir, suddenly wanted to champion him. Miss Moffett had that effect upon her. As the vicar's aunt, Miss Moffett thought she was the chief arbiter of their community's morals and brooked no opposition.

"I have not called as yet because there appears to be no female relative in residence, but both the General and Ned have made his acquaintance and consider him a sound man." Mrs. Wynstan hoped this endorsement by the General would quiet Miss Moffett but that lady was made of sterner stuff.

"Of course, gentlemen rarely take a censorious view of the wicked behavior of each other. But, surely you would not introduce Nicola to such a libertine."

"Better a rake than a prosy bore like your nephew," Mrs. Wynstan wanted to say. But she was in a difficult position as she did not know if Mr. Moffett had confided in his aunt that Nicola had refused his proposal.

"Nicola has already met the Marquis, quite by chance, on one of her rides."

"How unfortunate. Nicola is a charming girl but perhaps a bit headstrong. You must worry about her a good deal, long to see her settled."

Of course that was Mrs. Wynstan's chief aim but she would never admit that to Miss Moffett. "On the contrary, we enjoy having her at home." Mrs. Wynstan's ploys to deflect Miss Moffett were to no avail and the vicar's aunt gave her views on young women who had not taken advantage of a London season and caused their parents disquiet. Mrs. Wynstan clung to her hostess courtesy but finally had enough of the criticism.

"Since you are neither wife nor mother, Miss Moffett, you cannot, perhaps, understand my concerns."

While her mother was coping with little success against Miss Moffett, Nicola was doing her best to entertain her cousin, Julia.

"Do tell me about Mr. Pettifer, Nicola. Is he one of your beaux? Such an entertaining man. Where did you meet him?"

"In London. Adrian is a very inventive and intelligent man with some novel ideas. His latest project is a tunnel under the Channel. Quite revolutionary and exciting."

"A tunnel under the Channel! How enterprising, but is he

in trade and what do his people think of such a daring idea?" This was Julia's clumsy attempt to discover if Adrian was a man of means and proper background who might repay her interest.

"I have no idea. We have never discussed it." Nicola's tone was abrupt and Julia quickly changed the subject although she would return to it at a more opportune time. She was just a bit in awe of Nicola whom she both envied and despised.

"Do you suppose this Marquis everyone talks of will be at the Mumfords' tonight? Have you met him?"

"Yes, he's quite cosmopolitan and I cannot believe our country entertainments will attract him, if, indeed, he was invited. Lady Mumford disapproves of him."

"Oh, why is that? Is there some scandal attached to him?"

"I believe so. At any rate there should be plenty of young men for the dancing. I understand it will be a grand affair. The Mumfords have a house party for the dance."

"How thrilling. I so seldom have such treats, but I suppose I will spend my evening sitting with the chaperons," Julia, complained, seeking sympathy or at least a disclaimer.

"Oh, nonsense, Julie. Do try not to be so spiritless." Nicola had lost her patience with her cousin and thought the faithless Frank Lawson had shown sound judgment in ridding himself of such an incubus.

Whatever Julia's answer, and she was angered by Nicola's jibe, it was suppressed, for the gentlemen entered the room, and she would never be so gauche as to lose her temper before them. Adrian went right to Nicola's side.

"You must give me the first dance and the supper dance, Nicola. I will be in the midst of strangers and need support." Then, realizing his duty, he included Julia. "And you, too, Miss Overton, must honor me with a dance."

Julia simpered, "Of course, Mr. Pettifer. I would be pleased." However, she harbored dark thoughts. Why should Nicola have so much of his company? Still, it behooved her not to make any display of pique before Mr. Pettifer.

"Well, what about it, Nicola?"

"The first dance, certainly, Adrian, and then we will see." Nicola stood up and crossed the room to her brother who was chatting with Roger Forrest. Ned was a kind fellow and realized Mr. Forrest felt shy, not knowing how to go on. He was explaining to Ned that he dreaded the dance, not being a good performer, and had little experience with grand entertainments.

"You'll be fine, Mr. Forrest. This is only a country party. Nothing to tax your social skills," Nicola explained, hoping to put him at ease.

"You are too kind, Miss Wynstan."

"Oh, do call me Nicky. You will be living with us for some months while you cope with Father's book, and we must not stand on formality."

"Stop casting lures at Roger, Nicky." Ned teased his sister, noting that Forrest was completely under her spell.

"Pay no attention to my brother, Roger. Brothers have no respect. Have you any sisters?"

"No, alas, I am an only child. I have missed all that companionship."

"Fortunate chap. Sisters can be the very devil." Fond as he was of his sister, Ned was a staunch defender of the men she attracted. Poor fellows. They could not withstand her, and she seemed to enjoy their discomfort. Ned's hope, like his father's, was that someday she would meet her match.

"Come, come, we must not keep the horses waiting." The General marshaled his forces. It was time to take off for the Mumfords'. They would travel in two vehicles since it was a large party and the drive was at least an hour.

Nicola managed to persuade Ned to ride with her, Julia, and Adrian, leaving her parents, Roger and the Moffetts to the comfort of the family carriage. Reginald Moffett cast her a reproachful glance as she stepped into the brougham.

* * *

It was a mild evening and the ladies needed only their Norwich shawls for the journey. Nicola immediately entered into a discussion with Adrian about the tunnel while Ned was left to entertain Julia, a task he pursued with cheerful patience although vowing to rake his sister over the coals for placing him in such a position. He was not unaware that Julia had designs on him but he was too experienced to be caught in her toils. By the time the party arrived at the Mumfords' imposing Tudor mansion, he was quite out of temper, but he hid it well. Nicky gave him a wry glance of sympathy. The Guards had trained her brother in the social niceties as well as military maneuvers. She hoped he would find some appealing partners.

The Mumfords stood just inside the Great Hall where the dance was held, welcoming their guests. A hospitable couple they enjoyed entertaining and Lady Mumford, a dedicated matchmaker always hoped her parties would produce a romance and an engagement. She looked imposing in a violet satin gown, a matching turban and a fine display of diamonds. Sir Charles, the host, was among Nicola's favorites, a jolly man of wide girth, a fringe of grey hair about his bald pate, and an eye for the ladies.

"As beautiful as ever, Nicola," he greeted her. "Can't understand why some deserving chap has not persuaded you into wedded bliss by now."

"Ah, Sir Charles, if I could find a man like you I would succumb in a trice." Nicola was well used to his extravagant compliments and enjoyed sparring with him.

"You are a minx. Good evening, Wynstan, and Prudence, you are in fine form, I see."

Mrs. Wynstan introduced the strangers in her party, Roger and Adrian. Julia and the Moffetts were acquainted with the Mumfords. The moment she took the floor, having surrendered her shawl, Nicola was surrounded by eager claimants for a dance. Laughing, she allowed her card to be filled, saving only the supper dance for Adrian, to the disappointment of the young men who begged for it. She was happy to see there was a good contingent of men, a group of naval officers from Portsmouth, always a jolly addition, and saw several young women she knew from Chichester. It looked like being a fine evening. And thank goodness she had avoided a future dance with Mr. Moffett.

About to be drawn onto the floor by Adrian, for the first set was beginning, she was interrupted by the Marquis.

"May I claim a dance, Miss Wynstan?" He looked the epitome of fashion in his black superfine coat, white linen, and a subdued waistcoat. Obviously he did not favor the flamboyant dress of the dandies and sported no jewelry except a gold fob.

"I'm afraid my card is full," she said sweetly while Adrian stood by barely restraining his chagrin.

"Oh, I am sure one of these puppies will be persuaded to cede his claim to mine." And without a by your leave he crossed out Roger Forrest's name and substituted his initials for the fourth dance, a waltz.

Reduced to a furious glare at his high-handed action, for she could not create a scene on the dance floor, Nicola decided she would get her revenge later. Smiling at Adrian she allowed him to lead her into the middle of a set for the quadrille that traditionally opened a dance in the country.

Equally angry at the Marquis's assumption of privilege, Adrian had not dared interfere. He remembered that this haughty peer might yet endorse his tunnel and he could not afford to offend him no matter how fainthearted he appeared in Nicola's eyes. The quadrille proceeded with little conversation between the pair and afterwards there was no time for him to explain his attitude for Nicola was immediately claimed by a naval officer, a former beau.

After a rousing country dance Nicola was eager for a respite. Her next partner, Algernon Danville, a young baronet and member of the Mumford house party, whom she had met in London, suggested that they take a stroll on the terrace.

Nicola considered Algernon a fribble and had discouraged his attentions in London, but he would serve now as a method to escape the Marquis. She would enjoy cutting his dance.

"Well, Algy, tell me all the London on dits," Nicola insisted as they strolled up and down the terrace. They were alone although in view of the ballroom windows. Nicola walked down the steps toward the garden, and Danville followed her with eagerness.

"It's all very flat since you've retired to the country. When are you returning to brighten the scene?"

"Perhaps in July. It depends."

Danville, a fatuous young man with an unjustified conceit of his looks and breeding, felt this was too good an opportunity to miss. He had proposed several times to Nicola, intrigued as much by her probably healthy settlement as her obvious beauty and charm. She had refused him, to her mother's dismay.

"If it depended on me you would return tomorrow." Algernon was encouraged, as they were now out of sight of the dancers and he thought he might chance his luck again. He had drunk just enough champagne and port at dinner to spur him to outrageous lengths. Putting his arms around Nicola he stammered another plea for kindness and bent as if to kiss her. She averted her head but before Algernon could pursue his intentions he found himself lying spread-eagled on the ground. He had been felled by a blow from the Marquis who stood looking at him with contempt.

"You had best take yourself off, Danville. The lady finds you objectionable." The Marquis stood over him, looking disdainful and bored.

"You have no right, sir . . . ," Algernon sputtered, dragging himself to his feet.

"Don't be a fool, Algy. You had better douse your head in some cold water." Nicola, humiliated that the Marquis had come to her rescue, would have liked to send both her tormentors to the devil.

"Sorry, sorry, mistook the situation . . ." Algernon stammered and made a perfunctory bow, ignoring the Marquis entirely and hurriedly took his leave.

"What a siren you are, Miss Wynstan. I feel quite sorry for the poor clodpole." The Marquis seemed amused at the contretemps.

"Algy was a bit castaway. Nothing I couldn't have handled, but I must thank you for the rescue, I suppose." Nicola's gratitude was grudging. She loathed being under an obligation to the Marquis.

"Perhaps you would have preferred I did not interfere."

"Oh, don't be so cynical. I only wondered why you bothered. You probably believe the matter was my fault."

"Not at all. Your charms are so obvious, I can't blame the poor fool. I might even have been tempted myself under the circumstances." The Marquis was looking at her in an odious considering way that Nicola disliked exceedingly.

"In fact, my dear girl, I think you need a lesson." Before she could gather his intention he took her in his arms and kissed her skillfully. Then he stood back awaiting her reaction.

"Would you like to slap my face? I should warn you if you do I will kiss you again. I quite enjoyed it."

"Well, I did not. And if you have finished your assault, I would like to return to the ballroom." Nicola was determined not to show any emotion, to let him feel he had made an impact.

"But, of course. I believe this is our dance." With aplomb the Marquis offered his arm and Nicola had no recourse but to accept it and enter the ballroom, only praying that her face did not reveal her discomfort and chagrin.

Seven

As she might have known, the Marquis was as skilled at dancing as he was at dalliance. As they twirled about the floor in the intimacy of the waltz Nicola chatted coolly with her partner. She would not give him the satisfaction of knowing he had caused any disturbance to her senses. If his clasp was tighter than she considered proper she ignored it, as she did the envious gazes of the females who followed their every move. Silly fools, if they thought this dance signaled the Marquis's particular interest in her. When the dance ended she indicated he could return her to the chaperones' corner where her mother sat chatting with a distinguished looking matron who was a stranger to Nicola. But not to the Marquis.

"Ah, Cousin Annabel, I see you have made the acquaintance of Mrs. Wynstan. I have not had that pleasure."

Mrs. Wynstan had meant to look disapproving. She had not liked the Marquis making a spectacle of her daughter on the dance floor, but courtesy insisted she acknowledge Mrs. Sturbridge's hurried attempt to rectify the omission.

"My cousin has just come to pay me an extended visit and take charge of my household, give it an aura of respectability," the Marquis informed them with a bland smile. "Cousin, this is Miss Wynstan."

Greetings were exchanged and Nicola acknowledged them prettily but was vastly relieved when her next partner appeared to claim her hand. Without another look at the Marquis, who remained talking to her mother and his cousin, she took the floor for the country dance.

As she moved through the intricate paces of the dance, she hid her anger at the Marquis's suave and successful attempt to inveigle his way into her mother's acceptance. What his object was she could not fathom. She doubted the man had any interest in her except as a passing flirtation. His consequence could not allow any female to view him unkindly. The man was a conceited, condescending libertine and her every instinct was to have nothing more to do with him. But if he had persuaded her parents to accept him, she might find this difficult.

For the rest of the evening she gave the appearance of a popular belle enjoying her triumphs. Her intention of snubbing the Marquis if he approached her again was not put to the test. He never came near her. At supper while enjoying York ham, chicken patties and jellies with Adrian, Ned and his partner, she noticed the Marquis seemed to have transferred his attentions to a luscious brunette, a stranger to Nicola, who must be one of the house party the Mumfords had invited. She gave the couple only a passing glance. She must not appear to notice the reprobate. Ned, who rarely lost a chance to tease his sister, was not so easily dismissed.

"I saw you waltzing with our august neighbor, Nicky. I assume you do not find him so repugnant now?"

"Don't be ridiculous, Ned. The man forced himself upon me and rather than cause a scene I consented to the dance, but it will not be repeated."

"I don't know why you have taken him in such dislike. He's a fine fellow and the company appears quite honored by his joining our country festivity."

"I am surprised the Mumfords asked him. I understand that Lady Mumford thinks he is reprehensible."

"Lady Mumford never scorns a title, you know. The Marquis of Cranbourne is a notable acquisition to her guest list."

"Oh, enough of the man. If this community was not so

provincial it would not be impressed with him, just because he is a peer."

"With the biggest rent roll in the county, remember."

"Oh, Ned, I had no idea you were such a snob. I am disappointed in you."

As the brother and sister sparred, Adrian looked on, hiding his irritation. Could Nicola be attracted to the Marquis? He doubted that the man was seriously interested in her, lovely as she was, but if she took against him that would complicate his own arrangements. He wanted Nicola as his wife, but he also needed the Marquis to sponsor his tunnel. He had not decided what attitude he should adopt when the supper came to an end, and Nicola's next partner appeared. Adrian went off to do his duty toward Julia Overton, distracted by this latest contretemps. Julia did little to soothe his exacerbated feelings although she made every effort to interest him. Of course, she could not help throwing a barb at Nicola.

"I suppose you noticed Nicola waltzing with that Marquis everyone is so impressed by. I never waltz. My mother thinks it a bit fast." Julia did not think it necessary to mention that no one had asked her.

"Lady Jersey approves of it and allows the waltz at Almack's and when one of society's doyennes rules, society must follow," Adrian said, thinking what a fatuous female Miss Overton was and how stupid to show her envy of Nicola.

"Well, I am just a country girl. We do not endorse those sophisticated pleasures in Sidmouth," Julia simpered. "But, of course, Mr. Pettifer, you follow the lead of the haut ton, I expect." She realized belatedly it would not do to disparage Nicola to her partner. Men disliked anything of that nature.

"The waltz is very popular." Adrian barely hid his boredom and left Julia wondering not for the first time why she could not interest men in her conversation or herself. She felt quite aggrieved that he made no effort to continue their discussion. He hurried her back to Mrs. Wynstan without asking for another dance or even if she would like some refreshment. It was not just her indifferent looks that kept Julia a spinster, but she had never realized this, puzzled that girls with equal plainness but sweeter characters managed to snare husbands.

Finally the orchestra played Roger de Coverly, the signal that the dance was ending. Nicola did not see the Marquis on the floor. Having had his small divertissement he had probably left, bored with the rustic revels. The Moffetts, too, had departed early with some other guests so that Julia and Nicola were able to travel home with the General and Mrs. Wynstan, the latter pleased with her evening and wishing to discuss every nuance while the General nodded in the corner of the coach. He had spent most of the evening playing whist in the card room and imbibing freely of the brandy cup.

"I suppose I will have to call on Mrs. Sturbridge now that she has arrived to add some tone to the Marquis's establishment," Mrs. Wynstan informed the girls.

"I thought you had vowed never to accept the Marquis." Nicola knew very well that her mother was not proof against the temptation and once Mrs. Sturbridge had come on the scene she had an excuse to recant her previous decision.

"Well, my dear, we cannot be on bad terms with our neighbors in the country. The General thinks the Marquis is acceptable so I must be agreeable." Mrs. Wynstan knew that her daughter disapproved of currying favor so blatantly but Mrs. Wynstan, watching her daughter waltz with the wicked Marquis, had been visited with a splendid vision of Nicola donning the tiara of a Marchioness. Not that she would be so foolish as to confide this dream to her daughter.

Nicola shrugged, having some idea of what her mother was thinking. The woman was obsessed with marrying her off. It would serve her right if she eloped with a Detrimental. Nicola smiled. She was behaving in a rag-mannered fashion. Her mother was only doing her duty as she saw it.

"Did you enjoy yourself, Julia?" Mrs. Wynstan asked, recalled to her responsibility as a hostess.

"Oh, yes, Cousin Prudence. It was such a treat for me. I

rarely see such elegant company in Sidmouth, you know.
Thank you so much for taking me."

Why was it Julia managed to make Nicola feel a veritable
mean shrew? Whether she was flattering or criticizing, Julia
was equally annoying. Nicola vowed to try to behave with
more charity toward Julia, although it would be a hard task.
Toadying or vicious, Julia managed to alienate most people.
Nicola thought her mother was a saint to endure her, but she
was not a saint and wondered how long Julia would be a guest.
She concentrated on Julia's character because she was not
ready to contemplate the effect of that disturbing interlude
with the Marquis. How that man intruded on her life.

Just then the General snorted and came awake.

"I hope John has a wary eye out. That highwayman might
still be in the neighborhood and this road is not much fre-
quented."

"Oh, no. You have given me a horrid fright." Mrs. Wynstan
reproved her husband.

"Sorry, my dear. I wasn't thinking. Nothing to it. I was just
reminded because Mumford and a few others mentioned it
again to me. It seems the knave held up a coach outside of
Chichester the other day, couple returning from a rout, and
made off with some handsome jewelry and a bag full of guineas."

As if on cue the night reverberated with the sound of shots.
Mrs. Wynstan screamed, Julia moaned, the General cursed
but Nicola remained silent, straightening her back and clench-
ing her hands. The coach lurched to a stop, the General struggled to his feet, but before he could make a further move, the
door opened and the Marquis leaned in, his right hand holding
a pistol.

"No need to stir yourself, General. I rode off the rogues
with a little help from your footman, brave boy. I'm afraid he
took a flesh wound in his arm." The Marquis appeared calm
and confident, as if dispatching highwaymen was his usual
sport.

"Oh, how brave of you, my lord," Julia simpered. "We could all have been killed or worse."

By worse Nicola supposed the foolish girl meant ravished. Little chance of that, she thought.

"What about Ned?" Mrs. Wynstan, now that she knew the danger had been averted thought of her son, always her chief concern.

"I believe, ma'am, that the carriage with the men was quite a ways ahead of you. I wonder if the highwayman had some prior knowledge and realized that your coach would be carrying passengers with jewelry."

"You are implying, Cranbourne, that he is a local man." The General flushed with anger and shock at the suspicion that he and his family could be accosted in their neighborhood. Then, remembering his duty, "I must see to John and that footman."

The Marquis stood aside for the General to step from the coach. He leaned negligently against the doorway and contemplated Nicola with a mocking gaze she refused to meet.

"How did you come to be so opportunely on the scene, my lord?"

"I sent my cousin off in my coach as I had ridden to the Mumfords' with Gavin McCloud, an old friend who is visiting me. He is helping your coachman with the wounded man. We were not a hundred yards behind you when we saw two figures loom up out of that copse and suspected they were up to no good. Sensibly your men were armed and refused to pull up when the highwaymen called, 'Stand and deliver.' The young footman let off a volley and they returned the fire, but before any more damage could be done, Gavin and I scared them off with a few shots of our own."

"Do you usually carry a pistol when you go to a ball?" Nicola said a bit astringently. If they had to be rescued why hadn't Ned or Adrian been the one to accomplish it? She did not like being obligated to the Marquis, petty of her, no doubt, but she wished anyone else could have come to their aid. And her temper was not improved by sensing from the sardonic smile he gave her that he knew exactly what she was feeling.

"I had heard about the highwayman and it's always best to be prepared. I regret a cavalier more to your taste could not have been your savior, Miss Wynstan."

"What are you thinking of, Nicola, upbraiding the Marquis in that fashion? We are very grateful to you, sir. Just before the shots rang out the General mentioned the highwaymen and put a fright into us. You must forgive my daughter." Mrs. Wynstan gave Nicola a look that boded no good when they were in private.

"Miss Wynstan has made a correct reading of my character, ma'am, and believes I am only acting true to form." He laughed.

Before Nicola could indignantly defend herself, the General appeared at the Marquis's side. "Young Fowler seems to be a bit shaken but not seriously hurt, the bullet went through his arm, which McCloud has tied up. John can't do much. He has to hold the horses. We are much obliged to you, Cranbourne. The knaves ambushing us—it could have been disastrous."

"No harm done, I am only sorry the ladies have been frightened, although your daughter seems to have enjoyed the skirmish." The Marquis gave a wicked glance at Nicola who was flushed more from irritation than fear.

"Oh, Nicky is a stout heart, a real soldier's daughter. It would take more than a highwayman to shake her, isn't that right, Nicky?" The General approved of her stoic behavior and cast a scornful glance at Julia who continued to wring her hands and moan at their providential escape.

"McCloud and I will escort you the rest of the way, sir. Only about five miles, I believe. But I don't think the villains will try again. It must have seemed an easy jape to them and they were not expecting any interference."

"We are in your debt, Cranbourne." The Marquis stood aside and the General entered the coach, taking up his wife's hand and giving it a sympathetic squeeze. Julia continued to twitter and eye the Marquis with awe. He closed the door with a bow and disappeared into the night.

"Damn scoundrels, excuse my language, my dear. But if we are not safe practically on our own doorstep measures will have to be taken." The General fulminated all the rest of the way home about the brazen attempt of the highwaymen to accost them.

"Cranbourne is a good man in an emergency. We were indeed fortunate he was on hand. And that friend of his is a competent chap, bound up Fowler's wound and reassured John."

When the coach finally arrived safely at the manor, the General insisted his rescuers come in for a brandy. The Marquis handed Nicola down, having performed the same service for Julia who cooed her thanks.

"You have my gratitude, my lord, "Nicola said grudgingly. She owed him that courtesy, at least.

"And I know it's a burden to you, Miss Wynstan. Cheer up. Perhaps you'll have the chance to repay me some day."

She ignored that sally and followed her mother and Julia up the steps and into the house where Paxton was waiting to receive them, having heard from the General about the adventure. Not waiting to say more than a muttered good night Nicola ran up the stairs. She had had enough of the Marquis for one evening and thought fleetingly that she would have preferred to have been robbed by the highwayman than rescued by that supercilious lord.

Betsy was waiting to help Nicola undress and wanted to hear all about the dance, the gowns, the jewels, the supper and any other details her mistress could remember. What Nicola chiefly remembered was the Marquis's kiss in the garden. She could hardly mention that to her abigail. But she did give Betsy a much abbreviated report on the attempted robbery by the highwaymen.

"And the Marquis came to your rescue. How romantic," Betsy sighed. One of the great advantages of her service was to learn, firsthand, these tales of the quality.

"Not romantic at all. It was very mundane, except for poor Albert suffering a flesh wound in his arm. We never even saw the highwaymen, just heard the shots."

"Ooh! Weren't you frightened, Miss Nicola?" Betsy was far more fascinated by Nicola's reactions than Albert's injury although he was her cousin. Betsy thought Albert would be insufferably proud of his wound and she could hear all about it in the servants' hall.

"Not very. It was all over in a few moments."

"I bet Miss Overton carried on." Betsy had a poor opinion of Julia, who was apt to be demanding and querulous with the maids. Even Paxton, who rarely criticized the guests, had been moved to speak slightingly of Miss Overton who had little idea of how to treat her inferiors.

"She did a lot of moaning, thought she might be ravished," Nicola giggled, remembering her cousin.

Betsy nodded. That Miss Overton was always trying to gain attention. A real ninny, with none of Miss Nicola's spirit.

Finally, Nicola was able to dismiss her maid. However, she had barely settled into bed with her candle and book when her mother entered her room, still in her gown from the dance.

"Nicky, I must speak with you."

"Yes, Mother, of course." Nicola repressed a sigh, laying down her book. She had expected a visit from her mother, who would not retire until she had exhausted every nuance of the evening. But Nicola was surprised Mrs. Wynstan did not launch into a tirade against the highwaymen. Instead, she upbraided her daughter for treating the Marquis so rudely.

"I was quite ashamed of your manner toward Lord Cranbourne, Nicky. He behaved with such courage and daring. He could have been wounded by those villains. And you barely thanked him. He deserved your gratitude and you behaved abominably."

Since Nicola had no intention of describing the Marquis's liberties in the garden she had difficulty in defending herself. But she tried.

"Really, Mother, I don't understand this sudden affection

for the Marquis. You told me he was an unacceptable man and not a suitable person for me to meet. Now you behave as if he was all gallantry and courtesy." Nicola believed the best defense was to challenge her mother where she was most vulnerable, in her notions of propriety.

"Your father thinks highly of him, and now that his cousin has come to preside over his household I will call. Mrs. Sturbridge is a very respectable widow with the best credentials. If she has forgiven the Marquis for his youthful follies, it is not our place to judge him less leniently."

"I doubt if you would feel that way if he were not a Marquis with a tidy fortune and a fine estate."

"Don't be impertinent, Nicky. The Marquis is very eligible."

At last her mother had admitted to the reason she was prepared to look with charity on the Marquis. If Nicola was amused by this volte face she was also annoyed. She had a good idea of what her mother was planning and she wanted no part of it.

"Mother, I do not like the Marquis and he finds me equally intolerable. Whatever maggots you have in your head about arranging any match between us, forget them. I suspect he is not a marrying man. He has a poor opinion of women and even less of young females who defy him."

"Oh, Nicky. He danced with you."

"Only to be annoying and there were several others he honored with his attention. That Marsha Huntley, for example. He appeared to be charmed by her. She's a very sophisticated brunette with tonnish connections, much more his style."

"Yes, I noticed her at supper with him, a very pushy type of girl, I thought. Bold and forward in her manner. Did you know her in London?"

"She is very much the rage, created a stir at every ball and was besieged with partners."

"No more than you, Nicky." Mrs. Wynstan believed her daughter was a Nonpariel and only sighed that she would not take advantage of her assets.

"Mother, I realize you are an incurable matchmaker, but you would be well advised to lend your talents to getting Julia off. She would be most grateful, I know."

"I expect her mother sent her here with just that in mind. But, it will not be easy." Mrs. Wynstan had a shrewd suspicion that Nicola was correct, but Julia was a far more challenging figure than Nicola when it came to the marriage stakes.

"Not beyond your powers, I'm sure. Mother, I know you worry about my lack of interest in marriage, but I promise you when I meet the proper man you will be the first to know. Just concentrate on Julia in the meantime. Now, I'm tired and want to go to sleep."

"You really are the most unobliging girl, Nicky." Her mother accepted defeat for the moment but would return to the fray at the least encouragement, and comforted herself with the remembrance that girls often married men they had originally taken in dislike.

"Good night, dear. Sleep well. I'm fit to drop myself." Mrs. Wynstan reached over and gave her daughter a kiss on her cheek and left her to her dreams.

Nicola could not be angry with her mother for long. She realized that her mother's self-esteem was threatened by Nicola's spinster status. She felt she had failed in her duty. She dreaded Ned falling in love with some girl and foisting her on the family, but she would welcome almost any man who could persuade Nicola to wed. Well, she was not about to marry to satisfy her mother. And any ploys Mrs. Wynstan had for throwing her in the path of the Marquis would be thwarted. She could manage her mother and, for that matter, depress the noble lord's intentions, whatever they might be. Marriage was not on his mind, she was convinced. He wanted to take his revenge on her for her obvious disapproval of his august person. That kiss had been a punishment, not an expression of affection. Well, she could handle the Marquis, too. Having some wicked ideas on how she might manage that, Nicola blew out her candle and fell immediately into an untroubled sleep.

Eight

At breakfast the next morning the General was loud in praise of the Marquis and his conduct the previous evening. Ned was chagrined to have missed the adventure, but if Adrian and Roger did not share his disappointment they kept their own counsel. Ned agreed to accompany his father into Chichester to lay the matter of the highwaymen before the authorities. He wanted a detailed account of the attempted robbery and the General obliged.

"I am sure you would have dealt with the villains as easily as Lord Cranbourne if you had come upon them," Julia twittered at Ned. She was constantly trying to ingratiate herself with her cousin, who largely ignored her.

"I doubt it. I was not carrying a pistol." Ned turned off her comment abruptly. "But I believe it will be best to be armed when riding at night from now on."

"Oh, Ned, do be careful," his mother implored, always fearing some harm might come to her son.

"Not to worry, Mother. I am sure our local highwaymen cannot be more defiant than the Frenchies."

"Quite right, my boy. Most of those knaves are the most errant cowards when faced with any opposition. They prey on innocent passengers who will offer no defense." The General had little use for opponents not in uniform.

"One of the reasons we are having this outbreak of crime is because the government refuses to aid the discharged soldiers. They are thrown on the countryside without money or employment and have recourse to the only way they know of surviving, violence. The late war is responsible for that." Nicola had a well developed social conscience and was not averse to airing it.

The General, a fair man, had some sympathy for the veterans who had served in the Peninsula war, but any rebellion against the establishment roused his patriotism.

"Nonsense, Nicky. Robbery is not the answer. These fellows must be apprehended and deported. We can't have the country threatened by felons. We fought the war to keep England safe and prosperous."

Adrian agreed with Nicola but was too prudent to argue with the General. He had a request of his own to make. "Could I travel with you to Chichester, sir? I have some business I should settle there." His own concerns always took precedence for Adrian.

The General nodded a brisk assent and was about to continue the discussion with Nicola. However, wishing to distract her husband and Nicola from what could be a tiresome argument, Mrs. Wynstan hurried to explain her own plans for the day. "I am going to call on Mrs. Sturbridge today, Charles. It will give me an opportunity to thank the Marquis for his brave actions last night and I find her a most superior woman. Now that she is at the Hall we can contemplate neighborly commerce between our households." She gave her views in what she supposed was a decisive manner. "I want you to come with me, Nicky."

"Oh, no, Mother. I have seen enough of the Marquis for the moment. I will give him all credit for his rescue last night but you can tender our gratitude without my assistance."

"Gets under your skin, our noble lord, eh, Nicky?" Ned never lost a chance to tease his sister and he had soon realized the best way of doing that was to praise the Marquis.

Not willing to admit to Ned that the Marquis did just that, Nicola remained silent. In her duels with her brother silence was sometimes the best weapon.

"I will be happy to accompany you, Cousin Prudence,"
Julia offered. She was not averse to show nobility when Nicola
would be placed at a disadvantage.

"That is kind of you, Julia, but I feel Nicola should make
the effort."

Her mother seldom demanded that Nicola fall in with her
wishes and when she did insist her daughter felt she must
comply or live with an uncomfortable feeling of guilt.

"Oh, all right, Mother, if you insist."

Julia, who often took umbrage when none was intended,
decided that on this occasion she would swallow her irritation.
Cousin Prudence was the kindest of women but she could
take offense when pushed to unacceptable limits. Julia had
no intention of being sent home in disgrace because she had
offended her hostess.

"Perhaps your luck will be in, Nicky, and the Marquis won't
be at home." Ned was beginning to believe that his sister's
antipathy to their neighbor went beyond the bounds of reason
and wondered if her apparent dislike masked some other emotion. Could Nicky at last be engulfed by an unwanted passion?
He would not like to see her hurt or disappointed by falling
in love with a man who scorned her whatever the justice of
her being caught by that emotion she had dismissed in the
poor fools who had fallen under her spell. Ned doubted that
the Marquis was a man any woman could play fast and loose
with and his sister might find herself a victim of this experienced libertine. As a man Ned found him enjoyable company,
knowledgeable, sophisticated and daring, probably a good
man in a fight. But he was also arrogant, ruthless and strong-
minded. He would be more than a match for Ned's spirited
sister. Ned was concerned and as he and his father rode toward
Chichester at a comfortable jog he could not resist asking,
"What do you think of Cranbourne, Father?"

"Capital fellow. The old Marquis was a good landlord but
toward the end was not up to the business. I understand Cranbourne has dismissed that agent. Never did trust the fellow,

thought he was feathering his own nest. Just as well that this man has taken over the estate."

"Yes, I agree but he's a cynical devil, has a jaundiced view of his fellows, I believe. Not a comfortable chap."

"Comfortable, what use is that? And he has plenty of bottom. He handled those highwaymen smartly last night."

The General's judgment of a man was apt to be formed by qualities he had valued on the battlefield—courage, initiative, the ability to carry out orders. Not exactly the traits to fit him for domestic life. Ned did not pursue the matter, but he wondered how Nicky would fare at the hands of such a man. Still, it might not come to such a pass. With his usual optimism he decided he could leave possibility of Nicky's involvement with the Marquis to the future. He trusted his sister not to make a fool of herself.

Nicola was giving that sound advice to herself as she readied herself that afternoon to accompany her mother to Cranbourne Hall. She took extra pains with her appearance and donned a twilled cream sarsenet faced in blue with a matching velvet spencer and a peaked bonnet with blue ribbons. When she appeared downstairs her mother nodded in approval.

"You are looking quite smart, Nicola." Then, aware that some warning might be advisable she added. "See that you behave as well. I do not want Mrs. Sturbridge to think you are bold or inclined to put yourself forward."

"I'll be the very epitome of meekness, I promise. Is Julia coming?"

"Yes. I think her feelings would be hurt if she were left behind. Really, she can be trying, always taking a pet." Mrs. Wynstan, charitable as a rule, found even her patience tried by their cousin. Before she could enlarge on the subject Julia tripped down the stairs looking presentable in a serviceable hunter green ensemble which, unfortunately, emphasized her sallowness and bony figure.

"Oh, you look so fashionable, Nicky. I suppose you bought that outfit in Paris. You quite put me in the shade."

Unwilling to pander to Julia's constant self-abjection, Nicola thanked her and repressed a moue of boredom. She feared this expedition would try her own not very well developed patience. She had not her mother's tolerance.

As she feared, Julia spent the short ride to the Hall complaining about her lot, lack of friends, suitors, and fortune. With a captive audience she could not miss the chance to induce pity in her more fortunate relatives.

Both Mrs. Wynstan and Nicola were relieved to reach the entrance of the Hall, a massive grey stone edifice, its facade stark and relieved only by some impressive Doric pillars flanking the marbled steps. The hall had been built in Tudor times but significantly altered in the generations since, the small-paned windows replaced by wide expanses of glass which caught the late April sun. Two long wings, in the Queen Anne style, branched out from the main building and a great swath of green lawn spread on either side of the mile-long driveway lined with beeches. Julia was vehement in her praise of this impressive establishment, and conceded that Devon had no mansion to equal it.

Mrs. Wynstan had sent a groom with a message to Mrs. Sturbridge signifying her intention to call in midafternoon if that met with the lady's approval, and a note had been sent in return allowing the visit. Both Mrs. Wynstan and her daughter had been frequent guests in the old Marquis's day but it had been some time since they had been to the Hall. Andrews, the old butler, remembered the Wynstans, received them with his courtly manner and conducted them to the small drawing room. Nicola was relieved to see Mrs. Sturbridge alone beside the fireplace, sitting erect on a Sheraton sofa. The room was a comfortable blend of French and English furniture, the chintzes a bit shabby, and the velvet draperies faded but elegant. Obviously, the Marquis had not spent his few months in any refurbishment.

Greeting her guests, Mrs. Sturbridge ordered tea, and settled down for a sensible cose. Although stern of aspect she enjoyed a good gossip and was prepared to unbend toward these callers.

"As you can see, Mrs. Wynstan, the house has been allowed to fall into a deplorable state. The old Marquis took no interest in decor. But I believe my cousin intends to rectify matters." The two ladies were soon involved in a discussion of fabrics and furniture during which Nicola, mindful of her mother's strictures, kept silent, and Julia was too intimidated by both Mrs. Sturbridge and her surroundings to utter. Mrs. Sturbridge was a woman of the old-fashioned school, in her dress, deportment and manner. Her spine was stiff and she gave off an aura of hauteur which dispelled any attempt at familiarity, but she seemed to welcome Mrs. Wynstan's inquiries. Seeing that her mother had soothed the dowager, Nicola finally sought the information she had been impatient to learn.

"I know the Marquis is your cousin, Mrs. Sturbridge. Do you remember him when he was a boy? He rarely visited the old Marquis, I think."

Mrs. Wynstan frowned at her daughter. Such curiosity was not polite.

"Unfortunately, not very well. My home is in Hampshire and my brother-in-law, Jocelyn's father, lived in Somerset. We saw little of the family, and, of course, after he came down from Oxford, Jocelyn almost immediately fell into the difficulties that forced him abroad." She looked at Nicola with a forbidding stare. Surely this young woman could not want her to gossip about that long-ago scandal.

Mrs. Wynstan, hoping to avoid a reproof to her daughter, hurried to interrupt before Nicola could pursue the matter. "I am from Hampshire myself. I wonder if you knew my people. My maiden name was Atherton."

"Of course. The Athertons, of Ramsey." And to Nicola's disappointment the two women were off into the maze of relationships and ancestry which so delighted the gently bred who only felt secure in company they recognized.

Just when Nicola thought she would expire from boredom,

the door opened and the Marquis strode into the room in his usual domineering fashion.

"Good afternoon, Mrs. Wynstan, Miss Wynstan. Andrews told me you were visiting. How kind of you to call." His tone was pleasant but Nicola thought she caught a mocking glint in his eye. Mrs. Wynstan, who had met him at the ball, greeted him in a measured manner and introduced Julia, who was most overcome by the honor.

"McCloud and I have been going over the estate," the Marquis informed his cousin. "I hope he will consent to become my agent."

Mrs. Wynstan, always able to judge the proper moment to make her adieux, gathered her reticule and signified that they must depart.

"As I am sure my cousin has informed you, Mrs. Wynstan, I have not yet had time to refurbish the Hall. As soon as the property is put in order I will attend to it, and then I will be pleased to give you a tour."

"Surely you would be advised to await your wife's wishes, Lord Cranbourne," Julia simpered, hoping to learn if the Marquis had marriage in mind.

"I'm not sure I can wait upon a wife, Miss Overton. No suitable female has appeared on my horizon so I will just have to be guided by Cousin Annabel." He gave Julia a haughty stare as if to say what business was it of this rather pathetic female. She subsided into blushes and protests that she meant nothing. Nicola, who deplored the Marquis's manners, felt sorry for Julia. Stupid she might be, but she did not deserve a set-down.

"You must excuse my cousin, Lord Cranbourne. We females are always concerned with matchmaking."

"Somehow I doubt that my bachelor status concerns you at all, Miss Wynstan. But, come, we are keeping your mother waiting. Let me escort you to your carriage." Having routed both Nicola and Julia, he politely offered his arm to Mrs.

Wynstan and escorted her from the room, trailed by a disconsolate Julia and a furious Nicola.

The Wynstan barouche was drawn up at the entrance and the Marquis handed first Mrs. Wynstan and then Julia into the coach. Then he turned to Nicola.

"How kind of your mother to call on my cousin. I am sure she had to overcome some scruples about entering the domain of such a practiced libertine," he quipped.

"Not at all, my lord. My mother is a neighborly sort and she approves of your cousin."

"Well, now that we are on neighborly terms perhaps I can expect to see more of you."

"I doubt it, my lord. I don't believe we are in sympathy with one another." Nicola, believing she had the last word, entered the coach and turned her head aside, conscious that the Marquis was laughing at her. Odious man, he really brought out the worst in her character. He might be rich, well-born and courageous, she would give him those assets, but he had no idea how to behave in proper society. Besides, he was also too fond of his own way. Nicola suppressed the notion that when he entered the room he brought with him an aura of excitement. She would not succumb to his efforts to tease and charm her, since she knew he was just exerting himself to bring another female under his spell. He had already proved he was not to be trusted, was a philanderer and took liberties that were not warranted. She promised herself she would stay out of his way in the future.

Both Mrs. Wynstan and Julia did not share Nicola's misgivings. In fact Mrs. Wynstan seemed captivated by the Marquis and extolled his virtues all the way home. She was ably seconded by Julia and if she noticed Nicola's lack of enthusiasm she decided that her daughter was just being contrary. Mrs. Wynstan was satisfied that the Marquis was attracted to Nicola and the thought that finally her daughter might make an exceptional match cheered her. Of course, she was too wise to express her hopes.

On arriving home, Nicola hurried to her bedroom to digest the results of this latest meeting. A sudden idea had come to her in the coach. Despite the Marquis's valiant rescue of the previous night, she wondered a bit about his role. It was quite possible, she decided, that he was not the gallant savior that he appeared. He might even be the highwayman himself and had warned off his confederates in order to put himself in a good light with his nearest neighbors. The more she thought of him as a rogue the better it pleased her. It was just the kind of undertaking he would enjoy. Playing the arrogant lord of the county on one hand while conspiring with thieves and cutthroats on the other.

Delighted as she was with the thought that the Marquis might be a villain, somehow she could not wholly endorse the idea. Why would he need to rob coaches? Supposedly he had inherited a tidy competence. Of course, he might have joined the criminal fraternity as a jest, a fillip to relieve the boredom of acting the country lord. Yes, that was most likely his reason. No doubt he missed the challenges of the gaming table or the exchange where he had made his previous fortunes. How was she to unmask him? A man who would assault a defenseless female in a friendly garden was capable of anything.

Despite her best efforts Nicola had not been able to dismiss that kiss. She had been kissed before, shocking as it was to admit, by one or two of the beaux who had courted her in London. But on the whole they had been chaste affairs, arousing little more than amusement. There had been nothing amusing in the Marquis's kiss. It had left her shaken and excited although she hoped she had revealed neither of these disturbing emotions to her tormentor. It had been difficult meeting him today and adopting a cool and distant demeanor. She suspected she had not completely convinced him of her indifference. The man was an enigma, behaving on the one hand as if he cared nothing for the opinion of his neighbors, on the other installing his cousin to give a semblance of respectability to his household. He had succeeded in winning over her mother who had been one of his severest critics, and Lady Mumford must have decided to accept him or he would not have been invited to the dance. What was his purpose in maneuvering himself into a commendable position in the community?

She disliked him and distrusted him and she would be careful not to put herself in a position again where he could take advantage of her. She must expose him if he were indeed the highwayman. And whom could she enlist to help her? Ned would only laugh and her father would scoff at the suggestion that the Marquis was not what he seemed. Perhaps Adrian might prove a willing ally? In all the turmoil she had almost forgotten Adrian and his scheme. He had shown some interest in enlisting the Marquis's patronage for his tunnel, but if he was rebuffed he might join her in a plan to paint the Marquis in his true colors.

Satisfied that she had solved her immediate problem, she rang for her abigail. After dinner tonight she would seek Adrian's cooperation and swear him to secrecy. The Marquis's perfidy would not go unpunished. Whether that perfidy concerned his role as a highwayman or his effrontery in kissing her in the Mumfords' garden she was loath to admit.

Nine

Nicola, the most candid of girls, would not have made a good conspirator. Now that she had conceived this idea of the Marquis in league with the highwaymen, if not their leader, she could barely contain her impatience to reveal this startling thesis to an appreciative audience. As a young child she had always taken her troubles to her brother, but in this case she realized that Ned would scoff at her suggestion. He would not be a trustworthy confidant, and would laugh at her notion as well as make it a topic of hilarity at the dinner table. Her parents seemed to have taken a liking to their new neighbor. Besides, her father rarely accepted a view from a female as having any worth.

That left Adrian. Not perhaps the wisest choice but she had to discuss this idea with someone who would at least listen to her. Nicola understood that Adrian had his own interests to further, and shrewdly supposed that he would not want to antagonize her. Whether he would help her to unmask the Marquis was another matter. She suspected he would not be eager to challenge the man whom he hoped to enlist in his own cause. Nicola's respect for Adrian's tunnel scheme did not blind her to his imperfections. That he was ambitious and somewhat of a social climber she could not deny, and she intended to use both these traits to further her own ends.

With some difficulty she avoided her mother's efforts to enlist her aid after breakfast in going to church to arrange the flowers. Mrs. Wynstan was head of the ladies' altar guild and took her duties seriously. She was constantly trying to persuade Nicola to join her in whatever charitable responsibilities she thought suitable.

"I do wish you would come with me, Nicola. So much better for you than careening recklessly about the land on that mare of yours. One of these days you will encounter trouble, since you rarely have a groom with you." This was another constant complaint of Mrs. Wynstan's.

But Nicola had cannily provided a good excuse to avoid visiting the church. "But you must see, Mother, it would be embarrassing for me to meet Mr. Moffett after what has transpired between us. I have to meet him on Sundays, but he could hardly renew his proposal in front of the whole parish. I really think it best to avoid him on any other occasion." She implied but did not say that if her mother had not foolishly allowed Mr. Moffett to offer marriage to Nicola she would not be in this position.

While this conversation was going on in the morning room Julia had been hovering within earshot. Not one to ignore a situation that might rebound to her own advantage, she interceded.

"Dear Cousin Prudence, I would be delighted to assist you with the flowers. Such a genteel occupation for a lady." She preened, implying that her cousin Nicky's occupations for the most part were far from decorous. Nicola would not quarrel with her about that conclusion.

"A splendid idea, Mother. Julia is so much cleverer with her fingers than I am. She will be the greatest help to you."

Outmaneuvered, Mrs. Wynstan agreed, knowing she was no match for her stubborn daughter. Julia could not resist giving Nicola a triumphant look as she left the room. She had not the nous to realize she had been manipulated for Nicola's ends, but felt she had achieved some kind of victory. For some time Julia had thought of Mr. Moffett as a possible husband, and had not been discouraged when she learned that he had been refused by Nicola. Julia's one aim was to secure a husband. Affection and common interest would mean little in the alliance since she was at the stage when desperate methods were necessary if she were not to be forever a spinster. Her efforts with Ned had proved fruitless and she would have to look elsewhere.

Nicola waved off the flower arrangers in the pony cart and then asked Paxton to find Mr. Pettifer and tell him she wished to see him. Paxton did not wholly approve of his young mistress having interviews with single gentlemen alone, nor was he entirely happy about Nicola's preference for Mr. Pettifer, but he could not refuse her. She would only go boldly to seek him out herself even if that meant invading his bedroom. Paxton had long thought that the General and Mrs. Wynstan were unable to handle their daughter and fond as he was of her he decried her independent reckless ways. She should be married to some strong minded yet kind man who would appreciate her qualities but exert some restraint over her more outrageous behavior. He did not see Mr. Pettifer as this man. He let his disapproval be known by a stern look but Nicola just laughed at him and said, "I know, Paxton, you think I am impossible."

"Not at all, Miss Nicola. I just wish you would behave in a more prudent fashion occasionally."

"Not my style, Paxton, but do be a lamb and find Mr. Pettifer."

As usual, Paxton's stern visage relaxed under Nicola's teasing and he went away, shaking his head, but smiling at her wiles.

Adrian came into the morning room a few minutes later looking a bit harassed. Still, he took time to compliment Nicola on her appearance, which was as fetching as the early May morning. She was wearing a sprigged muslin frock and carrying a light cashmere shawl, her curls held by a fillet off her face, which glowed with mischief and excitement.

"Now what do you want to see me about, Nicola. I cannot spare much time. I have an appointment with the Marquis at half after eleven." He said this with an air of gracious conde-

scension that annoyed Nicola but she was prepared to overlook it in view of her eagerness to tell him of her suspicions.
She realized that he might not be receptive if he had decided
it would behoove him to treat the Marquis carefully in case
he agreed to sponsor his tunnel scheme.

"Well, I am glad to hear that. It will give you an opportunity
to observe him after I have told you my suspicions." Nicola
then proceeded to explain why she thought Lord Cranbourne
might be the mastermind behind these incursions by the highwaymen.

Adrian heard her out tolerantly, but raised his eyebrows to
signify he thought her ideas were nonsensical.

"Really, Nicky, what put this maggot in your head? The
Marquis is a man of wealth and standing. Why would he endanger his position by such a foolhardy jape? He does not
need the money."

"He's an adventurer and probably bored with playing the
role of a country squire. What could be more exciting than
robbing coaches? I have heard that several young sprigs of
the gentry have tried their hand at it. It's not so outrageous. I
think it might be great fun."

"Not to a man like Lord Cranbourne, believe me." Adrian
had a dilemma. It was not in his interest to antagonize Nicola,
but neither could he accept her wild notions about the Marquis. He wanted the man to invest in his tunnel.

Nicola, who could easily read his thoughts, hastened to
reassure him. "Of course I think it would be marvelous if he
did sponsor the tunnel, but I really doubt it is possible. I know
you must treat him with care, but you might also be able to
ferret out some indication that he was involved with the highwaymen."

"In the first place he could hardly have robbed your coach
the other evening when he was the man who rescued you."
Adrian felt this was a reasonable stance to adopt.

"Oh, he might just have done that to lull our suspicions.

Ours was probably the wrong coach and he realized it in time to warn his confederates."

"Unlikely." Adrian was now worried that Nicola was serious about this latest bee in her bonnet and must be discouraged. He thought the best way to distract her would be to tell her of the latest developments about the tunnel.

"As soon as I have seen the Marquis I must be off to London. I have already informed your parents that I will be absent for a few days on business. You see, my partner has discovered the original plans of Albert Mathieu who suggested the tunnel in 1803. Detailed plans, they are for two parallel tunnels each large enough for the grandest coaches with ventilation chimneys at suitable intervals. Midway there was to be a man-made island with food, lodging and stables. But you know all that. Now we have his ideas on how to solve the engineering problems which are formidable."

"That's exciting, Adrian. And you can use these plans as a selling point with the Marquis. He might just be intrigued enough with the tunnel to give up his criminal activities."

"Oh, Nicky, I think you must disabuse yourself of that idea." As Adrian spoke the words he realized he was making no impact. Nicola disliked the Marquis, which was in itself an encouragement, but she must not create a scandal by bruiting her notion of him as a highwayman around the neighborhood.

"Unless you have proof you could create a scandal and he might even sue you for slander, which your father might take in disgust."

"Don't be so cautious, Adrian. And, of course, I know we must have proof. If you will not help me find it I will endeavor to do so myself." Nicola was disappointed at the reception of her brilliant idea to link the Marquis to the highwaymen's depredations.

Really worried now, Adrian pleaded. "Promise me you will do nothing definite until I return and then I will try to help you, although I think you are wrong. You know how much I value your support and I would do nothing to make you take me in dislike but this whole business seems unlikely to me." Adrian was determined to cover all his bases. He had been startled by Nicola's suggestion concerning the Marquis but he must keep in her good graces. So much was at stake.

"Well, I can't promise that, Adrian, but I will promise to go carefully. Now good luck with your interview. Have you had your phaeton brought around? You must not be late. I suspect the Marquis is a man who would not appreciate unpunctuality."

"Yes, indeed. Now, try to stay out of trouble." Adrian grasped her hand and wondered if he should take further liberties, but before he could venture any, Paxton appeared at the door to announce his vehicle was waiting. Nicola waved him off feeling a bit let down, but quickly recovered her spirits. After luncheon she would go for a long ride and plot her next move.

Julia returned from church with high praise for the courtesy and attention of Mr. Moffett. She even had a good word for Miss Moffett, whom she thought the epitome of Christian benevolence, a description Nicola found amusing.

In the midst of her own concentration of the unmasking of the Marquis she had spared little time for her cousin. Now it occurred to her that Julia had her sights set on Reginald Moffett as a possible husband. Much as she thought they deserved each other she could not contemplate the idea of having Julia as a permanent member of their small society. Then she reproved herself for such uncharitable thoughts. Julia was definitely in pursuit of a husband and if Reginald was the only candidate on her horizon, who could blame her. Far better she concentrate on the Rev. Mr. Moffett than continue to annoy Ned with her simperings and sighings. Nicola considered her cousin a trial but realized the girl had not had an easy life, the companion of an irritable and complaining mother, little money and less charm. Good luck to her in her attempt to attach Mr. Moffett. However, she struggled to contain her patience when her cousin insisted on engaging her in a confidential chat about her prospects, not that she put it quite so bluntly.

Mrs. Wynstan escaped to her myriad household duties and left the girls alone, saying brightly to Nicola, "Nicky, you really have been most lax in your duty toward your cousin. She has been with us for over a week and I know she has much to discuss with you." This motherly advice was given with a stern glance, a reminder that she expected her daughter to behave with forbearance toward their guest. Since Julia was always very careful in her attentions toward Mrs. Wynstan that lady had rarely seen the darker side of her character, the malicious envy and caustic comments that Nicola had often endured.

But today Julia was all sweetness. She wanted information from Nicola and was prepared to swallow her resentment to obtain it.

"Nicky, do tell me about Mr. Moffett. I certainly have no wish to embarrass you, but I gather he has paid you some attentions." Julia managed to inject a girlish plea into her voice in an attempt to disarm her cousin.

"Well, yes, you could say that. He made me an offer which I promptly refused, so you might say he is available. I think he needs a wife. That vinegary aunt of his must be a trying companion and she does not add to his consequence with the villagers." Nicola, anxious to get to the stables, was not prepared to encourage a roundabout approach to what she sensed was on her cousin's mind.

"Of course, I can see you might not suit, but he appears to be a very respectable devout man."

"Yes, and he possesses a small private income, always an attraction in a vicar."

"The vicarage is a pleasant house, commodious and well finished. And he keeps three servants and a carriage so I thought he must be well established." Evidently Julia had learned a good deal in her short visit to the church.

"I really know very little about him. He has only been here a few years, came while I was still at school, and appointed by the old Marquis who held the living." Nicola nobly resisted saying that she thought him a prosy bore with an undeserved good opinion of himself and a patronizing view of women.

"Do you think it will take him some time to recover from your rejection of him?" Julia was shrewd enough to realize that few men would consider her a suitable substitute for her cousin in the marriage stakes.

"No time at all. I believe he badly needs a wife. A bachelor vicar is not much of a draw in a small village and a wife could take many duties off his shoulders."

"Oh, I agree. And what could be more satisfying than having the opportunity to serve the less fortunate in a Christian way as a helpmate to a man of the cloth."

Nicola, accepting that Julia now saw it as her role to don a cloak of piety, was not mean enough to accuse her cousin of hypocrisy. On consideration she thought that Mr. Moffett and Julia were well suited.

"I think your best plan, Julia, is to make yourself agreeable to Miss Moffett. She can be difficult but I am sure once Mr. Moffett sees your adaptability he will be attracted."

Julia did not know quite how to accept this advice. Her immediate reaction was to give some scathing reply, but for once, prudence held sway, and she bit her tongue.

"Well, of course, I would not want it to appear that I am husband hunting, so unattractive, but I do think we would suit," Julia simpered. Nicola thought she was very good at deceiving herself and excellent at simpering, but the whole subject of Julia's efforts to lure Mr. Moffett into the parson's mousetrap caused her little concern. Of course, having Julia permanently on the doorstep did not appeal.

"If you are sure you don't mind, or want to change your mind," Julia spoke tentatively.

"Not at all, Julia. I would be delighted if you could bring yourself to accept Mr. Moffett. Don't consider me for a moment, and now I must be off. I know you don't like riding or I would ask you to accompany me." A downright lie, for Nicola could think of little that held less appeal.

"You know I am a very indifferent rider, Nicky, not having your opportunities to learn at an early age."

Ignoring this innuendo that as a poor relation Julia lacked her cousin's advantages, Nicola said, "Well, I'll be off then." She barely restrained adding "Good hunting" for she knew Julia had no sense of humor.

Sometime later, cantering out of the stables on Bluebelle, she thought back on the conversation and gave a chuckle. Poor Julia, her options were not many. She could not blame her for trying to take what advantage she could from the situation. Nicola was sensible and perceptive enough to accept that her own lot had fallen on kindly paths, manageable parents, plenty of money and through no efforts of her own, a beauty and personality attractive to many men. If she were in Julia's position she hoped she would have a little more resolution, offer herself as a governess or companion, although both those positions held perils. For most girls a respectable marriage was the only answer, and she could not fault Julia for trying to secure one even if she thought her cousin a drab and a bore. Men seemed to prefer amenable wives and cared little for their characters. Actually Julia was at last evidencing some sense in trying to settle her future. She would do what she could to assist her.

By the time she had decided on this charitable effort she had ridden almost to the boundary of her father's estate. This time she would not chance a meeting with the Marquis but stay on the Wynstan boundary of the woods. A large crop of mature oaks spread beyond the last tilled fields, the dividing line between the Cranbourne property and the Wynstan's, unmarked in the small forest. It was shadowy and mysterious in the woods but not as silent, as small animals and birds made their presence felt.

Nicola had always found the woods soothing but today she

felt an unusual nervousness. She could not account for this unfamiliar reaction. She enjoyed riding alone and had never felt fear of any kind. Perhaps her unsettled state of mind was due to recent events, the aborted attack of the highwaymen, the pathetic quest of her cousin for a husband, but most of all, she laid her unrest at the Marquis's door.

The man was a menace, criticizing her, teasing and sneering and then the ultimate transgression, that kiss. He was capable of incivility and worse. Certainly her suspicion of his illegal activity was not beyond reason. But how was he to be brought to justice? Ambling along on Bluebelle, not noticing her surroundings, Nicola was unprepared for her mare suddenly rearing before a dark figure that loomed out of a dense thicket to the right of the path. He reached out a hand and jerked Bluebelle's reins, causing her to rear and throw Nicola to the ground.

"What have we here, a pretty little maid ripe for the plucking, eh?" he leered standing over Nicola as she struggled to her feet and then grasping her with one dirty hand.

He was a frightening figure, rough, unshaven, with uncouth features and menacing bloodshot eyes. She struggled from his tightening hand and let out a piercing scream.

"Whatcha want to bawl like that for? All I want is a little kiss." And the man drew her closer putting one dirty callused hand over her mouth. Nicola kicked out at him, her booted foot making contact on his shins and he dropped her with a curse. Before he could take any revenge, and she knew that was what he intended, the sound of a horseman broke the silence and suddenly he turned and ran. Nicola stood shaking, wondering who her rescuer could be. She stamped her foot in vexation as she saw the Marquis ride onto the path. Whatever fear she might have felt was swamped by her humiliation in once again being in a situation he would turn to his advantage.

"In trouble, Miss Wynstan? That was a scream I just heard."

He reined in his horse and looked down at her with some emotion she could not decipher.

"A man burst from the woods and grabbed Bluebelle's reins. She bucked me off and he was about to assault me when he heard your horse and rushed off over there to the left." She tried to sound composed, as if being attacked by a rogue was an ordinary occurrence not beyond her powers to handle, but the Marquis was not deceived.

"I never knew such a girl for having adventures. I thought you had learned your lesson. What are you doing romping about without a groom?" Not waiting for her answer, he leapt from his horse and tied the animal to a tree, coming up to her and looking searchingly into her face.

"I like riding alone and I would never suspect my father's woods to hide a varlet. I wonder what he was doing here. He might have been one of those highwaymen." She had banished any fright and determined to behave as if assaulting men were somehow the Marquis's responsibility.

He laughed. "I think you believe I imported the man here for my own nefarious purposes."

Since that was exactly what she thought, Nicola had difficulty in hiding her suspicions.

"I've ridden here for years and never met any strangers."

"We live in perilous times. There are lots of vagrants and discharged soldiers living rough on the road. One probably wandered in here looking for game or perhaps he was a local poacher. You have no one but yourself to blame, acting as a hoyden. But come, you have had a fright. I should not be upbraiding you. Allow me to escort you back home."

Not reassured by his explanation, Nicola was about to demur, but her horse had recovered her surprise at the recent incursion and nuzzled her mistress as if in apology. Before the Marquis could intervene, Nicola had mounted her mare without assistance and prepared to turn back.

"Thank you, my lord, but I am sure I will encounter no other villains."

"Aside from me, you mean. You are an ungrateful girl, but I will overlook it." The Marquis appeared to find the whole incident amusing, which forced Nicola to retreat into aloofness. She ignored him as he trotted amicably by her side from the woods and toward the Wynstan fields.

Ten

"I do approve of a female who doesn't chatter foolishly, Miss Wynstan, but don't you think a few words might be appropriate?" The Marquis gave her a look she had no trouble interpreting. He not only enjoyed teasing her but now he was faulting her manners. Actually, she was yearning to ask him the result of his interview with Adrian but she would not give him the satisfaction of rebuffing her again.

"I find I have little to say to you, my lord. Aside from thanking you once again for coming to my rescue. Courtesy demands that I do that."

If the Marquis felt annoyed by her coolness he ignored it. "This sparring is all very well for a time, you know, but after a while it becomes tedious. I cannot imagine what I have done to put you in such a pet."

Reddening but determined not to flare out at him, Nicola held her temper. "I am not in a pet, my lord, but I do not like being patronized nor finding myself an object of your amusement."

"Oh, dear, I can see you have taken me in some dislike. They do say that gratitude is an uncomfortable emotion for the one who owes it."

"You are an uncomfortable man." Nicola realized she had gone beyond the bounds of courtesy and tightened her lips. She would not say another word. All he did was twist her arguments and try to humiliate her.

"Well, you know, I have to admit you are quite correct

there. But I am really trying to place myself in your good offices."

"I can't see why." Despite herself Nicola blurted out this rejoinder.

"I don't think I will tell you why just now. Perhaps when our acquaintance has deepened I will oblige. And here we are at your home. Just in time or I might be in danger of rousing you to further criticism of my character. As it is I am most undone."

You are not, Nicola said to herself. *You enjoy putting me in an untenable position. And now I will have to invite you in for politeness demands no less.*

Two grooms came running to relieve them of their horses and this time the Marquis was prompt to assist her to dismount. Placing his hands on her waist he lifted her easily from the saddle. She refused to admit that proximity to the man stirred her senses, and told herself that anger made her flush.

"Do come in, my lord. I am sure my father will want to hear all about your rescue of me. Once again, we are in your debt."

"Nicely spoken, Miss Wynstan, although I can see it pained you to offer those kind words. I do wish to see the General."

Paxton, who had appeared the moment they reached the steps of the house, indicated that the General and Mrs. Wynstan were in the drawing room entertaining Sir Charles and Lady Mumford.

"Thank you, Paxton. If you will announce Lord Cranbourne, I will just go upstairs and change." Nicola had adopted a stiff hostess air. Surely the Marquis would not mock her in front of Paxton. He gave her an understanding look but meekly followed Paxton toward the drawing room as Nicola ran upstairs. On the landing she turned and saw him watching her with what she considered an enigmatic smile. Irritating as he was, he also intrigued her, but she was reluctant to admit that. She hurried into her bedroom and hoped that by the time she had changed and joined her parents he would have taken his leave.

However, when she entered the drawing room a half an hour later, dressed in a demure white dimity frock laced with pink ribbons and flounced at the hem, he was sitting quite at his ease on the sofa next to Mrs. Wynstan and discussing Edmund Kean, the actor. He stood politely on her arrival but then ignored her. Both Lady Mumford and her mother, she noticed, appeared to be charmed by his conversation and his attentions. Evidently he saved his manners for the drawing room, Nicola decided, then smiled. She was in a pet, just as he had accused her of being.

"I do miss London," Mrs. Wynstan admitted, "but the General prefers the country."

"Dirty noisy place filled with a lot of peacocks and layabouts," the General never shied away from expressing his opinion.

"I never feel safe in London," Lady Mumford said.

Sir Charles insisted that London was no worse than the country. They had been discussing the highwaymen before the Marquis's arrival.

"This incursion is very recent, you know." Sir Charles went on to explain that they had never had much crime in their corner of Sussex. He took his responsibilities as a justice of the peace very seriously.

"Agitators are stirring up the farm workers. They come from the north and bring their seditious lies with them," said the General.

"Poor devils are starving. Look what happened at Peterloo," the Marquis suggested and earned a look of approval from Nicola. She was surprised that he cared about such matters. She decided he had said nothing yet about the man who had assaulted her in the woods. He probably did not want to alarm Lady Mumford and her mother.

"Now that my cousin is in residence I feel I must repay the hospitality I have received in the neighborhood. I am planning a dinner party and a small dance. I so hope you will all be able to attend," the Marquis invited the company.

"How kind," Lady Mumford approved. She was a very social woman and, like Mrs. Wynstan, yearned for another London season.

"Yes, indeed. It will be lovely to have the Hall open again to guests. During the old Marquis's declining years he was not up to entertaining much." The ladies were overcome with visions of splendid routs, dinners and balls in their country retreat.

"I think in about a fortnight, then. I will count on you all." The Marquis stood, signifying he would now take his leave. He bowed over the ladies' hands, including Julia and Nicola, and then turned to the General.

"There is a private matter I would like to discuss with you, sir, if you can spare me the time."

"Of course, of course." The General welcomed this signal that his advice was valued. Since the Marquis and the General would be occupied, the Mumfords politely decided that they must call for their carriage and be on their way. Farewells were said, and promises of a meeting soon. Mrs. Wynstan accompanied the Mumfords to the hall and Nicola and Julia were left alone in the drawing room.

"I do think the Marquis is handsome, and fascinating, too, don't you, Nicky?" Julia asked.

After the Marquis, Nicola could understand Mr. Moffett might seem less appealing.

"I don't think he's a marrying man, Julia."

"Oh, Nicky, what a tease you are, as if he would ever look at me. But I think he is so romantic."

Thoroughly disgusted with Julia's arch comments about the Marquis, Nicola had little interest in pursuing the conversation. However, Julia had not exhausted the topic.

"I think it's ever so exciting that he is planning a ball. Of course, I have attended few such high-flown occasions. And I have nothing elegant enough to wear, not that anyone will notice me. You have so much experience in these affairs, Nicky, you must tell me how to go on," Julia beseeched ingratiatingly.

"It's not a ball, Julia, just a country dance and nothing to tax either your social skills or your wardrobe. Now, I must write some letters." By giving this time-honored excuse, Nicola was able to make her escape.

Crossing the hall she met her father who had just waved off the Marquis. Remembering the subject of his recent conversation he beckoned his daughter.

"I want to have a talk with you, Nicola."

Oh dear, when he called her Nicola she knew she was in for a raking about her lonely rides. She sighed and reluctantly followed her father into the library. He sat down behind his desk and looked at her as if she were a rebellious subaltern who had disobeyed orders. For once, cajolery and smiles would not help, his attitude promised.

"Sit down. I am most dismayed at what the Marquis had just told me. It seems we are no longer safe, even on our own property. This rogue who attacked you could have seriously injured you, or even worse." The General was really disturbed but had no intention of voicing his secret fear, that his daughter could have been violated by the ruffian. The Marquis had made it clear that he thought the General was too obliging a father and must keep a tighter rein on his wayward daughter. The thought of what she had just escaped appalled the General but he was reluctant to explain to Nicola just what her reckless behavior might lead to. Still, he was a man who never shirked his duty.

"Nicky, you must see you cannot ride about without a groom in this harum-scarum manner. With highwaymen in the district and idle vagrants you are in danger."

"Oh, I do see, Father. I'm not stupid, but until today it never crossed my mind that any strange ruffian would invade our land." Nicola did not want to admit she had been thoroughly frightened by the man's attack, and was indeed grateful to the Marquis for her rescue.

"You must promise me that you will take George or one of the other grooms with you when you ride. I don't want to forbid you riding. I know how much you enjoy it but until these villains are apprehended you must take care. I think we won't tell your mother of this latest incident. She would worry herself into a megrim."

Fair-minded, Nicola had to accede and promised her father she would take a groom with her in future although she hated the curb on her freedom. She realized she should be grateful to the Marquis but she disliked him for being the cause of her restrictions. She could imagine what he had said to her father and how embarrassed the poor man had been by this criticism of his parental responsibility. She wished with all her heart that the Marquis had remained on the other side of the world. He was causing her all sorts of problems.

The General, reassured, rose from his desk and gruffly embraced his daughter. "I couldn't bear it if anything happened to you, Nicky."

"You're an old bear, but I love you, Papa," she said, calling him by the name she had used in childhood. They parted affectionately. But her father's concern and embarrassment just added to the list of shortcomings she attributed to the Marquis. She would not allow the man to dictate to her as he seemed determined to do. But she had to accept her father's strictures. She did not want to cause him worry. Despite the General's outward facade of a resolute domineering character he was really softhearted and manageable, a victim of his real affection for his children, and Nicola would not cause him pain.

The Marquis, riding home slowly and reviewing his talk with the General, wondered if he had been vehement enough in his warnings. He had told the General he would take precautions himself and try to discover the whereabouts of the ruffian who had attacked Nicola. But, really, the girl was a hoyden, with no idea of how to go on. After two seasons in

London where she had been a nonpareil she thought she could ride roughshod over every man she met. She ignored the rules of proper behavior and was then surprised when her actions resulted in ugly situations. She refused to accept her vulnerability. He admired her spirit and independence but she needed to be protected no mailer how much she scorned such need. She was an unusual girl who had stirred his interest, much as he loathed the thought.

Nicola was correct in her assessment to Julia. He was not a man who intended to be caught in the parson's mousetrap. Foolish passion had scarred his youth and he was too wily now to surrender to a fleeting attraction. For years he had dodged eager maidens with marriage on their minds, and managed demanding mistresses without ever engaging his heart. He would not be embroiled in a country romance where the only outcome would lead to just that unenviable state. Too bad that Miss Wynstan was such a respectable girl with protective parents. She would have made a fascinating member of the muslin set, but he was too experienced to be lured into a net of her contriving. Then the Marquis gave a somewhat bitter laugh. The girl disliked him and offered no threat. He was a fool to consider her in any role. Spurring his horse he rode recklessly forward determined to banish all sorts of the disturbing Miss Wynstan from his mind.

Both the Marquis and the General would have been alarmed and their worst fears justified if they had known of the rendezvous being held by the highwaymen and their leader not ten miles from their estates. Nicola's attacker was indeed one of this company and had escaped from the woods to meet his confederates in an abandoned isolated farmhouse near Cranbourne village.

"You're a fool, Jeb, wandering around that lord's land, and just fortunate that the nob didn't follow you. Then you'd've been for the chop." One of the miscreant's companions growled at him. "And what's worse you could have led us all to the hangman."

"Just for a silly mort, too. There's plenty of them about. No need to cast your paws on one of the gentry."

"Quite right." Their leader added his complaint to the general muttering. "We're in this to get gold, not women."

"No harm done," Jeb excused himself. He didn't like the reproof. "And about that gold. Haven't seen much since the Chichester doings. Maybe we ought to move over to Portsmouth."

"Too dangerous. There's soldiers there and we don't need the damn army on our tails."

Another bottle was cracked and arguments ensued as to their next robbery. The three rogues were discharged veterans of Wellington's "infamous army" and found peace not to their taste after the brutal excitements of campaigns and battle. But they were in some awe of their leader, a different type, who had brains and energy. A clever cove, and they were under his spell. The trio settled down between hearty quaffs to listen to his plans. He treated them with contempt for they were mere instruments in his grand plan to amass enough money to finance his real intentions, of which they had no inkling.

"We failed in that last venture because of His Lordship, but our next job will be more successful—the London mail."

Some doubts were offered as to the feasibility of this raid but the leader quickly quashed any rebellion and told the villains just how the robbery would be managed. Then, eager to rid himself of their brutish company, he left them to their drinking. He had more important interviews to conduct.

But as he rode away from the rendezvous, some of the concern he had hidden from his cohorts surfaced. He did not like this business of Jeb attacking the girl in the woods. Jeb had tried to explain that he was scouting the land in preparation for a robbery, but the leader was not convinced. Stupid lout, probably had every intention of raping the lady, and that would have altered all his careful arrangements. He had not connived and masqueraded so masterfully to have his intricate plot brought down by some crude rogue with animal passions. Well, he had enough guile and skill to defeat that noble lord and anyone else who interfered with his mission. Satisfied with his own ingenuity and armored with conceit he rode on toward London. Before long he would be able to rid himself of these stupid villains and be set for life, his dreams realized and a fortune in his pocket. No perishing lord or foolish female would prevent him attaining his goal.

Eleven

A fortnight had passed since Nicola had been attacked in the woods, and true to her promise she had allowed George to accompany her on her daily rides. She had not encountered the Marquis on these outings. She understood from his cousin, who had come to tea, that he had gone to London. Nicola, relieved to hear this, did not connect the feeling of flatness she had been experiencing lately with his absence. The incident of the rogue in the woods had only strengthened her belief that Lord Cranbourne might be the leader of the highwaymen. Why else was the man lurking around his estate? She confided her belief again to Adrian who also had a budget of news.

"You may be right about the Marquis, Nicky. There does seem to be evidence that rather favors him in the role, but somehow I can't envisage it."

"Is he in London checking up on your tunnel proposition, do you suppose?" Nicola had been all agog to hear of Adrian's interview with the Marquis but he had been strangely reticent on the meeting.

"Perhaps. He's a sardonic devil, didn't show much interest in sponsoring the tunnel, but neither did he turn down my suggestion that he might invest in the company being formed to promote it. He must have a tidy fortune. He appears very knowledgeable about the spice and tea trade in Asia. He'd be a sharp bargainer in any trade, I'm sure. Rather odd that most aristocrats think collecting money beneath them. They are only interested in spending it."

"I suppose the Marquis had to earn some, after his family cast him off due to the scandal." Nicola was honest enough to admit that she thought the Marquis had shown a lot of courage and cleverness in making his way in a hostile world. She was not so mean and petty as to deny him his due. And she remembered, too, that the late Marquis had appeared to admire his heir despite his youthful sins. "Shows some spirit and determination," he had confided to Nicola. "My brother was a straitlaced Puritan, never forgave the boy, but I thought he showed enterprise." The late Marquis, with whom Nicola was a favorite, had been eager to discuss his heir's business acumen but carefully never discussed the scandal that had driven him to such exertions. He might not have been as priggish as his brother but he was an old-fashioned courtly gentleman who had strict ideas about protecting young females. Nicola, thinking of the last lonely days of the old Marquis, wished he could have known his heir. They would both have benefited from the companionship.

"Well, he made it quite clear to me he would not think of investing in the tunnel scheme until he had investigated it more thoroughly. Can't blame him for that and he did not definitely refuse me." Adrian cut across Nicola's musings with a report of the interview and then went on to describe his own efforts in London to secure the original plans of the tunnel and seek other financing. In that, she suspected, he had not been too successful.

For some reason Nicola found her own enthusiasm for the project waning. She wondered if Adrian had the wits to see the scheme through. He did a lot of supposing and projecting but she noticed that he had really accomplished little toward his goal. And she was beginning to wonder, too, how long he intended to remain at the manor. Her parents were hospitable but he had been here now over three weeks except for the few days he had been in London. He would not be realizing his dreams by idling in Sussex. London was where he should be, unless he had some reason to suppose the Marquis could be persuaded to advance him money. Nicola discounted this possibility. From what she knew of the Marquis it seemed extremely doubtful.

As if Adrian had sensed her withdrawal he mentioned that he might be returning to London very soon. "I would not want to outstay my welcome," he insisted one evening at dinner, casting a wary look at the General. Despite his best efforts Adrian was aware that Nicola's father had never accepted him. Even Ned, who normally was the most gregarious of fellows, kept his distance.

"We hope you will at least stay until the Marquis's dance this Saturday," Mrs. Wynstan said, her kind nature touched by Adrian's attempts to please and the knowledge that he had not been received with any enthusiasm by the men of her family.

"Oh, yes, Mr. Pettifer, you would not want to miss the Marquis's dance. There will be a full orchestra, I understand, and over a hundred guests." Julia could not imagine how any right thinking person, fortunate enough to be included in such an affair, could possibly refuse.

"And don't forget the lobster patties and jellies, Julia," Nicola could not resist twitting her cousin and then, as was her usual reaction, felt ashamed of herself.

"Well, the lobster patties are an inducement, Miss Overton. And if my generous hosts do not think I have become a nuisance I would very much like to attend, and dance with you, too."

Julia blushed and preened herself. She thought she might have to reconsider her pursuit of Mr. Moffett if Mr. Pettifer showed any interest. He was more appealing if not quite safe. Safety was an important asset in any man booked for the husband stakes, Julia had decided. Her efforts to lure Mr. Moffett into a proposal had borne some fruit but as yet he had not taken the final fence.

Adrian, during this discussion of the dance and his remaining for it, had carefully not glanced at the General. Actually he was a bit afraid of the old soldier, who had such antiquated ideas about modern life but managed somehow to instill respect and affection in his son and daughter, neither of them meek or subservient by nature. Whatever his faults the General did not lack courage, and Adrian suspected he had a shrewd knowledge of men. That was what caused him concern. It suited his purposes to remain at the manor for some time so he would do nothing to antagonize the General.

"Did you hear, Father, that there had been another robbery? The highwaymen attacked the mail coach on the Lewes road, and this time Lord Cranbourne was not on hand to drive them off." Ned ignored his father's frown. He saw no reason why the topic should not be introduced at the dinner table. It was common gossip in the village and stable.

"Of course, I heard, Ned, but I did not want to alarm your mother."

"It's more than twenty-five miles away. Could they be the same ruffians that held us up?" Nicola asked.

"Possibly. It's only a few hours ride on good horses." Ned viewed the whole highway robbery menace as an adventure, and rather admired the audacity of the perpetrators.

Nicola was silent but she was thinking that the Marquis had been absent for some days, plenty of time to lead this latest foray. The mail coach robbery deepened her suspicion of him.

"There's talk of calling out the army," Ned continued.

"Stupid idea. How could the soldiers be alerted in time to catch the robbers? Unless they had some advance notice of where the attempts would be made." The General had a certain respect for the intelligence service of the army, but thought the deployment of the forces on such a fruitless task a waste of time.

"Well, at least they have left our neighborhood," Mrs. Wynstan commented.

"I wonder if they have learned of the Marquis's entertainment. Lots of ripe pickings from the guests on that night, I vow." Ned delighted in stirring up excitement.

"Oh, Ned, why would you want to frighten us so?" wailed Julia.

"That's enough of that, Ned. Can't have you upsetting the ladies. There is no danger, my dear," the General assured his wife and frowned at his son. "It's less than an hour to Cranbourne's and you can be sure we will be looking out for any trouble."

Later that evening Nicola drew Ned into the morning room while the rest of the company was still in the drawing room and tried to learn more of the incident of the mail coach. He was happy to oblige, but belatedly remembered his father telling him about the attack on Nicky in the woods. His father had warned him not to discuss the matter but he could never keep a secret from his sister.

"Are you afraid because of what happened in the woods, Nicky? I know it was a dreadful experience and most providential that the Marquis was on hand."

"But was it providential? Could not the Marquis be involved with the highwaymen, even their leader? He might need money or even just do the business for the thrill of it." Nicola was prepared for Ned to laugh away her idea, but to her surprise he appeared to consider it.

"I shouldn't think he was short of funds, made quite a fortune in the East, you know. But he may have done it for the adventure. I happen to know of two young noble sprigs who tried it in Hampshire. Not beyond the realms of possibility."

"If he is involved we should expose him. It's our duty. We have to consider the neighbors like the Mumfords."

"Nicky, I am surprised at you. I never thought you were a girl for the proprieties. I seem to remember tales of a curricle race in Hyde Park that raised a few eyebrows," Ned teased.

"A harmless jape. Had the parents in a bit of a fret but Elizabeth and I committed no crime." Nicola defended herself and the friend whom she had challenged to the race.

"What has happened to Elizabeth? I thought her quite a promising girl and expected her to be visiting you during my leave." Ned tossed out this supposition casually. It would never do for Nicola to think he had any but the vaguest interest in her friend.

"I invited her but she was promised to the Redmonds in Dorset and then Julia arrived. Sorry you are disappointed." She looked slyly at her brother wondering if he had a tendresse for Elizabeth. She would look with favor on a match between them.

"Not really, although I wouldn't mind meeting her again. And I agree asking anyone to visit while Julia is here would be demanding a great deal from the friendship."

"Poor Julia. If only we could marry her off."

"What nodcock would have her? Imagine facing that simper across the breakfast table for the rest of your life." Ned gave a mock shudder.

"You'd best be wary, Ned. Don't let Julia lure you into a compromising position. I think she still has you in her sights, despite Mr. Moffett."

"Ugh," Ned shuddered. "She really is too much. Mother lets her familial obligations overcome her at times. And if she marries Moffett we will have her playing the role of the whingeing vicar's wife on our doorstep."

"True. Poor Julia, no one wants her." Nicola sighed, realizing that every discussion about her cousin ended up with the "Poor Julia" tag, damning if true. Abandoning Julia she tried to interest Ned in some plan to expose the Marquis as a highwayman but concluded he did not really seem convinced that their noble neighbor was the culprit.

While Nicola was plotting to gain allies in her efforts to reveal the Marquis's perfidy as a highwayman, her adversary, ignorant of her object, was having luncheon with Henry Addington, Viscount Sidmouth, Home Secretary in the Liverpool cabinet.

The two met at White's, which despite Lord Cranbourne's checkered past, had admitted him as a member when he inherited the title. The ton forgave the most blatant sins when the culprit was a handsome, wealthy and titled member of society. The Marquis was not on easy terms with Addington who was a bit of a prig, but the tunnel scheme came under the Home Office and the Marquis believed in going to the top for information. Not that he had much in common with the conservative Sidmouth, the minister responsible for the repressive actions taken after the Peterloo Massacre that had aroused the nation.

"This tunnel business is all a hum, you know, Cranbourne." Sidmouth spoke with scorn while picking at his beefsteak. He suffered from dyspepsia.

"You mean it's a pipe dream. My informant insists it's perfectly possible, has the engineering designs to prove it."

"Nonsense. His Majesty's government would never allow it. We don't want the French brought into Sussex. We fought a costly war to keep them in their place, which is across the Channel. Even if some fool could raise the funds to build it, it would be doomed. The Duke is strongly opposed, you know."

"Then the investors would never recover their money, another South Sea Bubble perhaps." The Marquis was referring to the giant failure in the previous century in which several members of the aristocracy had lost not only their fortunes but their reputations.

"An apt analogy. But, believe me, don't waste your guineas. It has no chance at all. Pitt favored it in 1802 but wiser heads prevailed. A great minister, Pitt, but no sense where finance was concerned." Sidmouth pursed his lips. His was a conservative cast of mind, not eager to entertain a project that hinted at change in the status quo.

"Well, I must be guided by your superior knowledge, although I do believe someday we will have the tunnel." Cranbourne found Sidmouth's politics and general mien not to his taste but he was much too suave to give any hint of his dislike.

"Believe me the tunnel will never happen. Now, tell me, how are conditions in Sussex? Any trouble with your agricultural workers?" Sidmouth always feared another uprising from these disenfranchised and poorest members of the country.

Taking a deep draught of his claret the Marquis assured Sidmouth that his farm workers were causing no trouble. "The only disturbance in the neighborhood comes from highwaymen. We have had a rash of robberies."

"Yours is not the only report. We must insure safety on the public roads, and the local magistrates seem helpless. It may be a case for the army." Sidmouth was always in favor of putting down any disturbance with force, not accepting that economic or social conditions could be the root cause of crime. The Marquis could not agree but saw no use in arguing with such a hidebound Tory.

They parted with mutual expressions of esteem that hid their real feelings, Sidmouth to return to Whitehall and the Marquis to idle the afternoon away at the gaming tables where he had an unusual run of luck.

Returning later that evening to his rooms in the Albany, he decided he had done his duty toward the tunnel scheme and, whatever its merits, it appeared the project was a losing proposition. He had made some intensive inquiries into Adrian Pettifer's background and nothing he learned improved his opinion of that opportunist young man.

As he dressed for an evening at Astley's the Marquis wondered if Miss Wynstan was seriously interested in Pettifer. He had more faith in her intelligence than to think she would be taken in by what he now believed was a mountebank. Pettifer might be persuaded as to the worth of the tunnel but the Marquis was convinced the man saw the scheme as a vehicle for increasing his personal coffers. Any money raised would go

to provide Pettifer with a comfortable competence and his
investors would find themselves without a tunnel and their
money lost.

Unlike many of his fellow aristocrats the Marquis had no
disgust of trade or business. He had been quite clever along
those lines himself, but he recognized fraud when he met it.
Pettifer and his tunnel had a bad smell. He only hoped the
General had not been beguiled into endorsing it, but he had
a healthy respect for that old soldier's acumen. It was his
daughter that worried the Marquis and he found his irritation
rising at the knowledge that she was occupying too much of
his time and interest. What he needed was some frivolous and
undemanding feminine companionship and set out to find it.

At the manor before dinner that evening Adrian had an
uneasy feeling that his various plans needed some revision.
Affairs were coming to a climax and although he had an un-
warranted opinion of his ability to further matters to his advantage, his interview with the Marquis had raised doubts.
Lord Cranbourne was too astute, too experienced in matters
of business to be gulled. If he investigated Adrian's bona fides
it might mean trouble. Perhaps he had been unwise to approach the man for aid. Adrian walked a very fine line between
fraud and legal dodgy business practice. He was desperate for
money and thought his best method of achieving it would be
to make a provident marriage. A decent settlement could solve
his immediate problems. And if it also brought him an attractive and complaisant wife so much the better. It would be no
hardship to propose to Nicola but he must not delay. He believed she would accept him. She was fascinated with the
tunnel scheme and because of it found him a contrast to the
idle frivolous beaux who had courted her. She might be a bit
too spirited, but surely marriage would tame that reckless
streak. He had every faith that he could control her. His instinct told him she found him intriguing. Why else had she
invited him here? The General was far from approving, but
Adrian had noticed that Nicola managed her father to a treat.

Even if the General refused his consent she might be persuaded to elope. Once they were wed he doubted that the General would cast her off.

That mawkish emotion called love did not enter into Adrian's mind. Passion and the pleasures of the bed could not be denied but any deeper sentiment did not concern him. A man of little perception and much conceit, it never occurred to him that he could be disappointed.

Twelve

As the members of the Wynstan household prepared for the Cranbourne dance a few days later Nicola and Adrian were not alone in feeling a sense of anticipation. Julia was almost beside herself with excitement. Few such elegant entertainments had come her way, and she was determined to enjoy herself, despite some fears that she might spend the evening in the chaperones' corner. Nicola had given her a cerulean silk gown of exquisite cut with clever insets of seed pearls. The color flattered her and made the most of her limited assets. Seeing her in such a beautiful gown might impress Ned and Adrian and they would look upon her in a more favorable light. If they failed to appreciate her stylish appearance surely Mr. Moffett would be struck by her attractions and finally come up to the mark.

Ned, who had no idea that Julia entertained any thoughts of luring him into some declaration, and would have ridiculed the notion, was looking forward to renewing his acquaintance with the delectable Elizabeth Shillingford, one of his sister's bosom bows. She had written Nicky that she would be a house guest of the Mumfords for the dance and might then come to the Wynstans for a visit. He approved of the plan. Ned always enjoyed dancing, especially with a special partner. He would wear his regimentals. Girls were always impressed with a uniform.

Mrs. Wynstan, as always, thought of dances as an opportunity for Nicola to discover the man who might win her as a wife. Secretly she had hopes of the Marquis, although her daughter had made it quite evident she disliked the lord. But so often girls ended up marrying a man whom they at first had found unacceptable. Aside from her dreams of Nicola's impressive alliance, Mrs. Wynstan enjoyed the opportunity to preen in Nicola's reflected glory. Her daughter was always the most sought after partner at these affairs, either in London or the country. Other mothers envied her Nicola's popularity.

The General looked forward to a challenging evening of cards and airing his opinions of the state of the nation to his contemporaries, feeling that his martial experience gave him a commanding position in the county. He also looked forward to the supper that he expected would be lavish and the wine that he expected would be superior. He had a very good opinion of Cranbourne's taste. The General, too, was proud of his daughter and liked to see her as the belle of any gathering she attended. Unlike his wife he was in no hurry to see Nicola wed. He would miss her and felt that few men were worthy of such a prize. Thinking of future sons-in-law, he frowned. He hoped Nicola was not serious about this Pettifer fellow. There was a touch of the opportunist about the man. The General usually distrusted young men who had no visible means and had not served in the army. He could not see why Nicola found the chap attractive. He hoped Pettifer would be leaving before long. He had outstayed his welcome.

For Roger Forrest, donning his somewhat shabby evening clothes, the evening loomed as an ordeal. He did not dance well, and his status as a humble secretary in the Wynstans' home did not inspire much hope that any fair partner would honor him. He had wanted to refuse the invitation but the Wynstans' would have none of it, being unaware of his insecurity and fear of humiliation. They had been most kind to him, treating him as a member of the family, but others might not be so tolerant. Roger liked his work for the General and once over his first awe of his employer had developed a real fondness and appreciation of him. But he knew he did not shine in company and he wished he could have remained at home.

Adrian, shrugging himself into his black superfine dress coat, wished he had the means to employ a man. A valet would add to his consequence and would advise him on dress. He was not completely sure of this silk embroidered waistcoat. Beau Brummel had set the fashion for plain unadorned clothes and perhaps this one had a touch of vulgarity about it. So much depended on this evening. For Adrian had decided it was the perfect setting for his proposal. He had been a bit frustrated that Nicola had refused him the supper dance in advance. When he asked she had turned off his request that she did not want to commit herself. "There will be several old friends at the dance, I understand, and I want to hear all the on dits."

This reminder that there were other claimants for her hand did not please him. He had forgotten that Nicola had her pick of partners in the heady days of her London seasons. He would have several rivals. Still, he was on the scene, a decided advantage. Adrian had an inflated opinion of his standing with Nicola but occasionally doubts surfaced. He realized he would have to leave the Wynstans after this party and before he went he wanted Nicky's promise to marry him. He would tread carefully.

Nicola was approaching the evening with a certain apprehension. On the one hand she wanted to see the Marquis again, for despite her protestations that the man was impossible, arrogant and critical of her, he was challenging. Of course, she had no romantic emotions toward him. But somehow when they engaged in their duels she felt alive, involved, and fascinated. Foolish, really, for the man brought out the worst in her. Instead of reacting to his gibes she should remain poised, cool, aloof, slightly amused, but somehow she never managed to bring off this desirable manner.

She was relieved when Betsy arrived to help her into her gown, an ivory silk of gossamer lightness, with a silver gauze overdress. Even Miss Moffett would approve for the dress accented her youthful charms and was the fashionable color so admired by the critical arbiter. The gown had a modest décolletage and slight puffed sleeves. With it Nicola wore her matched pearls and a simple silver fillet holding back her curls. Betsy's approval, as usual, was unrestrained.

"Oh, Miss Nicola, you look lovely. Every man will want to lead you onto the floor. That poor Miss Overton has done herself up well, but she's not a match on you."

"Thank you, Betsy. I think I will do."

"No one to touch you, miss. Now, here's your reticule and your shawl." She handed her mistress a small beaded purse and a wrap of silver tissue, then stood back in admiration. Betsy thought herself fortunate to have such a lovely mistress, and kind besides, not forever carping like that Miss Julia, of whom Betsy had the poorest opinion.

Ned and Adrian were to take Ned's curricle, leaving the family chaise for the parents and the girls so there would not be a crush. Roger Forrest was riding alone to Cranbourne Hall. Adrian had not liked this arrangement but thought it prudent not to insist on riding in the coach. He would have liked the chance to settle the question of his dances with Nicola but sensed she would not be receptive to any insistence on his prior claims. Well, after this evening, all that would change.

Nicola was strangely quiet on the ride to the Hall, barely hearing her mother and Julia atwitter with their anticipation of the evening. Her father noticed her unusual silence.

"Not looking forward to this entertainment, Nicky?" he asked, wondering if she were sickening or something for it was most unlike her.

"Oh, it will be nice to see Elizabeth and some of my London friends again. I have been out of touch for some months and letters are not the same."

Could she be pining over some young buck? The General did not like the thought, especially if it were that Pettifer. But surely the fellow had not disappointed her. If only he could be certain of how she reacted to the man. The General sensed that his would be an unenviable position if Pettifer asked him for Nicky's hand. Of course, he would refuse, but perhaps she really cared for the chap, and the General hated the idea of quarreling with his daughter. Tonight she would renew her acquaintance with those London bucks and might realize that Pettifer was not so grand after all. The General had found the weeks of biting his tongue about Pettifer a strain and longed for his departure. But if he were Nicky's choice what could he do?

As the Wynstan coach approached the Hall several carriages were before them proceeding in stately fashion up the long drive gaily lit with flambeaux that highlighted the huge grey pile. It was not a distinguished house but it was impressive, with its two low wings and a porticoed entrance. As she stepped down from the carriage Nicola had a sudden expectation that this evening would be climactic. Then she smiled at her fancy. It was just another dance of which she had endured scores, neither more or less important than the others. She was a ninny to dramatize the occasion. She followed her mother into the marbled entrance hall and handed her shawl to a liveried footman.

At the top of the great staircase that led to the ballroom, the Marquis and his cousin stood to receive their guests. Large urns of roses flanked the stairs and many were the gasps of appreciation from the company that preceded them. A footman announced the names in a ringing tone as each guest approached Mrs. Sturbridge and the Marquis. Nicola was impressed, for Lord Cranbourne certainly had spared no expense to make this dance as elegant as any she had attended in London.

Much had been done to redecorate the Hall in just the few weeks since Nicola had come to tea with her mother. Fresh paint and gilding on the walls and ceiling, new crimson carpeting on the wide stairs and new livery for the servants were

just some of the changes. However, she was now face to face
with the Marquis who was looking as elegant as his house in
a black superfine coat of impeccable cut, a plain silk waistcoat
and an intricate cravat tied in the Mathematical mode. He gave
Nicola a raking glance, and complimented her on her gown
as if she had worn it just to please him. Accustomed as she
was to moving in the highest circles of the ton and rarely
unnerved in society she found herself blushing, to her dismay.

"I do hope you will honor me with a dance or two, Miss
Wynstan."

"Yes, of course, my lord," Nicola answered demurely and
was about to pass on when he stopped her with a hand on her
arm.

"A waltz and the supper dance, please." The Marquis held
out his hand for her dance card, which she had received from
a footman. The Marquis scrawled his name in bold strokes
across the spaces. Behind her she could hear the murmurs of
guests, wondering about their host's interest in this attractive
girl. Mrs. Wynstan, briefly with Mrs. Sturbridge, had noted
the exchange too and swelled with pride in her daughter. Nicola, a bit overset by the attention, only nodded, and hurriedly
greeted Mrs. Sturbridge, leaving Julia to the mercy of the
Marquis, but inwardly she was fuming that he had made her
the object of gossip. Mrs. Sturbridge, looking stately in a lav-
ender silk and matching turban, gave her a wintry smile and
then, at last, Nicola was free to enter the ballroom. It, too, had
been embellished for the occasion with large urns of yellow
roses decorating the niches in the various recessed areas, yellow and cream-striped satin upholstering the French chairs in
the chaperones' corner, and hundreds of cream wax candles
lighting the scene from three huge Venetian chandeliers.

Nicola's arrival was the signal for several gentlemen to
crowd about her requesting dances. Adrian was among the
first. He was not comfortable in this assembly. His waistcoat
was a mistake, he decided, having noticed the Marquis's aus-
tere garb and feeling that he might be dubbed a dandy. Ni-

cola would only allow him one dance, a country reel later on in the evening, and insisted that she wanted to open with her father. The General, pleased by her choice, offered her his arm and they joined one of the sets forming for the minuet, a staid dance of bows and courtesy which the General performed with studied concentration. In his younger days he had fancied himself as a skilled performer and thought he did credit to his much admired daughter. Adrian had to make do with Julia, believing that it might be best to get that onerous chore dispatched early so that he would be free to besiege Nicola later. The ballroom was already warm and he hoped to lure her into the gardens where he would make his proposal.

Ned had made straight for Elizabeth Shillingford, a sprightly brunette whose attraction rivaled Nicola's. She was surrounded by eager claimants but Ned persisted and won her hand. Nicola gave her friend a smile as they passed in the intricacies of the dance, indicating they would meet later for a chat.

The orchestra, established in the minstrel gallery overlooking the floor, was as expert as any in London. Nicola suspected the musicians had been imported from town for the occasion. She was surprised that the Marquis had organized such a splendid spectacle to introduce himself to the ton of the county. She mentioned in a teasing tone to her father that she was sure he would have his lobster patties for supper and no doubt some superior claret or brandy. The evening promised to be as sophisticated as any ball she had attended in London, an evening that would be discussed in surrounding drawing rooms for some time. She wondered what had impelled the Marquis to make such an effort. She did not think he was a man with social aspirations, determined to puff up his own consequence.

He did not appear on the floor until after the first few dances had been completed and his first partner was properly his cousin. Mrs. Sturbridge accepted the honor with gracious dignity. She was a woman who paid a deal of attention to her consequence but did not appear overwhelmed by the honor. By the time the Marquis came to claim his dance just before supper Nicola had decided the evening was a resounding success.

"You have certainly provided an elegant entertainment for us, my lord." For some reason she felt nervous and unsure of herself, a position she rarely suffered, as they whirled onto the floor.

"I have done my best. And I do wish you would call me Jocelyn, for I intend to call you Nicola. As a near neighbor as well as an experienced dueler in our several passages at arms I consider formality between us ridiculous."

"Do you? Well, I suppose I must consent, Jocelyn." Nicola felt at a disadvantage, a situation she observed she often encountered with the Marquis. Determined to take the offensive she rushed into unconsidered speech.

"This dance is far from a little country gathering. It would be remarked upon even in London. You have spared no expense, I see."

"And you wonder if I have depleted my coffers to impress my neighbors? One of the many qualities I admire in you, Nicola, is your forthrightness. No shilly-shallying. Let me assure you I can well afford it."

"You will be the object of much conjecture and envy in the county, Jocelyn."

"That was not my intention. Perhaps I only wanted to impress one disapproving female. I am delighted to have at last made a gesture that wins your approbation." His tone was suave and smooth but she knew he was laughing at her. All of her practiced social skills came for naught with the Marquis.

As the waltz drew to a close, she was relieved to slip from his confining arms. His clasp had not been unduly personal but the intimacy of the waltz with such a disturbing partner had left Nicola flushed and uncertain. Somehow the Marquis provoked unsettling emotions in her to which she had never before been prey.

"Shall we sample the lobster patties? I understand that your father finds them the chief attraction of the evening."

She laughed, grateful to have been provided with such an innocuous subject. "Yes, indeed. I am equally as greedy. There are Ned and Elizabeth Shillingford. Can we join them?"

"Of course. Is Miss Shillingford a friend?"

"Yes, we were at school together in Cheltenham and I saw a deal of her in London. We had some merry times together and some shocking ones. I suppose you have heard of our curricle race. We created quite a scandal."

"I would expect no less of you." The supper room was crowded but the Marquis secured a table without difficulty and summoned Ned and Elizabeth to join them. Although Nicola would have liked to quiz the Marquis about his recent absence, hoping to find some hint that he could have been involved with the highwaymen she welcomed the addition of Ned and Elizabeth. She settled down to a good gossip with her friend but kept one ear on the conversation between the two men. They were discussing the recent robbery of the mail coach.

"They are a slippery bunch, always able to evade capture. I wonder if they are receiving some kind of inside information." Ned thought Nicola's suspicions about the Marquis were unfounded but he was not averse to humoring her in her quest to tie the Marquis to the miscreants. He understood Nicola quite well and believed her eagerness to find evidence against the Marquis stemmed from her ambivalent feelings for the man rather than any real sense that he was a criminal.

"Could be," said the Marquis. "And who do you think this informer could be?"

Ned had a wicked impulse to say, "It could be you," but caution prevailed. "I think it must be someone recently arrived in the neighborhood, for until a few months ago our area had never been bothered with highwaymen."

"Well, aside from myself, who has arrived recently?" He gave Ned a quixotic smile as if he realized what Ned was implying. "I believe both Pettifer and that young secretary of your father's are also recent arrivals."

"By Jove, of course. They must be suspects," Ned agreed with some haste.

"And myself. In my younger days I might have thought such a jape good value, but I regret that age has brought some caution. Somehow I don't think these local highwaymen are aristocratic sprigs out for a thrill. They appear to be too organized."

Ned, thoroughly embarrassed because he sensed the Marquis knew exactly the reason for his seemingly idle questions, silently cursed his sister. She had forced him into this unenviable position.

"You know, Wynstan, I think your sister suspects me of all kinds of devilment and I am probably her chief candidate for leader of these villains." The Marquis had just spiked Ned's guns and he kept his composure with some difficulty.

"Oh, Nicky often gets wild bees in her bonnet. You shouldn't take her too seriously."

"But I do, Wynstan. She's a very determined female and for some reason, I have incurred her disapproval." The Marquis did not appear to find that worrying. "Let's ask her, shall we?"

He waited until there was a pause in the conversation between Nicola and her friend and said suavely. "I suspect, Miss Wynstan, you believe me quite capable of being the leader of these wretched highwaymen who are causing so much concern."

Nicola almost choked on her lobster patty, shocked by the Marquis's bold challenge. But she was not going to be routed by his unexpected attack.

"Well, my lord, I understand some daring members of the ton think it great sport to behave as robbers and villains. And

I do believe you might get some sort of thrill by such daring escapades."

"How exciting, a highwayman who is also a nob," Elizabeth thought the idea had merit and chuckled.

"You must not be influenced by Nicola, Miss Shillingford. No calumny is beyond me in her eyes."

"I know you are funning." Elizabeth responded intrigued by this view of Nicola's relationship with such an exceptional parti. Elizabeth had been party to several of Nicola's more questionable exploits but this was beyond all. Could there be some attraction between the two? Her curiosity was aroused and she was determined to quiz Ned about their relationship. Until now she had thought Nicola's preference was for Adrian Pettifer.

"Pay no attention to the Marquis, Elizabeth. He delights in discomforting me. I think it's time to return to the dance. My next partner must be waiting."

Nicola had no intention of showing her vexation at the turn of the conversation but she gave Ned a dark look, promising retribution later. She stood up, preparing to abandon her companions and courtesy demanded that the Marquis follow her lead.

But he had the last word. "We must continue this fascinating supposition at a later date. I believe I have a dance later." His bland tone did not deceive Nicola. She knew he would demand an accounting and she wasn't sure exactly how she would handle the matter. Fortunately she could postpone that problem for Adrian had arrived to claim his dance. As they walked away from the supper room, Nicola had the impression that the Marquis was plotting some wicked revenge and she must thwart his efforts. She barely heeded Adrian when he suggested that they avoid the dance floor and walk in the gardens. Before she realized it they had wandered out onto the terrace.

"You seem somewhat distrait, Nicky. Has the Marquis said

anything to upset you?" He asked, rather annoyed that she appeared unaware of his presence.

"No, he's just rather mocking and it irritates me. It was so warm in the supper room. It's a relief to be out in the air, and such a fine night, too." She marched ahead, hardly realizing that they were distancing themselves from the house and soon were alone in the shrubbery beyond the terrace. The gardens of Cranbourne Hall were intricate and lush, the scent of roses pervading the balmy May night. Just the scene for his proposal, Adrian thought, and halted her with a hand on her arm as they entered a small plot shielded by lime trees.

"Nicola, listen to me. I have been trying to get you alone for days now but someone is always about at the manor. I have something very important to ask you and it must be tonight for I fear I must return to my various duties in London." He paused as if waiting for some response but Nicola was silent. He plunged on. "You must know how much I have come to admire you, yes, love you. I know I have not as much to offer as many of your other admirers but I feel we have a special bond which could be the foundation of a lasting and felicitous relationship. I want you for my wife." This pompous speech had not emerged with the sincerity and ardor Adrian had planned and to his dismay Nicola did not receive it with appreciation. She laughed.

"Really, Adrian, you are ridiculous. Whatever could have given you the idea we would suit? I consider you a friend, of course, and I am intrigued with your revolutionary idea for the tunnel but marriage is not in the question." If Nicola had not been still bemused by the Marquis's uncomfortable accusations she would have handled Adrian's proposal with more kindness and skill.

"I supposed you would not have invited me to meet your parents and honored me with so much of your confidence if you had not felt some warm emotion toward me."

"Well, you were wrong. If I have given you any idea that I might care for you it was unintended. I am not in love with you. I really don't know what love is but I know I must marry for love. I regret disappointing you but my answer is no. Now, let us return to the ballroom."

Adrian, furious and humiliated by this rebuff, then showed his true colors. "I suppose I am not good enough for you, available for flirtation but beneath you in fortune, breeding and status. Well, you need a lesson." And he took her roughly into his arms and pressed wet hot kisses on her resisting face ignoring her efforts to escape. Before she could take any decisive action, Adrian was pulled away and knocked to the ground. He lay there for a moment stunned and aware that his jaw was throbbing from a punishing blow. He looked up and saw the Marquis. His first reaction was anger then quickly followed by fear. He recognized that his position was perilous, but neither the Marquis nor Nicola paid the slightest attention. They were too absorbed in each other.

Thirteen

"Really, Nicola, I know you are a temptress but I wish you would take some care about whom you dally with in my garden." The Marquis looked at Nicola with his usual acerbic expression. He continued, "I have warned you I might not always be available to rescue you from your follies."

"Not my follies. It never occurred to me that I should have to fend off an assault just because I agreed to walk in your garden." Why was it that whenever she found herself in disagreeable situations the Marquis appeared to extricate her? He was the last man she wanted to discover her in this embarrassing role, although she felt it was hardly her fault if Adrian had presumed upon their friendship to behave in such an outrageous fashion.

Adrian struggled to his feet and gave Nicola a look of reproach which she failed to see. He yearned to return the Marquis's blow, but assessing the Marquis's broad shoulders and clenched jaw thought better of it. He had best try to soothe the irate lord. Adrian would never admit he had behaved like a cad, but wisdom dictated that he put himself in as good a light as possible.

"You misunderstood, sir. I was asking Miss Wynstan to be my wife and under the stress of emotion, perhaps, I pressed my attentions too ardently. You interrupted a discussion that does not concern you," Adrian explained with righteous dignity but realized to his chagrin that neither of his companions seemed interested in his views. They were far more concerned with scoring off one another.

Paying no attention to Adrian's self-justifying remarks, the Marquis continued to upbraid Nicola. "You really must abandon this habit of luring gullible young men to express their admiration and then spurning them cruelly. I can quite see the entertainment value in the sport but surely you have enough scalps on your belt already. And I fear this popinjay is unworthy of your prowess." The Marquis looked at Adrian with contempt. If he blamed Nicola for the business he certainly had no sympathy for her admirer. Indeed, Adrian looked the worse for the reddening bruise on his jaw, which ached painfully, and a general disheveled appearance.

Ignoring both the Marquis and Adrian, Nicola struggled to replace the silver fillet holding her curls and restore her gown to some order. She did not know which of the men she despised more, Adrian for presuming on her friendship with his nauseating attentions, or the Marquis for rescuing her, then raking her up and down as if she had deserved such behavior.

Determined to defend herself, she launched into her own scathing rebuttal. "You make me sound like some Mideastern houri. If I cannot walk in your garden without suffering the unwanted attentions of a dance partner and your nasty castigation, I think it is shameful. I suppose in these regrettable circumstances it is commonplace to blame the female, but in this case I was not at fault. I have never given Mr. Pettifer any reason to think I would welcome either his proposal or his unwelcome kisses." Having delivered this explanation in a lofty tone, Nicola prepared to flounce off back to the ballroom, leaving the two men to their own devices.

Adrian, noticing the ugly expression on the Marquis's face, thought it might be prudent to follow her example but he was determined to have the last word.

"Since you have treated me so shabbily, Nicola, I will take my leave of you and your parents immediately and return to

London where I will be welcomed by more understanding and regard." He bowed and turned away.

"Very wise of you, Pettifer. Take my advice and abandon your tunnel, too. You seem to have a penchant for lost causes." Adrian pretended not to hear these parting words and walked away hoping that he had signified his rejection of this unjustified critique of both his person and his beliefs. Nicola wanted to escape herself but found she was restrained by the Marquis's hand on her arm.

Adrian, in the grip of a rage that barely masked his fear of being felled again by the Marquis's hard right hand, was in no state to consider his action. All he could do was mutter that neither Nicola nor her protector should be allowed to inflict such injustice without suffering. As well as rejection Adrian was feeling humiliation and he meant to see that others would pay for his miserable condition. He made his way to the ballroom and seeing Mrs. Wynstan in the chaperones' corner marched up to the lady and subjected her to his displeasure.

"Since your daughter has made it clear that my presence is an offense to her and has ridiculed my proposal of marriage, I have no recourse but to return to the manor, pack my cases and take my leave. I will not thank you for your grudging hospitality for I know you have always disapproved of me as beneath your touch. I will only suggest that you try to keep your daughter in better order or there will be a scandal before long."

It looked as though the scandal had already happened. Avid eyes and ears had gathered that Nicola had made herself the object of conjecture. Mrs. Wynstan, mortified by being the cynosure of her fellow chaperones and those guests near enough to hear Adrian's complaints, had too much dignity to engage in any dialogue with this angry, ill-bred young man. She had treated him with every kindness and this was how he repaid her. She did not deserve his censure.

"I regret you feel you have been treated badly, Mr. Pettifer, but that does not excuse your manner to me in this company. The sooner you take your departure the better." She turned her back on him, her shoulders stiff and her chin raised. Mrs. Wynstan was not without a certain courage, and well able to protect herself from social snubs. She had been gravely mistaken in her reading of Mr. Pettifer's character. Even more galling, she must allow that her husband was correct in his estimate of the man, a parvenu and an opportunist.

Adrian, aware that he had allowed his rage to master him to no avail, was conscious of the cold stares from the guests who had been privy to this disgusting display of bad manners. He might have known they would all bond together against the obvious outsider. He must make as dignified and rapid a retreat as possible. Unfortunately he had come to the dance in Ned's curricle and now must insist that the young man, who would surely champion his family, drive him away from this unhappy scene.

Ned, who had observed his mother's encounter, but had not heard Adrian's bitter accusation, was not prepared to be obliging. Normally the most tolerant of men, he did not appreciate Adrian embarrassing his mother before the other old tabbies.

"Take the curricle, Adrian, and be off with you. I will find another way home, but please be careful with my horses." Ned turned away, dismissing Adrian as the most paltry of fellows, not a gentleman. Adrian's anger, and the knowledge he had not behaved well, only added to his frustration, but he saw no help for it but to slink away, rebuffed on all counts. He would make them pay, the whole blooming lot of them. In the grip of his unbridled passion, Adrian retreated to vulgarity that was inbred. Nicola, Ned, the Marquis, and Mrs. Wynstan had all treated him with contempt. He had been spared the ire of General Wynstan, safely ensconced in the card room, and who only later learned of the shameless display of his unwanted house guest. He was not surprised, only justified in his original view that the man was a jackanapes.

While the ballroom was all agog with the rumors of a delicious scandal involving Miss Wynstan, the two most concerned were seated on a stone bench in the garden.

"I think you need some time to compose yourself before you join the company." Seeing Nicola's downcast expression and realizing that he had been too harsh with her, the Marquis was moved to make amends. "I am sorry you were exposed to that ill-bred fellow's assault. Perhaps I was too critical of your behavior which might be put down to innocence rather than conceit. Will you forgive me?"

Overcome by this gentle reproof coming from a man who had never lost an opportunity to put her in the wrong, Nicola was in danger of crying and that would never do. She could not let him see her vulnerability.

"I assure you, Jocelyn, I had no idea that Adrian entertained such ideas of me. My only interest in him was as a friend, a clever young man with his way to make in a cruel world. I guess I am not a good judge of character."

"At least this contretemps has brought you to the improbable state of using my name, and perhaps, reassessing my own character. I really could not have borne any more 'my lords' and much as I enjoyed our recent passages at arms, I think we have entered into a happier relationship now." He seemed sincere with no mockery evident in his calm even voice.

"Well, your reaction was very lordly just now but I am grateful, much as I hate to admit it." Nicola rewarded him with a watery smile.

"So we have declared a truce."

"I can do no less in view of your gallant behavior. And I suppose I should apologize for suspecting you of being a highwayman. But you know, you really give the impression that such lawless conduct would not be beyond your talents." Nicola thought she should offer some excuse for her suspicions but she was not completely cowed by her recent experience.

To her relief the Marquis seemed to find this rather naïve admission amusing. "Actually, I might have chanced it at one time in my chequered career, but now I am much too staid and proper to risk my respectability for such a jape."

"I don't think of you as respectable, Jocelyn," Nicola gave him a cheeky smile with this assessment of his character.

"Very astute of you and just as well. I am not feeling very respectable at the moment." Indeed, Jocelyn was considering what would happen if he surrendered to his baser instincts. Nicola was a very fetching piece, but he would be little better than her recent attacker if he gave into his instincts. Strangely her friendship and good opinion was beginning to matter to him.

Divining his intent, Nicola stood up nervously. "Perhaps we had better return to the ballroom. I am sure my absence has caused some speculation. Mother will be annoyed."

"Let us hope that your unsavory houseguest has removed himself. If not, I will be forced to evict him."

"Yes, I cannot understand what impelled Adrian to behave so badly. I have certainly never given him any cause to think I would welcome his advances."

If the Marquis was inclined to point out to her that opportunistic young men faced with the chance to win both money and beauty could be tempted by Nicola's open and friendly air to make just those advances, he wisely held his tongue. Despite her two successful London seasons she was still an innocent in many ways. By encouraging Adrian's friendship and inviting him to her home she had acted rashly. Still, he did not want to endanger their recent accord, so he kept silent.

Entering the ballroom on the Marquis's arm, Nicola was aware of the avid curiosity of the guests who viewed their entrance with raised eyebrows and some whispering. She indicated that she would join her mother, and the Marquis escorted her to the chaperones' corner, where he blandly made his explanations to Mrs. Wynstan.

"Nicola felt the heat of the ballroom and we have been taking a stroll about the grounds. I fear we forgot the time and she may have disappointed her next partner. All my fault, I confess."

"Not at all, Lord Cranbourne. Nicola has behaved carelessly." Mrs. Wynstan had too much awareness of social protocol to upbraid her daughter in public and she was so gratified by the Marquis's defense of her daughter to feel really aggrieved. Jocelyn, cynically aware of what was passing through Mrs. Wynstan's mind, chatted a moment to Mrs. Wynstan and her fellow chaperones before leaving to attend to his duties as a host. He would leave it to Nicola to confide in her mother or not, as she wished. He made his way across the ballroom only to be intercepted by Ned.

"Thank you, sir, for rescuing my sister from Pettifer. I suspect he made an ass of himself. At any rate he has departed in my curricle and I hope has the sense to leave the neighborhood with all speed."

"I suppose we might have averted some scandal, but at least Pettifer has been revealed to Nicola in his true colors. I'm afraid she was greatly mistaken in her judgment of the man."

"Nicola can be overenthusiastic when she embraces some outlandish ideas. She was quite taken with the fellow's tunnel schemes, but I honestly believe she had no idea he entertained any such feelings for her."

"Well, we are rid of him now. But you might keep a prudent eye on her in the future."

Much as Ned wanted to defend his sister and disliked this haughty aristocrat implying any criticism of her, he had to agree.

Nicola's partners, not deterred by the rumors, kept her busy on the dance floor and she hoped that she had weathered the disagreeable episode without too much speculation. If some of the stricter matrons, envious of her success with the gentlemen, gossiped among themselves they were careful not to appear too disapproving. Lord Cranbourne was too important a figure to invite any criticism of his manners. Of far more interest was his apparent approval of Miss Wynstan. She had made another conquest. What would be the outcome? Was there a romance in the air? Whomever the Marquis claimed as his bride, the company was more than eager to accept her. It would never do to be at odds with the most distinguished and wealthy peer in the neighborhood.

Nicola, aware that she was the object of speculation, pretended to ignore the whispers and conducted herself with propriety for the rest of the evening. It took considerable courage and she knew she would have to endure some stringent words from her parents before the incident could be laid to rest. Fortunately, Ned, who claimed the final dance of the evening with her, cheered her with his support.

"You are well rid of Pettifer, Nicky. I don't think you will have to endure any more of his unwelcome approaches. He will leave the manor as soon as possible, but you should chalk up this little contretemps to experience. It never pays to take up with unknown fellows about whose background you know so little."

Meekly, Nicola agreed with her brother. In the past her experience had been with men of her own social circle, and although she could judge fortune hunters, Adrian's type had not previously come across her path.

"I hope I am not a snob, Ned, but, really, Adrian's ridiculous idea that I favored him as a husband was beyond the bounds. I will be more careful in the future."

"The parents will crow a bit, but since the Marquis has thrown the mantle of his protection over you, not much harm was done."

If Ned wondered just what the Marquis had said to Nicola, and if the recent imbroglio signified a change in his sister's attitude toward Lord Cranbourne, he kept his own counsel. He was beginning to believe that Cranbourne would be just the man to handle his mercurial sister but he would do nothing to suggest such an idea. Instead he talked with some enthusiasm of the coming visit of Miss Shillingford for whom he had his own plans.

The Wynstans rode home without any discussion of Nicola's brush with scandal for Mrs. Wynstan would not reveal her displeasure before Julia and that young woman was eager to discuss her own enjoyment of the ball. The General, full of brandy, dozed in the corner of the coach. Nicola, although both disgusted and disappointed with Adrian, was more concerned about her altered relationship with Jocelyn and what it meant.

Fourteen

Much as Nicola would have liked to avoid the family breakfast on the morning after the Cranbourne ball by pleading a headache she realized that would only postpone her explanations to her parents. Mrs. Wynstan had given a very edited account of the reason for Adrian Pettifer's sudden departure from their midst to her husband who was only relieved to see the back of the fellow. She did not intend to mention Adrian's proposal of marriage, for that would only rebound on her daughter. Julia Overton, however, was not so sensible. She suspected that Nicola had been involved in some outrage against the proprieties and was determined to learn all about it. But she had to tread carefully.

"What has happened to Mr. Pettifer, Cousin Prudence? He appeared to vanish from the ball last night soon after his dance with Nicola." Of course Julia had listened to all the rumors bandied about by jealous girls and their mothers, but she behaved as if she knew nothing. The ploy did not deceive Nicola nor her mother, who, sorry as she felt for Julia, often found her irritating. In this case she thought the girl was being deliberately provocative and had to remind herself sternly that Julia was a guest, however unwelcome at times, and must be treated kindly.

"Mr. Pettifer had to leave us suddenly. As you know, Julia, he developed a tendre for Nicola and was rebuffed, rightly we believe. He removed himself from an embarrassing situation for which we must be grateful." Mrs. Wynstan spoke with firmness and a certain look in her eye boded ill for Julia if she pursued the matter.

Cowed, for Julia had no intention of making herself disagreeable to her hostess and having to cut short her visit, she nodded and applied herself to her shirred eggs. Nicola looked at her mother with admiration. She wished she could learn to depress Julia's curiosity with such skill.

Ned, always willing to come to his sister's aid, turned the conversation by saying, "Just as well he's gone. Elizabeth Shillingford is coming to stay and I don't think she would appreciate him."

"We are so pleased Elizabeth can join us. Your former schoolmate will be company for you," Mrs. Wynstan suggested, further quelling Julia, who realized she had better keep her suspicions to herself, or she would be banished in favor of the delightful brunette whom her cousin Ned found so appealing. A bold and saucy piece she thought Miss Shillingford, but then men often mistook that flagrant flirting for the solid worth of less attractive girls. Julia fell into a brooding self-pity, her defense against rejection. Perhaps she had better concentrate on Mr. Moffett after all.

Having successfully avoided the trap Julia had set, Mrs. Wynstan finished her meal and suggested Nicola might join her in the morning room as there were several small duties she wanted to discuss with her about her friend's arrival. Pointedly Julia was excused from this conference, and she hastened to remove herself to sulk in the garden.

Ned winked at Nicola, showing his support and commiseration for the dressing down she would undoubtedly be receiving. The General, impervious to all these undercurrents, emerged from behind his newspaper, threw down his napkin, and informed his family he was off to the lower twenty-acre field. Ned decided to accompany him.

Nicky followed her mother into the morning room, resigned to some severe words, but certain she could talk her mother around. However, her mother surprised her. Settling in her usual chair she took up her tapestry and looked at her daughter with gentle reproof.

"I feel I cannot chastise you too harshly over the business with Mr. Pettifer, because I, too, was deceived by that young man."

"Really, Mother, I had no idea he entertained any but the most casual feelings toward me. He behaved in a shabby fashion and I regret causing you any embarrassment."

"You were fortunate that Lord Cranbourne happened on the scene. He seems most interested in you, Nicky."

"Aggravated, more likely. But, yes, he did rescue me from a most unpleasant situation. I may have misjudged him, but, Mother, please do not have any maggots in your head about Lord Cranbourne. We would never suit and I don't think he is hanging out for a wife."

"Probably not, but then most men aren't. Women marry men, not the other way around," Mrs. Wynstan suggested sagely.

"Mother, you shock me. Did you inveigle Father into a proposal?"

"Certainly not. No wonder Lord Cranbourne finds you aggravating. You are a most disturbing girl, never react as one might expect."

"Poor Mother, always disappointed that I don't submit to some suitable parti. Never mind. I will be lured into the parson's mousetrap one of these days. But what have you told Father about Adrian's behavior?"

"Very little. Just that he was very rude to me at the ball and I asked him to depart. Your father is only too happy to see the back of him. He never approved of him, as you know, and I must say we all should have listened to him. The man is a mountebank."

"Possibly. But I was interested in his tunnel scheme. I think he used his acquaintance with us to further his plans and when he found he could get neither money nor support from us and

Lord Cranbourne, took out his disappointment on me. I did like him but never thought of him as a husband."

"Well, we have seen the last of him. And Elizabeth Shillingford will distract your father. He likes pretty pleasing girls and she is certainly fascinating. Ned likes her, too, and she is very eligible."

Nicola could only agree and settled into a comfortable gossip with her mother about Ned's interest in her friend. Happy to put the episode with Adrian behind her, she could only endorse her mother's wish that they had seen the last of him, but somehow she lacked that assurance. She had refused proposals before and remained friends with the disappointed young men, but she feared that Adrian might not be so easily deterred from some kind of revenge. She would enlist Ned's aid in discovering if he had indeed left the neighborhood.

Nicola's fears were justified. Adrian had stolen away from the manor on his horse and returned to the Crown and Anchor in the village, knocking up the innkeeper and demanding his best room despite the late hour. He had no intention of leaving the area before he had completed his mission there.

Angry and humiliated as he was by Nicola's rejection his real fury was reserved for the Marquis, the agent of his downfall, he believed. That arrogant peer would regret treating him so scurvily. For the moment all ideas of promoting his tunnel had been abandoned. At best it had only been a scheme to provide him with a lavish income. From the beginning he had seen the tunnel as an opportunity to float a company to which eager investors would be attracted. He meant to take their money and abscond, having realized that the government would never allow the tunnel to become a reality. Now he had another source of income, one much less problematical. He would use his sudden access of funds to settle the Marquis. And he meant that Nicola should also pay for the heartless way she had deceived him. But he must be careful. He was

dealing with some dodgy colleagues, who required the clev-
erest of handling, not that he was not able to control them. It
might be best to take a flamboyant departure form the inn and
remove to less comfortable but safer surroundings where he
could direct the action to his satisfaction.

As he fretted and fumed about his revenge he failed to take
into account that he was opposing a man with a great deal of
experience in besting his enemies. Lord Cranbourne would
not so easily be deluded, but Adrian's conceit could not entertain such an outcome. He thought himself more than a
match for the Marquis. About Nicola he had not quite decided.
He had not enjoyed her contemptuous reception of his proposal when he had been sure she would accept. She had led
him to believe she cared about him. She might yet be eager
to marry him when he had her in his power. He comforted
himself that then she would be begging for him to insure her
respectability and the wretched Marquis would not be on hand
to interfere. Adrian nurtured his visions of revenge but he was
shrewd enough not to underestimate his victims. Over a hearty
breakfast he decided that the sooner he left the vicinity the
better it would be.

It was Roger Forrest who surprised Adrian as he was leaving the inn. Roger had been dispatched into town by the General after an early breakfast and had not heard the news of
Adrian's midnight departure. He hailed Pettifer cheerfully as
Adrian was about to ride away in the landaulet he had hired.

"Hello there, Pettifer. I had no idea you were leaving us."

Adrian, who had never paid much attention to Roger, believing him to be a negligible addition to the Wynstan household, bit back a curse and greeted him coolly.

"Press of business, old chap. I have been recalled to London unexpectedly. You are on some chore for your employer,
I suspect."

Not liking Adrian's condescension, Roger only nodded and
turned away. Accustomed to effacing himself from unpleasant
confrontations rather than challenging the perpetrator, he

thought it simpler to ignore Adrian's gibe but he wondered at this abrupt departure. Had Adrian offended his hosts in some manner? If so, Roger, always tactful, preferred not to be involved. Adrian frowned at his retreating back. He did not like being snubbed by a lowly secretary and he chalked up another score to settle.

Roger, completing his errand, returned to the manor, but soon became immersed in the notes he was compiling for the General's next chapter and forgot the encounter. At luncheon he was reminded of the meeting when the General informed his family that he was relieved to see the last of that bounder Pettifer.

"I believe Mr. Pettifer has returned to London, sir." Roger offered his news tentatively. He rarely entered into family discussions. "I met him in the village, leaving the inn with his effects in a landaulet."

"Is that what he told you, Roger?" Ned asked.

"Yes, I understood business recalled him suddenly." Roger was aware of some restraint and relief in the company and was at a loss to account for it.

"Well, I certainly trust we have seen the last of him." Mrs. Wynstan, too, had some doubts about Adrian's departure and could only hope that Roger's report was correct. Roger, puzzled by the family's attitude, inferred that Pettifer had committed some transgression that made him unpopular. They had seemed to accept the man and Nicola, in particular, had appeared on very friendly terms with him. Could Pettifer have made unwanted advances to her? Roger, himself, was most particular in keeping his distance from the alluring daughter of the house. A personable young man, he had met with some unwanted advances himself in his last post where the wife of his patron had taken an inordinate liking to him. It was highly embarrassing and resulted in his decision to leave before he was dismissed. Roger never lost sight of his equivocal position in the households he served.

"What are your plans for this afternoon, Nicola?" Mrs. Wynstan asked her daughter.

"Father tells me that Mrs. Wright's youngest is ill. I thought I might call and offer some comfort. She is such a good woman and I always enjoy a visit to the Home Farm."

"Be sure you take a groom with you, my dear." Mrs. Wynstan wanted no more wild escapades from her daughter. "And be sure to be home in time to welcome Miss Shillingford who will be arriving just before dinner."

"Suppose you have lots of work for me, Forrest, so we had better get down to it, eh?" The General pretended that Roger ordered him about ruthlessly when it came to the compiling of his history when Roger would not have dared make such demands.

"We should get on with the new chapter, sir," Roger suggested.

"I'll accompany you to the Wrights', Nicky, then you won't have to endure while George and I inspect that roof. Father thinks it needs more than a patch and might require more than just stop gap repairs."

Their dispositions made the family depart on their various interests, leaving Julia to entertain herself, a situation to which she was not a stranger. She would have liked to go with Nicola and Ned but accepted with some bitterness that her presence would not be welcome. Mrs. Wynstan decided to take a well-deserved rest and retired to her room so that it was Julia who received Lady Mumford when that lady made an afternoon call.

"I had to go into the village to match some wool, since my abigail, Nancy, seems unequal to the task, and thought I would just call unexpectedly," Lady Mumford explained, when Paxton ushered her into the morning room where Julia was idly leafing through some French fashion booklets.

"Aunt Prudence is resting. She was very tired from the ball, but I am sure she would want to see you, Lady Mumford. Should I ask Paxton to tell her you are here?"

"Don't bother, my dear. I will only stay a moment. I just thought we might have a cose about the Cranbourne ball. What a hum, with all the rumors about Nicola and the Marquis." Lady Mumford enjoyed a good gossip and was not too careful in whom she confided.

"I never listen to gossip and was not aware that there was any talk about Nicola and the Marquis," Julia spoke smugly, hoping that Lady Mumford would be tempted to tell her the story.

"Well, you might not have noticed, but Nicola left the ballroom with that Mr. Pettifer, and evidently he made some kind of advance to her and she was rescued by the Marquis who escorted her back to the ballroom, all attention, but only after a long interval. And that Mr. Pettifer was quite rude to dear Lady Wynstan, marched right up to her and told her in so many words that Nicola was a veritable jade. Prudence set him down smartly and then he disappeared. Has he left you?" Lady Mumford was determined to find out every detail.

"Yes, he seems to have departed very suddenly. Aunt Prudence said he had been called to London."

"In the middle of the night? How peculiar." Lady Mumford settled herself in her chair, prepared to pursue the matter, but just then, Mrs. Wynstan swept into the room, having heard from Paxton about her visitor.

"Moira, how nice to see you! I am so sorry I was not available when you arrived. Has Julia been entertaining you properly?"

"Yes, indeed Prudence. We were just discussing the ball."

Lady Wynstan had a shrewd idea just how the tenor of the discussion had gone, and gave Julia a baleful look. Since the damage had been done, she decided to minimize any aspersion on her daughter's reputation.

"Mr. Pettifer, in whom I was gravely deceived, made an unwelcome proposal to Nicky and was refused. He did not take it in good part and made his displeasure known, as you heard. We thought it best that Mr. Pettifer cut short his visit—

so embarrassing to have a rebuffed suitor in the house, don't you think?"

"Well, you should be used to that. Nicola has turned down scores of men, I gather. She seems difficult to suit, but perhaps she has her eye on the Marquis." Lady Mumford thought Nicola too particular in her taste and enjoyed her friend's struggles in getting her daughter settled into a proper marriage. "Of course Mr. Pettifer would not have done. I quite see that. The mistake was in inviting him to stay, my dear."

"Yes, I am afraid I misjudged the man, but Nicky can be so headstrong. The attraction was not Mr. Pettifer, but his tunnel scheme. She was so intrigued with it, and probably gave him the impression she liked him and raised his hopes. Of course, the General would never have consented." She knew that Moira Mumford had a very good idea of how little that would have mattered if Nicola had made up her mind to wed the man.

"I do sympathize with you, my dear. My girls were so obedient, accepted their first offers. Of course, they never had the chances Nicola did, not being beauties." Lady Mumford was avid to hear every nuance of Nicky's embroilment with an unsuitable young man. Then, because she could not help herself, "Do you think the Marquis is épris?"

"He and Nicola seem to have settled their differences. They did not get along well at first, but that is so often the case with young people, don't you find?"

"Perhaps. It would be quite a coup if she could attach him, and convenient for you, since he is a close neighbor. But he does not appear to be a marrying man." Having depressed Mrs. Wynstan's hopes and learned all she could, Lady Mumford took her leave shortly afterwards, leaving Mrs. Wynstan to take out her irritation on Julia.

"I do hope you did not tell Lady Mumford any wild tale about Mr. Pettifer's departure, Julia. All this gossip could be injurious to Nicky."

Having learned all she wanted to know, Julia turned a bland

sympathetic face toward her hostess. "Of course not, Aunt Prudence. But I do think Nicola is tiresome to cause you so much worry. She does not always behave prudently." Having delivered this rebuke with an assurance that she, herself, would never behave in such a fashion, she was quite annoyed that Mrs. Wynstan had the last word.

"But, then, you don't have Nicola's chances, do you Julia?" Mrs. Wynstan was ashamed of herself but, really, Julia was a thorn in her side, so jealous of her cousin, and so eager to cause trouble. Julia, her intentions discovered and suppressed, retired in order to brood over the injustice done to her and for the rest of the day behaved like a martyr, misunderstood by all.

Fifteen

Elizabeth Shillingford's arrival proved a much-needed tonic for a household of bored, restless, sullen and troubled inhabitants. The General, becoming edgy under the demands of Roger Forrest that he apply himself to his book, welcomed the sparkling brunette with the violet eyes. He always blossomed around an attractive female whatever her age. Ned enjoyed flirting with the cooperative Miss Shillingford who knew how to play the game. Mrs. Wynstan found their guest's winning ways a comfort after hours spent soothing the envious Julia. And Roger Forrest, usually afraid of sophisticated members of the ton whatever their sex, responded to her easy manner without embarrassment. For Nicola, Elizabeth's visit meant she had a contemporary whom she had always admired and who would listen to her confidences. Only Julia took exception to the introduction of such a rival to the gentlemen's attention, not that she had ever been of much interest to them. Her chief worry was that Mr. Moffett might cast an appreciative eye on the newcomer in their midst. Julia herself did not respond to Elizabeth's easy polite approach and conveyed her disapproval of Miss Shillingford's inclusion in their circle, not that the visitor appeared to find this defection unnerving.

She enlivened the dinner table that evening with a budget of news from friends in London and then surprised them all with an account of the latest attack of the highwaymen who had been terrorizing the neighborhood.

"I was quite relieved to arrive here safely especially since

I heard, when we stopped at Chichester, that another mail coach had been robbed. Of course, the Ellertons had kindly sent me and my abigail in their own carriage with two stalwart outriders so I did feel comfortable. It might have been quite a thrill to be robbed, a new experience."

"I am sure you would have charmed the villains and escaped without harm," Ned offered gallantly.

"I would have tried," Elizabeth quipped. Indeed, she looked quite capable at trying her lure on any male who crossed her path no matter how desperate and villainous they appeared.

Julia, casting a critical eye on Elizabeth who was wearing a low cut lustrous violet silk gown to complement her eyes, made her disapproval evident. "Surely you would not enjoy an encounter with such ruffians, Miss Shillingford."

"Oh, do please call me Elizabeth, Julia. And yes, I must admit it might have been exciting. Of course, I would not have liked giving up my jewels but I doubt that the highwaymen would have harmed me. I could have dined out on the escapade for months." She was joking, but Julia took her seriously and frowned at such levity.

"Did you learn anything about the highwaymen?" Ned asked. "They are a bold bunch. I think the authorities are at a loss."

"Old maids, unwilling to take any measures to catch the varlets," the General grumbled. "I'd like another chance at them."

Elizabeth had to hear all about the abortive encounter after the Mumford party and was all agog at the Marquis's rescue.

"I found the Marquis most intriguing and now I hear he was a hero. Do you see much of your august neighbor?"

For some reason Nicola found this interest of Elizabeth's in Jocelyn annoying and then reproved herself for such pettiness. How could it matter to her if he appealed to Elizabeth? During their seasons in London her friend had attracted almost as much attention as Nicola herself but she had never found this a troubling situation. Like many beautiful women she admired those who were equally attractive and never begrudged them their triumphs. Why should she suddenly feel that Elizabeth was a threat?

"We are on very friendly terms with Cranbourne. You will probably see something of him while you are here, my dear." The General answered her question with a smile.

"We will have to give a dinner for you, Elizabeth. Having just come from the Ellertons where you were greatly feted, I vow, you might find our little community a trifle staid." Mrs. Wynstan, always eager to entertain, suggested with enthusiasm.

"Not at all, Mrs. Wynstan. I am looking forward to a nice rest. The season was very fatiguing and I am looking like a hag after all the festivity. The Ellertons were too active in providing jollities. I want to ride and enjoy the countryside, have long coses with Nicky and restore my jaded spirits."

"You look far from jaded to me," Ned protested with an admiring glance. He had his own plans about the entertainment of their guest. He would leave it to Nicky to distract the Marquis, a chore she might be willing to undertake. Ned had noticed that the Marquis had made a definite impact on his sister and he wondered what the outcome of that relationship would be. Perhaps his sister had at last met her fate. He did not like Elizabeth's interest in their neighbor.

Julia, unwilling to be ignored, and seeing that her disapproval of the fast ways of Miss Shillingford would gain little support, hurried to retrieve any bad impression she may have made. "The Wynstans are so hospitable, Elizabeth. I know you will enjoy your visit. And how long will you be staying?"

A little surprised by Julia's rude question, Elizabeth arched a perfect eyebrow but before she could answer Mrs. Wynstan said, "As long as possible, I hope, my dear."

Julia retired, realizing she had put a foot wrong again. If her hostess did not see Elizabeth Shillingford as a threat to her efforts to snare the Marquis for Nicola this was not the time to mention it but she would manage to insinuate a suggestion later to Aunt Prudence. Julia was always eager to repay slights on her consequence although loath to admit she deserved most of them. She had her own agenda to pursue and Elizabeth would not be allowed to endanger any of her plans.

Later that evening, after preparing to retire, Nicola and Elizabeth gathered in the latter's bedroom for a good gossip.

"Tell me, Nicky, is the Marquis of Cranbourne a factor in your life? Be frank, if you have your sights set on him I will retire from the field. I wouldn't for the world queer your pitch." Elizabeth was sincere, for she was not among those girls who would sacrifice a friendship for a passing romance.

"We have become friends after an initial misunderstanding, but don't get nonsensical ideas, Elizabeth. I don't know how I feel about him. He can be quite maddening and is always taking me to task for something. Do you find him intriguing?"

"Of course I do, but I find George Ellerton, Lord Hastings, and your brother Ned equally fascinating so you see I am no rival. I enjoy men but I am not ready to make an alliance. It's much more fun to enjoy their attentions. Once you are married you have to behave, so dispiriting." Elizabeth laughed, but wisely surmised that her friend cared more for the Marquis than she was willing to admit.

"Ned has been eagerly anticipating your visit. I would love you for a sister, you know." Nicola thought she ought to further her brother's wooing although she was not sure what he really had in mind. She knew he was drawn to Elizabeth but how deep was his feeling she had not yet discovered.

"I am very fond of Ned, but I wonder if he is really hanging out for a wife?"

"No man really is eager to put his head in the noose, I expect. Mother says women marry men, not the other way around."

"Your mother is a wise woman. Now, tell me about your cousin, Julia. What a grim female she is."

"I try to exert patience with Julia, but she is a trial. She wants to marry, and I believe any man would do. She has her eye on Mr. Moffett, our vicar, who has already been refused by me, and she resents that, but I do feel sorry for her. She has a dim time of it in Devon, few prospects and a rather demanding mother. Naturally she wants her own establishment, poor dear."

"You are charitable. But be warned. I think she is out to do you harm, full of envy and other unpleasant emotions. Of course she is a drab but if she weren't so vinegary she might get a husband. I have known girls far less attractive who have pulled it off because of the sweetness of their dispositions or other desirable qualities. She is her own worst enemy."

"Too true. Julia is a cross my mother bears and we all try to be kind, but I am not sure I want her for the vicar's wife, continually on the doorstep exuding disapproval. But enough of Julia, tell me about George Ellerton and Lord Hastings. Are they both épris and whom do you favor?"

The two friends, both looking most desirable in their white lawn nightdresses settled down to a good gossip with much giggling and exchange of confidences. When Nicola finally left for her own bedroom she felt more cheerful than she had in a long time. Whatever the disquiet the Marquis had caused to her usual ebullient spirits had been banished for the time being. No mention had been made of Adrian Pettifer.

The next few days passed in simple country pursuits, but Mrs. Wynstan had plans for some more sophisticated entertainment. Five days after Elizabeth's arrival a large party was invited to dinner. Leading the guest list was the Marquis of Cranbourne who had not been seen since the night of his ball.

For the party Elizabeth chose a gown of ivory Italian crepe embroidered with shells of silver and wore a silver bandeau to hold back her curls. Nicola's choice was sea green gauze over a slip of white satin embroidered with seed pearls. Julia, whose formal wardrobe was more limited, favored a brilliant shade of spangled pink, intended to complement her sallow complexion and she prevailed on Nicola's abigail to arrange her mousy hair in an overelaborate coiffure that was far from flattering. She thought she looked very fashionable beside Elizabeth and Nicola whose simpler gowns were far more suitable for a country dinner. On comparing notes in the servants' hall later Betsy, Nicola's abigail, and Elizabeth's Polly tittered over that prosy Miss Overton's efforts to steal the limelight.

"I suggested her white dimity might be more appropriate, but she spoke up sharply and accused me of trying to make her look dowdy," Betsy confided.

"Not much trying. She's a plain old thing and so mean," Polly commented.

Conversation among the invited company, numbering twenty guests, was mostly concerned with the boldness of the highwaymen. Some of the guests who had traveled a considerable distance spoke of their fears of robbery and the men admitted they had come armed and had armed their footmen and coachmen. The Marquis, among the last arrivals, and accompanied by two friends from London, was besieged with questions when it was learned he had visited the commander of the regiment outside Chichester.

"Townsend and Leigh, here, know a great deal more of the army's dispositions. They are both officers of the 10th Hussars," the Marquis explained, introducing his companions. Although both men were in dark evening dress, not uniform, they looked very military and attracted many admiring glances from the ladies.

"But will the Hussars do anything to catch these villains?" the General asked.

"We are patrolling the roads around Chichester, sir," Major Townsend offered.

"That's the spirit. We can count on you fellows, I am sure." The General was delighted with the officers and monopolized them, much to their chagrin as both men were eager to meet Elizabeth and Nicola.

Captain Leigh thought himself a fortunate fellow to take Elizabeth into dinner, much to Julia's annoyance. Although

Mrs. Wynstan had thoughtfully arranged for Mr. Moffett to escort her, Julia would have preferred to have one of the dashing military officers on whom to work her wiles. Nicola drew the Marquis, which caused her a certain confusion. She was not sure what her attitude should be toward Jocelyn. He had made no effort to call after his ball and perhaps had no interest in pursuing their recent entente.

Sensing her withdrawal, he smiled. He had a very good idea of what she was imagining, probably regretting her artless confidences after the scene with Adrian in his garden.

As they waited for the turtle soup to be served, he asked her if Pettifer had removed himself from the neighborhood.

"Roger Forrest saw him leaving the inn in the village the day after your ball, but, somehow, I feel we have not heard the last of him."

"Perhaps not. He appeared to be a vindictive man." The Marquis believed in facing his fences head on.

"I feel his enthusiasm for the tunnel was just a ruse to gain entree into our household. I was gravely deceived," Nicola, always ready to face her own fences, confided.

"You are probably correct there. The man is a mountebank. He wanted to marry you, I suspect, and not entirely because of your position and money. Poor chap was enamored and forgot his careful wooing under the temptation of your charms." The Marquis was teasing and was gratified to see that Nicola blushed.

Angry at her lack of sophistication for she had much experience with such remarks, she rushed into speech. "Now you are blaming me again because I lured him into rash behavior. Not tactful, Jocelyn."

"You know you really are a minx. I cannot help but feel a little sorry for the man. But, come, I am mean to quiz you when I promised to conduct myself with every propriety."

"Hah, I doubt that." Nicola was enjoying their sparring but underneath all the bandying she sensed some other feeling. Was it disapproval or admiration? Did she want to encourage him? The Marquis was a challenge and she was not certain she wanted to take up the gauntlet he had thrown down.

After the serving of braised pigeons, she turned to her neighbor on the left, Major Townsend, and set herself to quiz him on his army duties. The Marquis perforce had to content himself with Lady Mumford on his right and he was received with flattering attention.

"Well, Lord Cranbourne, you are becoming most easy in our little company. I thought you might find country customs boring after your travels and would be off to London seeking excitement," she said archly. She meant to discover, if she could, what his intentions toward Nicola were. But the Marquis was a past master at eluding searching questions and parried her attempts politely, tuning the conversation to common friends. Balked, but not wanting to offend, Lady Mumford had to follow his lead.

After the savoury which followed the strawberries meringue, the ladies retired, leaving the men to their port. Lady Mumford, frustrated by the Marquis, made a beeline for Nicola hoping for a better reception.

"Well, my dear, with Mr. Pettifer gone you must be feeling bereft of followers. How are you managing?"

Accustomed to Lady Mumford's forthright manner when in pursuit of information, Nicola only smiled and parried, "Well, Elizabeth is here to keep me company, and we find it soothing to have a holiday from importuning gentlemen."

"And, of course, the Marquis is most attentive, I vow."

"Lord Cranbourne is always courteous, but we see very little of him. I understand he is occupied with settling the estate."

"And a most comfortable one it is. His uncle had let matters deteriorate a bit but I am sure the Marquis will correct all that. He is no doubt looking out for a wife to help him." She threw in the remark slyly, hoping for a response, but was disappointed.

"Oh, I don't think so. His cousin, Mrs. Sturbridge, seems to fill the role of hostess admirably."

Lady Mumford, conceding defeat, decided both the Marquis and Nicola were duplicitous opponents. She was sure that their relationship had prospered and wanted to be the first to know the outcome, but Nicola was equal to her challenge. Before Lady Mumford could continue her campaign the gentlemen joined them and Major Townsend hurried across the room to her.

"Your mother has sent me to request that you honor us with some music, Miss Wynstan. I understand you have a lovely voice and Miss Shillingford has consented to play for you."

Nicola had no recourse but to consent. She joined Elizabeth at the piano. The two girls made a delightful picture, and both Nicola's rendering of some country airs, and Elizabeth's accomplished playing received enthusiastic applause.

Both girls would have admitted that the evening, although pleasant, seemed a little flat. They had been monopolized by the two military gentlemen who appeared to be entranced to have discovered such delightful females in what they considered a rural backwater. Both the major and the captain tried to win a promise from Nicola and Elizabeth that they would ride out with them the following day, but the girls would give no assurances. Elizabeth was hoping that Ned might invite her to take a spin in his phaeton, one of the few opportunities for a couple to be alone without a chaperone. As for Nicola she was not sure what she expected from the Marquis. Now that they had settled their differences did she wish for a different relationship? She was unsure but a bit piqued that he made no effort to draw her into a tête à tête. That was not the reaction she expected with gentlemen she honored with her approval. He had behaved with unusual circumspection, talking easily to Mrs. Wynstan and Lady Mumford, but she had been conscious of his eyes upon her while she sang. She had returned his look with what she thought was the proper coolness but she had been aware of his gaze and it caused her some confusion. Surely she was not falling in love with Jocelyn?

The Marquis, a skilled campaigner in affairs of the heart, had a shrewd idea that his refusal to pay her attentions was causing some confusion. He avoided any attempts of Mrs. Wynstan to learn how he felt about her daughter, only expressing a tepid endorsement of Nicola's charms and listened with some amusement to her mother's tales of Nicola's London triumphs during two seasons.

"A most independent and spirited girl, who needs a firm hand," he conceded.

"Not biddable, that's true, but I believe Nicola would prove to be a most obliging wife to the right man. Unfortunately, she will not settle." Mrs. Wynstan sighed. Her hopes for the Marquis were rapidly dissipating.

"I'm afraid your best matchmaking is doomed to disappointment ma'am. Her judgment is often mistaken. She certainly made an error in her assessment of Mr. Pettifer."

"He turned out to be quite odious, and we had been so kind to him. I wonder if we have seen the last of him. There was a definite threatening quality to him. I must thank you for your coming to her rescue."

"I was fortunate to happen upon the scene. Any gentleman would have done the same." The Marquis was not to be drawn into any warmer expression of his interference between Nicola and Adrian. But he had learned what he wanted to know. As yet Nicola had not suffered any affront to her heart. Her trust in her judgment had been shaken, but only her pride had been affected.

As the company made its farewells to the Wynstans, the Marquis was able to have a private word with Nicola.

"I would like to take you for a ride tomorrow, Nicky. There are several things I want to say to you. Will you be available about ten tomorrow morning?"

"I think so. Of course, I cannot desert Elizabeth."

"I believe Ned has plans for your friend. At any rate, I will come around then. Until tomorrow." He bowed over her hand and missed the searching look she gave him. What did he want to say to her? Was it to be more comments on her behavior or had he another purpose in arranging a private conversation. She agreed to his invitation but could learn nothing from his bland expression. The Marquis was not a man whose emotions could be easily read.

Sixteen

For Julia Overton the evening had not been a success. Mr. Moffett had not paid her any particular attentions and the military gentlemen had preferred the company of Nicola and Elizabeth. Her sensibilities, always tender, were much wounded, a common occurrence with Julia. Determined to pursue Mr. Moffett, the next morning she offered to visit the vicarage with a message from Mrs. Wynstan to Miss Moffett. Not enjoying exercise she accepted the offer of the pony cart and set off for the few miles to the village, still brooding over her treatment. Halfway to her destination on a deserted section of the road she was hailed by a horseman. To her surprise she recognized Adrian Pettifer.

"A happy meeting, Miss Overton." He hailed her with a smile and appeared pleased to meet her. Julia appreciated his words and his evident interest.

"Why, Mr. Pettifer, I thought you had left us for London." Her curiosity aroused, she sensed a mystery that might give her an advantage.

"Well, I probably will in a few days, but I have some unfinished business in the neighborhood. And some of that business is an apology to you, Miss Overton. It was boorish of me to have cut our dance the other evening, but you may have heard that I had an unfortunate encounter with your cousin." Adrian's manner was a combination of contriteness and appeal to her womanly sympathies. As he had expected Julia, flattered that he seemed to be seeking her approval, responded eagerly.

"Of course I heard of your . . . er, disappointment. And you have my sympathy, but do not reproach yourself for missing our dance. I quite understood although I was looking forward to it."

"That is kind of you, Miss Overton. But I am holding you up and preventing you from completing your errand."

Basely abandoning Mr. Moffett with the suspicion that Mr. Pettifer might offer better value, Julie demurred. "Not at all, Mr. Pettifer. I just have a message to deliver at the vicarage for Cousin Prudence." She waited expectantly.

"Then, perhaps, you could spare the time to have some chocolate with me at the Crown and Anchor, if you think it a respectable enough establishment. I would not want to put your reputation at risk."

She was delighted and surprised, for in Julia's limited experience, gentlemen rarely considered her reputation or little else. Adrian's interest was raising exciting ideas in her bosom, unused as she was to such attentions. She could not help but contrast his behavior to that of Ned and the two military gentlemen of the evening past. Naïvely, she did not question why Adrian was taking such pains to cultivate her and she trotted off to the vicarage after agreeing to meet Adrian at the inn without any thought of Mr. Moffett.

Much subsequent trouble might have been avoided if any of the manor party or the Marquis had glimpsed this meeting between Adrian and Julia. However, Ned and Elizabeth had ridden out about the estate in quite the opposite direction and the Marquis, who had called for Nicola at the appointed hour, had secured her mother's permission to drive her to Chichester, an hour and a half distant, where he intended to give her luncheon away from the distractions of her family. Mrs. Wynstan, who normally would have wondered at the impropriety of allowing her daughter to be seen lunching without a chaperone at a hotel, was so overcome by the Marquis's interest in Nicola, that she gave her assent cheerfully. She hoped this tête à tête would produce some sign that the Marquis's intentions toward Nicola were honorable and would lead to a brilliant alliance. She put her recent miscalculation about Adrian behind her. She had been wrong in her reading of that young man's character but she had few doubts about the Marquis's prestige or his rent roll. She was determined to offer Nicola every opportunity to charm such an eligible parti. It was always difficult for unmarried respectable girls to find an excuse to be alone with any single man, and in London society, with its strict social code, almost impossible. But here in the country, rules of conduct could be relaxed a bit, and Mrs. Wynstan took advantage of the situation to assure the Marquis she trusted him to behave with every circumspection.

"I will take the utmost care of your daughter, Mrs. Wynstan, and have her home by late afternoon," he assured her, repressing a wicked desire to tell the obliging lady that he meant to abscond with Nicola to Gretna Green at the first chance.

Nicky, who had been standing silently by, wondered if her mother would have been so amenable if the gentleman seeking her company had not been a peer. She felt a bit mortified at such obvious angling and intended to set the Marquis straight on the subject once they were alone. She could not deny that she looked forward to a break from the routine of the manor and would welcome a day's outing but she was not prepared to show her pleasure in too gratifying a manner.

Once they were on their way in Jocelyn's phaeton, he anticipated any stringent remarks she might have made.

"Decent of your mother to relax her standards and allow this trip," he said, suppressing his amusement. He had easily divined Mrs. Wynstan's strategy.

Refusing to be embarrassed, Nicola spoke frankly. "She thinks you are an eligible parti and probably secretly hopes for an accident with the phaeton which will place you and me, too, in a scandalous position, and then you will have to make me an offer. But let me assure you even if we have to spend the night in an abandoned barn, you need not fear. I'm not so desirous of a husband that I will stoop to such devices."

The Marquis laughed. "Oh, Nicky, you never fail me. I might have known you would scorn such tactics. And I suppose you realize I am not the man to be caught by such ploys."

"Certainly not. You have probably evaded even more blatant attempts to lure you into the parson's mousetrap. Any man with a title, even if he is ancient, stooped, mean and ailing, is a target for ambitious mothers and daughters. Whatever my mother expects, you can rest assured I do not. So relax and let us enjoy the day. I haven't been to Chichester in ages and I enjoy getting away from the manor, whatever the means."

"Oh, dear, I am now just a means. How dispiriting."

"Not at all. You can be very pleasant company when you are not upbraiding me for some suspected japes."

"Thank you. But I don't think that is a sign of unqualified approval. I must study to make you view me in a more felicitous light."

And so the conversation continued as the Marquis's fast pair of chestnuts ate up the miles to Chichester. The two passengers were delighting in the verbal sparring, which masked their real feelings.

Conversation between Julia and Adrian in the Crown and Anchor's best parlor was of a far more serious nature. Both had grievances and Adrian hoped to use Julia's to his advantage but he had to tread warily. Accustomed to living by his wits, he had accurately judged Julia's relationship in the Wynstan household and her resentment of her single state. Although both the General and Mrs. Wynstan had always treated her with the utmost consideration, Adrian sensed they looked upon both Julia and her visits as a duty. And, of course, she did little to change this attitude, filled as she was with envy and malice. Adrian intended to make use of Julia by appealing to her feeling of being ill-treated and scorned. And he had encountered her at a time when her amour propre was injured.

"I can see, Miss Overton, that the Wynstans, although offering you hospitality, did not seem to appreciate your obvious qualities. I suffered from similar treatment myself. They did not think me good enough for their precious daughter."

"I thought Nicola's treatment of you inexcusable, leading you to expect she would favor your attentions and then, when you proposed, treating you so shabbily. She is a very spoiled headstrong girl, and I cannot think why gentlemen find her so attractive."

"I admit I was misled as to her true character and she behaved shockingly, flirting and encouraging me. I am well out of that relationship. I realize my stupidity in being lured by her outward facade and now seeing what a truly shallow vain creature she is. A woman with a kind heart and proper modesty would not have acted so." Adrian inferred that Julia, herself, would have behaved in a much more suitable fashion, a hint she was eager to embrace. By now Julia, under such flattering attentions, would have believed any nonsense Adrian suggested. He had chosen his conspirator well.

"I would willingly intercede with Nicola and the Wynstans in your behalf, Mr. Pettifer, but I doubt they would listen to me. They are not inclined to take my opinions as of any worth."

"Now that we have had this opportunity to cement our friendship, won't you call me Adrian?"

"And you must call me Julia." She was almost beside herself with pleasure at this thrilling encounter with a gentlemen who seemed to prefer her to her cousin, and she was prepared to take every obsequious remark as her due.

"Well, Julia, I think we could both benefit from a more intimate relationship. I plead guilty to not recognizing your obvious worth when I was blinded by your cousin's rather coarse charms. But I am willing to make up for my abysmal neglect if you will honor me with your regard."

"Of course, Adrian. I quite understand that you are an innocent victim of the Wynstans' arrogance." Thrilled at entering into an alliance with this personable young man, Julia would have promised anything he asked, by the time she finished her chocolate.

"I do want to see more of you, Julia, but I think any future meeting must be done in secret. The Wynstans do not approve of me and would not take kindly to your championship of one who was turned out of their house."

"Certainly, Adrian. I can only agree."

"You see the real villain in my ejection is Lord Cranbourne, a rake and womanizer of the worst kind. He has assumed a gallant pose in Nicola's eyes and she will get her just deserts if she tries her wiles on him. He is not a marrying man."

"Do you think he will make improper suggestions to Nicky, and that she will respond?" Julia was quivering with the delightful prospect of her cousin as a fallen woman.

"Possibly. Of course, I would not wish that tragic outcome but the Marquis is a haughty man who needs to learn a lesson, and I intend to teach him one." Feeling he had gone quite far enough for the present, Adrian turned the conversation to soothing Julia's sensibilities and persuading her of how much he preferred her gentle charms to those of her cousin. She was completely convinced. Later he would enlist her in his plan for revenge.

Jocelyn's business in Chichester took just a few minutes. He made a call on the commandant of the regiment stationed in the town, and made some suggestions for apprehending the highwaymen. He was received with all cordiality. Then he joined Nicola at the hotel where he had bespoke a private parlor and ordered a lavish luncheon. After fresh salmon with cucumber sauce, a salad dressed in the French manner and pineapple Nicky felt most replete.

"I like to see a girl relish her food. You have a healthy appetite, Nicky." The Marquis approved.

"Well, I would be a widgeon not to appreciate such a meal. Some say it is fashionable to pick at each dish, but I think that's nonsense. If you are offered a well-prepared meal it would be quite mean to the cook to reject it."

"Sensible girl. Now that you have been saved from starvation I have something of import to say to you."

For a moment a wild surmise rose in Nicky's mind. Was Jocelyn about to propose? Surely not. She folded her hands and tried to look composed.

Jocelyn, who noticed her rising color, had an idea of what was passing through her mind. "No, I am not about to make you an offer, at least not yet. I want to talk to you about that puppy Pettifer."

Nicky, wondering what he meant by that equivocal statement, "not yet," tried to look receptive, not disappointed. Her feelings were in a turmoil but she was determined to keep her composure. It would never do to look expectant.

"What about Adrian? He has returned to London and can no longer be of any concern."

"I think you are wrong there. From the beginning I have been suspicious of that young man. His tunnel scheme was all a hum to raise money. And the odd thing is he appears to have some kind of income. From what I can learn he does not come from moneyed people. What did he tell you about his family?"

"Well, not much really. I understand his parents are comfortably situated up north somewhere. I believe his father is a solicitor. He went to Oxford and was accepted by some men who introduced him to London society. I met him at the home of a hostess that Mother considers rather flashy but he was received in some good houses. How nasty I sound, like a real snob."

"Not at all, and your parents are quite wise to question his bona fides especially since you gave the impression you were interested in him as a possible husband."

"I never did. Where he had that idea I cannot fathom. It was the tunnel that intrigued me and I admit I used the scheme to tease Father. He's such a hidebound old dear, always scorning progress."

"I'm afraid Pettifer did not see it in that light."

"Well, he does now." Nicky was annoyed that Jocelyn implied that her conduct had not been all it should have been in that situation. But how could she have known that Adrian was a charlatan? She blushed now to remember she had told Adrian she suspected Jocelyn of being the leader of the highwaymen.

"I fear he intends to take his revenge on you or your family and possibly me. Furthermore I fear he may, himself, be involved with the highwaymen. These recent outbreaks only occurred when he arrived in the neighborhood."

"Oh, my goodness. That had never crossed my mind. Still, if that's true, they will cease now that he has returned to London."

"But has he? I am not so sure of that. He told Forrest that was his intention but can we believe him? And Colonel Wright just told me there was another hold-up twenty miles from here, a well-to-do merchant and his family returning home in their carriage from a visit to Southampton."

"Somehow I cannot see Adrian having the daring to lead a raid." Nicola was astounded at this picture of Adrian masked and brandishing pistols as he robbed innocent travelers.

"I don't think he does the actual robbery. I think he organizes the raids, and very skillfully—with advance knowledge he gains by some method or other."

"And what will you do to prove it?"

"Offer him a tempting bait?"

"What will that be?" Nicola was agog at this clever ruse to capture Adrian in the act if indeed he was the villain.

"I don't think I will tell you that. It would be most imprudent, knowing how you manage to embroil yourself in dangerous situations. What I am doing now is to ask you to promise me you will not expose yourself to peril by careening around the countryside unescorted. I know your father has spoken to you but I wonder if you will heed his advice?"

"Of course I will. I do not lack common sense." Nicola was outraged that he should think she was some heedless madcap, dashing about the countryside looking for adventures.

"Oh dear, you have taken me in dislike again. But you must understand that I cannot always be about to protect you from your follies."

"If you are deliberately trying to make me angry you are succeeding. I did not expect to find some strange villain in our own woods prepared to attack me and I did not encourage Adrian to behave like a nodcock and propose to me in such an outre fashion in your garden." Nicky was fast losing her patience.

"I don't think you are aware of how devastating your charms can be." He gave her an enigmatic look she could not decipher. One of the qualities she most disliked in Jocelyn was his ability to make these teasing remarks that hid his real opinion of her.

"Well, you seem to be able to ignore my so-called charms without difficulty," she snapped and then wondered if he thought she was being provocative.

"How wrong you are, Nicky. But this very respectable hostelry is not the place to display just how affected I am." He grinned at her, causing her to redden annoyingly whether from anger or pleasure she hardly knew.

"Seriously, Nicky, I believe Adrian may be the leader of the highwaymen, and I think he has a bolt hole in the neighborhood from which he plans some kind of revenge on you and possibly me, if he can. All I am asking you is to be on your guard. Don't be beguiled by notes luring you to a rendezvous, ride out without a groom or an escort, and let me know if you see any sign of a stranger in the village."

"You don't think he has returned to London then?"

"No, I don't. I believe he is both vindictive and vicious. You are in danger. I have alerted the army and hope the colonel will deploy some troops around the countryside. If Adrian sees soldiers he may cry off and give up his plot as too perilous. But I also think he is lacking in common sense, in the grip of some passion and who knows what he might attempt."

"Well, I will be on my guard. Have you spoken to Ned about this?"

"Yes, and he agrees with me, although your brother is apt to see life optimistically, and he also is quite sure of his own ability to protect you."

"I do believe you are exaggerating the danger, but I will be careful." She wanted to reassure him and was gratified that he cared enough to worry about her.

"Delightful as this interlude has been we must be on our way. I do not want to get in your mother's bad books by keeping you too late."

"Thank you for my lovely luncheon." Nicola was somewhat subdued by Jocelyn's grave warnings although they had not entirely convinced her. Of much more concern were his veiled allusions to his interest in her. Was he just toying with her, exerting his formidable charms to win her approval and more? She was fast falling under his sway and the emotion he evoked confused and almost frightened her. If this was love she was not sure she liked the feeling. However, on the ride back he behaved with every propriety, making no advances and entertaining her with vignettes of his life in the Far East. Just before they neared the entrance to the manor driveway he pulled his chestnuts to a stop and turned to her.

"When this miserable business is concluded I have a great deal more to say to you, Nicky. For now you must be content with this." And he took her in his arms and kissed her with a hot passion that demanded response. Releasing her, he gave her a wry smile and said, "I suppose you are offended. Spare me the usual outrage."

"I am not offended, only baffled." She was determined not to react in a missish manner. "To be honest, I really enjoyed it."

He laughed. "You are a rare female, Nicky. I can see I will have to watch my step."

Nicky responded with a wary smile. She was never certain what Jocelyn meant, although his kiss at least was evidence that he was not indifferent to her. But he had not spoken one word of love nor persuaded her that she had won his heart. It was a strangely subdued girl who bade him farewell at the manor's front door. He refused her invitation to come in and for that she was grateful. For the moment she wanted to be alone and consider what it all meant. All thoughts of the highwaymen and the perfidious Adrian were swamped by this new development.

Seventeen

Nicola intended to go directly to her room, but as she crossed the hall Paxton stopped her.

"The mistress is in the morning room, Miss Nicola, and wants to see you as soon as you return."

She sighed, knowing her mother would want a detailed account of her outing with Jocelyn. Nicola had no illusions about her mother's interest in her relationship with their titled neighbor. Mrs. Wynstan's chief aim in life seemed to be concerned with her daughter's marriage to an eligible parti. Nothing could deflect her from assisting in the process of bringing this about. Well, Nicky decided, she was accustomed to parrying her mother's questions. She had plenty of experience. When she arrived in the morning room she was relieved to see both Elizabeth and Julia with her mother having tea.

"Oh, there you are, my dear. Did you have a pleasant time in Chichester with the Marquis?"

Elizabeth gave her a conspiratorial look. She understood the nature of Mrs. Wynstan's apparently casual question. Julia, as usual, looked smug and disapproving. She had her own secrets.

"Yes, we had lunch at the Crown and Anchor, cold salmon and pineapple, very good." She hoped that would satisfy her mother but she should have known better.

"I wonder what his object was in going to Chichester? He seems to spend a lot of time there."

"He went to call on the Colonel and see how the search for the highwaymen is proceeding."

"And is it?" Elizabeth asked, eager to hear any developments.

"As far as I can tell the army is baffled. The only conclusion is that the highwaymen must have a great deal of local knowledge, some spy in the neighborhood who knows when travelers will be on the road. It's hard to believe. We have always been a most law-abiding neighborhood."

"Well, Ned is convinced the army will apprehend the villains." Elizabeth gave Nicola a wink. She was impressed at how Nicola had turned the conversation from the Marquis and his intentions, but meant to get more information from Nicola when they were alone.

"Where is Ned?" Nicola asked, determined to distract her mother.

"He and your father went to Arundel, some business with the Duke's factor," Mrs. Wynstan said impatiently. It was all very well for Nicky to behave so casually about the Marquis but she had hoped for some definite progress while the pair were alone. Not for the first time she felt her daughter did not take advantage of her opportunities. But Nicky was not prepared to discuss her relationship with the Marquis before Julia.

After a few moments she was able to extract Elizabeth from the tea table and leave her frustrated mother and Julia alone.

Following her friend into her bedroom Elizabeth sank down in a chair and regarded Nicola with an appraising air. "Now, tell all, did the fascinating Marquis make advances?"

To her embarrassment Nicola blushed. "Not really. I think he may be a philanderer. I can't really tell what he feels for me."

"And you care. Well, that's progress. Usually you have no trouble in thwarting your beaux with that touch-me-not manner you have cultivated." Elizabeth was teasing, but she wondered just what Nicky really felt for the Marquis.

"Oh, Elizabeth, the man is an enigma. Sometimes I think he is really interested in me, then he goes all cool and indifferent."

"Quite the right attitude to keep you fascinated. I knew it. You care for him, admit it."

"I suppose you think it would serve me right if I fell in love with him and he spurned me."

"Of course not, Nicky. I was only funning. If you have at last met the man you could marry I can only wish you every success in bringing him up to scratch."

Nicola laughed a bit bitterly. "You sound like Mother. Who knows what he feels? He's a master at deception. Anyway, it was a pleasant outing. That's all I can tell you."

Elizabeth took the hint and changed the conversation. "You know that Julia is up to something. She has been sitting around looking like a cat that swallowed the cream. Really, she's a most objectionable type. I don't know why your mother receives her."

"Mother feels sorry for her. Julia is a far better target for her matchmaking than I am, but I doubt if even Mother can find her a husband."

"Too true. She was making some very odd remarks about you this afternoon, implying that flirts eventually get their just deserts."

"I am not a flirt."

"Julia is a jealous cat and a bore, but she could cause trouble."

"Oh, I have been dealing with Julia for years. Don't take her seriously."

In this judgment of her cousin, Nicola was mistaken, and Elizabeth more sagacious than she realized. Julia was about to cause a great deal of trouble. She had made an assignation with Adrian in the village church. During the week it was usually empty except for the occasional visits of Mr. Moffett and the sexton, an aged, gnarled retainer who did little work but for whom the vicar felt compassion although he often became impatient with him. Old Jock was a cousin of Nanny and had always been viewed by that formidable woman as a scoundrel and a lazy varmint who spent too much time at the pub. Adrian had early taken his measure and won his allegiance by providing the coins for Jock to have a steady ration of ale.

The morning after Nicola's journey to Chichester with Jocelyn, Adrian met Julia in the church. She had left the manor surreptitiously, quite enjoying the secrecy, and believing that Adrian had conceived a passion for her. Julia's judgment was often at fault and she was easily influenced when it came to the matter of a possible romantic attachment. Despite past experience that should have taught her men found little in her appearance or character to charm them, she was convinced that only the spite of other females and unhappy circumstances prevented her from securing a husband. Adrian had replaced Mr. Moffett in her dreams and the fact that he had been disillusioned by Nicola and sought revenge only heightened her excitement and bolstered her hopes. She had no compunction in repaying the Wynstans' hospitality and kindness by abetting Adrian in his nefarious plot.

Looking about furtively she darted into the church. It was vital that neither of the Moffetts saw her, but there was small possibility of that. Miss Moffett did her village shopping early and she had seen the vicar ride off in his shabby pony cart, the only vehicle he could afford, to visit a parishioner on the outskirts of the village. She had to wait some time for Adrian, but she passed the time comfortably imagining her future role as Mrs. Pettifer. At last he arrived through the side door and hurried up to her where she sat in a pew toward the back of the church.

"Good morning, Julia. How kind of you to come, but it is such a pleasant morning I am sure you had no trouble in making an excuse to leave the Wynstans."

"Not at all. I just left, not telling anyone of my reasons.

Have you had a long ride? You look tired," she cooed, with all sympathy.

Adrian had no intention of telling Julia where he was staying. The less she knew about his direction the better. He spent a few precious moments in flattering her, realizing that he must not betray his repugnance at her simpering efforts to please him. When she had served his purpose he would discard her without any regret, but for the moment she was a tool that suited his nasty designs.

"You are a very clever girl, Julia. I know you have every reason to despise Nicola as I have. But you will see that she suffers what she deserves."

A little chill fell over Julia as she looked at his menacing expression and heard his bitter words. Seeing her slight withdrawal he soothed her. It would not do to arouse her suspicion.

"I mean only to throw a fright into Nicola, not cause her any harm except to her reputation. She has queened it over other females, far more worthy, such as yourself, for far too long. She needs to realize she cannot behave in a heedless fashion toward men who honor her with their regard. That's all I intend to make her see."

"I quite agree. She is a bold and uncaring tease. What do you have in mind?"

"It's best you do not know exactly, so that if questioned you can answer sincerely that you have no idea of my actions. All I want is some knowledge of her daily routine. I know she usually rides out often in the mornings. And she rarely takes a groom, so it will be safe to approach her. But I must know when she goes."

"Most mornings she rides about ten o'clock after doing the flowers. Of course, with Elizabeth Shillingford visiting, her plans are not so set."

"Does Miss Shillingford accompany her?"

"Sometimes, but she often goes with Ned when he visits the tenant farms. That Miss Shillingford is another who is a flirt and no better than she should be. She has her talons into

Ned, wants to marry him, I am sure." Julia spoke bitterly. Ned's resolute avoidance of her she laid at the door of the visiting belle and would like to see her suffer equally with Nicola, but Adrian was not interested in Elizabeth.

"Well, with your help I can settle Miss Nicola. Now this is what I suggest." And Adrian went on at some length to explain what he required from Julia. He hoped she was reliable and would have enough sense to keep her own counsel. To ensure her secrecy he went to some lengths and ended the interview by pressing her hand suggestively and assuring her yet again of his admiration and respect. Leaving her hugging her expectations if she managed to please him, he finally slipped out of the church, careful not to attract any attention. Julia sat on for a moment savoring the encounter, a sly smile adding little to her meager attractions.

Julia's implausible dreams of her future as Mrs. Pettifer engrossed her but she realized she had small chance of achieving them if she did not fulfill Adrian's demands. She enjoyed their conspiratorial meetings and would have been happy to delay the climax of Adrian's coup to revenge himself on Nicola but she sensed he was becoming impatient as the days passed. She temporized by explaining that Nicola's daily rides were sometimes canceled. But she realized that Adrian's irritation was growing and she would have to report some more definite information or he might abandon her for a better ally. In the past she had managed to bring a man almost up to proposing, then for some reason he retreated. She sensed that Adrian might be capable of treating her in a similar fashion but she was clever enough to understand that she had the power to betray or blackmail him. Julia had few scruples when her future was at stake. The driving motive of her life was to gain a suitable husband and she was not above any tactic, no matter how sordid, to achieve her aim. So, convinced that her strategy could not fail, she barely hid her satisfaction, arousing some speculation on the part of the Wynstans.

Elizabeth Shillingford had been wary of Julia from the beginning and kept insisting to Nicola that her cousin was up to some ploy. Even Mrs. Wynstan, the most easily duped, began to comment on Julia's changed manner. But it was Roger Forrest who supplied the evidence. Although he was the most retiring of men, never eager to put himself in a position to be noticed, he was also observant and he had also early taken Julia's measure. One evening, sharing a game of "beggar my neighbor" with Ned, Nicola and Elizabeth, he mentioned his concern about Julia.

"Did you know that your cousin has been leaving the house every morning on some mysterious errand?" he asked Nicola.

"I try to avoid Julia whenever possible and have no interest in her odd habits."

"Well, she scurries out of the house every morning soon after breakfast. I almost followed her the other day but the General called me to some chore and I could not."

"What do you think she is doing, Roger?" Elizabeth was intrigued. She suspected Julia of some chicanery and was anxious to have her suspicions confirmed.

"Could she be meeting a lover?" Ned quipped, not believing for one moment that was conceivable.

"Oh, Ned, don't be ridiculous. Do you think she and Mr. Moffett are having romantic trysts in the church? Surely he is too proper and staid to lend himself to such conduct and why would he? He could court her openly. In fact, Mother would give him every assistance." Nicola had little faith that even the prosy Mr. Moffett would be attracted to Julia.

"She's up to something, Nicky. I have been telling you that for days."

"Well, I think you are wrong. If she were spying on me I might believe you, but she has been avoiding me lately for which I can only be grateful."

"Use your charm on her, Roger, and discover what she's up to," Ned suggested thinking this idea of Julia involved in some dubious activity all a hum.

"Now, don't take umbrage, Roger. Ned is only funning. We

are so used to Julia's moods and megrims that this latest whim is of little interest. I must say I cannot look forward to her snaring Mr. Moffett for then she would be on our doorstep forever, and as the vicar's wife we would have to be polite to her. Perhaps she is meeting Mr. Moffett secretly because she knows his aunt would never countenance a match which would mean her dismissal from the vicarage."

"Somehow I don't think it is Mr. Moffett she's meeting, Nicky," Elizabeth said.

"Well, I suggest Roger pursue her when he has the chance and then he can reveal the whole business."

"I find any discussion of Julia without merit. Shall we have another game?" Ned really wanted to lure Elizabeth out onto the terrace. It was a balmy June evening and he thought a little romantic dalliance with their delectable guest much more to his taste than any discussion of his dreary cousin. The matter of Julia's mysterious errands was forgotten. Only Roger Forrest remembered and wondered.

Nicola was feeling a bit out of sorts for she had seen little of the Marquis. He had called one afternoon but aside from a brief visit with them all, had retired to the library where he was closeted with the General for some time. Nicola decided that his momentary interest in her had vanished. Perhaps she had been too easy a mark, allowing him to kiss her on the ride home from Chichester.

Unfortunately, Nicola was having some trouble in forgetting that lapse of decorum. What was his purpose in attracting her and then ignoring her? Was the man a cad and just entertaining himself because no other likely female was in the neighborhood? The idea was very lowering. Concerned with her own troubled state of emotions she had no time to spare for Julia and her possible intrigues. The morning after Roger's warning she decided that she would try to rid herself of her blue humor by a long ride, always a tonic when she was depressed. At breakfast she informed her family of her intentions. Politely she asked Elizabeth to accompany her. Her friend was a skilled horsewoman and enjoyed racing about the Wynstans' acres.

"No luck, Nicky. Elizabeth has promised to accompany me to Arundel. Father is involved with the Duke on some scheme to corner the apple market and I have to meet with the Duke's factor about the matter. Would you rather come with us?" Ned politely tendered the invitation, hoping his sister would decline. He anticipated an intimate day with Elizabeth without his sister's knowing eye upon him. But Nicola was easily able to read her brother's wishes and saw no reason to interfere with the development of what she hoped would be a serious understanding between her friend and her brother.

"No thanks, Ned. Enjoy your day." She gave him a wry glance, signaling that she knew what he wanted.

"Be sure to take a groom, Nicky," her mother warned. "Those highwaymen are still about, I am sure."

"You do have a bee in your bonnet, Mother, about my safety, but I have promised not to ride alone while the villains are roaming about so I will take George. He loves escaping from his stable duties."

While this discussion was proceeding, Julia kept her eyes downcast but she was listening avidly. This would be information Adrian would welcome. At last he would be able to get his revenge on Nicola and the instrument of his scheme would be Julia. She thought he would be exceedingly grateful for the news and might at last reward her efforts on his behalf with the coveted proposal.

As the various members of the family left the breakfast table in pursuit of their plans for the day, Nicola to do the flowers before riding, Ned and Elizabeth to journey to Arundel, Mrs. Wynstan to interview the cook, the General to the library to write letters and look over Roger's notes, only Julia and Roger were left. The General had given his secretary a free morning. Roger suspected that his employer was losing his enthusiasm for the book which entailed more work than he had expected. Roger admitted he may have been pushing him too hard but he was a conscientious young man and wanted to acquit himself well. Also he had become fascinated by the material. Still, he was relieved to have a few hours to himself. An observant man, he had noticed Julia's air of excitement, badly concealed, and wondered what her complacent mask hid. She was up to some scheme, he was convinced, and today he would follow her if she snuck away on her odd errand. He found her a most unprepossessing female and was not deceived by her toadying and meek demeanor.

"Do you have any plans for today, Miss Overton?" he asked, pretending some interest.

Julia wondered if the shy secretary was about to ask for her company. Usually she would have found that flattering, but today she could not allow herself to encourage him.

"Oh, no, Mr. Forrest. I make myself available to Cousin Prudence. She always has some little task for me. I try to help her about the house since Nicola and Miss Shillingford never appear very obliging," Julia responded snippily.

"Well, I have some pressing duties, so I will leave you to get on with yours."

He had no intention of allowing Julia to believe he had a free morning. He left her with a kind smile to get on with whatever she intended. Roger meant to follow her this time and discover exactly to what purpose she took those daily walks. He did not think it was exercise.

Julia scurried away, hoping to avoid Mrs. Wynstan for she could not be delayed with some trifling task this morning. She only hoped that Adrian would not be late for their meeting. Who knew how long it would take Nicky to do the flowers? On her way to the side door she peeked into the flower room and saw Nicky dutifully arranging some roses and noted that three or four vases stood ready to be filled. She had plenty of time. Not waiting to fetch a bonnet or shawl, for it was a warm morning, she scuttled out the door, looking behind her to make sure no one noticed her departure. Roger Forrest was too clever to show himself, but wondered if she were stupid enough not to sense that these strange absences had caused comment by some member of the family. Of course, Julia was used to being ignored.

On the whole he had found the Wynstan household happy. Julia was creating the only false note and he thought, not for the first time, that the Wynstans were too tolerant of this spiteful cuckoo in the nest. It would never occur to them that Julia would repay their hospitality by any malicious act. He suspected that she detested them all, believing they treated her with contempt and would do what lay in her power to cause them all trouble. But what could she do? Were these mysterious errands devoted to that end? Well, he would find out.

Eighteen

For once Adrian was early for his rendezvous with Julia, and crept into the church after a careful surveillance. She was quite right to think he was getting tired of waiting for her to produce some information that would help him achieve his revenge on Nicola. As he sat fuming, adding up his grievances, he wondered if his cultivation of Julia had been a mistake. Was she just procrastinating, hoping to keep his attention, and unwilling to give up these meetings, which the foolish woman thought was based on his regard for her?

If only she knew how much he despised her. How could she believe that any man would prefer her dubious attractions to Nicola's? She had no beauty, no charm, and a very unpleasant character. But females were easily gulled. He had made a mistake with Nicola, who had badly damaged his conceit, but he had managed Julia cleverly. He would tell her today she must produce the needful or this would be the end of their relationship. He would have to be careful for it would never do for her to confess to the Wynstans that she had been meeting him secretly. His musings were interrupted by Julia sliding into the pew beside him, breathless and excited.

"Today could be the day, Adrian. In about a half an hour Nicola will be riding out. She announced it at breakfast and that Elizabeth, who has beguiled Ned, will not be with her. She and Ned are going to Arundel."

"Fine, excellent. You have done the trick, Julia." All

Adrian's doubts had vanished. At last he would repay Nicola for spurning him, and take his revenge on the Marquis, too.

"I think she deserves what you plan for her, but remember, Adrian, that my part in all this must never be revealed. The Wynstans would toss me out, never to be invited again."

"Of course, Julia. I understand, and you will not lose by your kind cooperation and warm compassion toward me. You know that I have been grievously wronged and want to see justice done."

Impressed as she was by these glowing tributes, Julia expected more than gratitude. "I had hoped you had a matter of more personal concern to discuss with me, Adrian." She looked at him coyly, waiting eagerly for the proposal that would reward her for her betrayal.

Adrian knew what she expected and had no intention of providing her that solace, but he was too shrewd to reveal his real feelings.

"Of course, Julia, but first I must make these arrangements as I discussed with you. Our affairs will have to wait upon that, but be assured I will never forget your generous loyalty to me, and at a later date we will seal our compact."

Julia felt that at last she would achieve her heart's desire, a husband, and one she need not be ashamed to claim. She would be the perfect helpmate to Adrian in his important work with the tunnel and their life together could not begin too soon for her.

"Naturally, you must deal with Nicola. I quite see that. I hope we can put this all behind us soon."

"I am exceedingly grateful to you, Julia, but now I must leave you and take care of the details. Don't worry. Your part in this affair will never be revealed, but you must pretend shock and surprise when the Wynstans learn what has happened to their dear daughter. I know you can behave with all circumspection." He rose on the words and without any token of affection slipped out of the church. Julia, relaxed and pleased, had no idea she would never see him again. Smugly she sat on, dreaming of her future, without any compunction about her part in Nicola's ugly fate.

Roger Forrest had not dared to enter the church, for fear of being discovered, but he had seen enough. Julia was meeting that meretricious Pettifer and he had little doubt they were plotting some skullduggery involving the Wynstans. He watched Adrian hurry away, concealed behind a large yew in the church-yard, and he waited for some time before Julia emerged and scurried away looking furtively around.

But what was Roger to do with his information? His obvious confidant would be Ned, but that young man had ridden off to Arundel. He probably should approach the General, but would his employer take his news seriously? He would bluster and condemn but probably decide that Julia was just carrying on a clandestine relationship with that puppy Pettifer and if that was what she wanted, good luck to her. He would never be convinced that Adrian had some nefarious purpose in cultivating Julia, for the General was an honorable, although simple man. No, the man to see was the Marquis. He would return to the manor and secure a horse to take him to Cranbourne Hall.

When Roger reached the Hall some time later he found the Marquis in his library attending to his correspondence. His natural awe of the haughty aristocrat was submerged in his conviction that Cranbourne was the only person to deal with this situation. He was received politely and asked the nature of his business.

"Well, sir, it's a dashed tricky affair, and you may think I am being overly suspicious. But Adrian Pettifer, the fellow that behaved so badly to the Wynstans, has been meeting Miss Overton in the village church. I believe they are planning some wicked scheme against the Wynstans."

"I thought we had not heard the last of that preposterous young man. I knew he had a vindictive nature. Have you informed the General of this fact?"

"No, sir. I thought it would not come well from me and

you would be the person to make the General see the serious-
ness of the matter. He might think that Miss Overton was just
having a romantic tryst with Pettifer, but I believe she is conspiring with him to bring harm to the Wynstans, especially
Nicola, for she envies and dislikes her cousin. She is a very
jealous and spiteful type."

"And you want me to approach the General with this information. I agree it sounds ominous, but what exactly is your
plan to thwart Pettifer?"

"Well, that's just it, sir. I thought you would come up with
some scheme. Pettifer must be hiding somewhere in the neighborhood. He came to the church on foot, sneaking through
that copse of yews to the north. If he had a horse nearby I
neither saw or heard signs of it." Roger felt he had fulfilled
his part in counteracting Adrian's plot and was content to be
directed by the Marquis for further steps.

"Where is Miss Wynstan this morning, Forrest?"

"She was doing the flowers when I left to follow Miss
Overton, but she mentioned taking a long ride afterwards. Of
course, she will take a groom. She promised her parents since
the scare about the highwaymen that she would not ride out
alone."

"Well, that's some comfort, but you know she is perfectly
capable of ignoring that promise. She likes her solitary rides.
We must go immediately to the manor and try to learn her
whereabouts." The Marquis spoke calmly but he feared the
worst. He had almost been expecting some attempt by Adrian
to repay Nicola for what he thought was her cruel rejection
of him. Throwing down his pen he rang for his man and ordered his horse. Roger followed him to the wide steps of the
Hall where the Marquis waited, giving no sign of his concern.
Since Jocelyn had been convinced for some time that Adrian
was involved with the highwaymen he felt that the fellow
would enlist his confederates in whatever plan he had hatched.
Despite his best efforts Jocelyn had not been able to discover
their headquarters. He was hindered by not knowing the area

well. Until he inherited the title his visits to Cranbourne had been few and brief. But surely the General would have knowledge of the local terrain.

If the Marquis and Roger had taken the longer route through the woods separating the Cranbourne acres from the Wynstans they might have surprised Adrian in his kidnapping, but they took the shorter route, along the road.

The General, who had been napping over the newspaper in the library, was startled from his slumber by the eruption of the Marquis and his secretary. He had thought Forrest was enjoying a respite from his duties, and here the fellow was accompanied by the Marquis, and both of them looking grave.

"General, we have reason to think that Nicky has ridden into an ambush planned by that rogue, Pettifer." The Marquis spoke with conviction, having little patience to explain the whole business to the General.

"Nonsense, she's about here somewhere, I am sure."

"No, sir, we asked Paxton. She has ridden out already."

"Well, she will be perfectly safe on our grounds. And she took a groom with her, I presume."

"He would be of little use if she were attacked by three or four men."

"And you think that may have happened?" The General could not believe his ears, but he was impressed by the Marquis's concern. "Well, we must try to find her. She probably rode toward the woods. That is one of her favorite haunts. What makes you think she's in danger?"

"Forrest, here, saw Pettifer sneaking away from the church. We think he was meeting Miss Overton there and she has been his spy in your household."

"Julia! I can't believe that. She would never betray our trust in such a shabby way and I doubt that Pettifer would enlist her in any plot. She has no more sense than a pea goose."

"We are wasting time, sir. I would like to question Miss Overton but I feel we must first try to find Nicky." The Marquis was eager to get on the trail of Pettifer and had little patience with the General's feeble protests.

"I do think the Marquis is right, General. We should be marshaling a force to find Nicola." Forrest, too, was anxious and impatient.

"All right. You two start the search and I will gather some of the grooms to help. Damn Pettifer. If he has harmed Nicky he will answer to me."

"If we catch him, sir." The Marquis, followed by Forrest hurried from the room. Every minute was precious. The General, now thoroughly alarmed, was not far behind them, calling to Paxton, who had been hovering in the hall, aware that some crisis had occurred. The General called for his horse and watched as Forrest and the Marquis mounted their horses and rode away.

"Did you see Miss Nicola leave, Paxton?" the General asked his worried butler.

"Yes, General, some time ago. George brought her mare around and went with her. They rode down the back drive, heading for the north woods. Has something happened to Miss Nicola?"

"I hope not, but it looks as if she may have been waylaid. Don't mention this to Mrs. Wynstan. I don't want her alarmed."

"Of course not, sir." Paxton would have liked to hear more, but he could see the General was disturbed and anxious to begin the search. A groom appeared with his horse, and he rode off toward the stables to gather more men. Paxton shook his head. Such upheaval was foreign to the usual even tenor of the household and he could not understand what it meant. If anything had happened to Miss Nicola he would be as devastated as her parents. He was very fond of his young mistress. He stood irresolute, not knowing what he could do to help.

* * *

Adrian had lost no time in returning to the small cottage some ten miles from the church and gathering up his cohorts. The three men had been playing cards, idly discussing their successful forays on the carriages they had robbed. They were not evil men, but greedy. Bart, Joe and Reg, were all veterans of the late wars and had returned to a country which had not rewarded them for their prowess on the battlefield. Bitter at their inability to find work, they had been recruited by Adrian, who had masterminded their raids, providing the information, the guns and the horses, and taking the lion's share of the illegal proceeds.

They were somewhat in awe of their leader, who had shown such skill in protecting them from arrest. And they had become careless, believing they were invincible. But they were not so sure about this latest caper. Adrian had convinced them that the ransom he intended to collect from the kidnapping of Nicola would be substantial and they could all retire with a fortune. He was holding most of the proceeds from their recent raids, suspecting if he gave them all their share, they would squander it in taverns and quickly come under suspicion. They would not desert him without their shares. Still, they had qualms about carrying off a lady of quality and feared their fate if Adrian's scheme went awry.

Bart, their spokesman, a cross-grained, sturdy chap, too handy with his fives, made their objections known when Adrian commanded them to mount up for their ride to intercept Nicola.

"Don't like this kidnapping, squire. Have the whole country on our trail. And what will we do with the mort when we get her? This be no place to hide a female." Bart looked about the rude cottage with scorn. All right for the likes of them, but squalid and dirty, with few comforts. He didn't like the notion of restraining some squalling female who would cause trouble. Females always did.

"Not to worry, Bart. Haven't I proved to know what I am doing? Come on. We must hurry."

"Well, carrying off a female is a vast difference from robbing some nob's carriage and facing a cowardly coachman. Who is this mort who you intend to grab? And won't her family be on the warpath?"

"Not if they wish to secure her safety. It's foolproof. Now, let's get going."

Grudgingly, the trio followed Adrian. Past successes had led them to trust him and the promise of more guineas was too much of an inducement. But Bart muttered to the other two as they mounted their horses. "Don't like it, have a bad feeling about this caper."

Adrian deployed his men deep in the woods, which he was sure Nicola would enter. Julia had told him this was her favorite ride and he relied on her information. The silly woman had assured him that Nicola often went in that direction because she liked to gather the wildflowers growing in the depth of the copse. He hoped she would not be accompanied by a groom, but was certain he and his men could handle any stableboy. They all donned masks, which added to their formidable appearance and would prevent any future trouble if the groom tried to describe them.

Julia had returned from her rendezvous with Adrian in time to see Nicola descending the stairs dressed in her riding costume.

"Oh, there you are, Nicky. Off on your ride? You have a lovely day for it." Julia greeted her cousin with spurious camaraderie that did not fool Nicola.

"Where have you been, Julia? Mother was asking for you."

"Oh dear, I am sorry. It is such a fine morning I took a little walk. I will go to her now."

"You seem to take a great many walks. I don't remember you being so eager for exercise in the past." Nicola looked at her cousin sharply. The girl looked as if someone had just given her a great prize. Could Mr. Moffett have proposed at last? No, if that were the case Julia would be bubbling over with the news. I wonder what she is hiding, Nicola thought, then dismissed her idle curiosity. Whatever it was Julia could hug her secret, it held little interest for her.

Julia watched her leave with a smug expression. In a short time her cousin would not be so sure of herself. Julia wished she could witness Nicola's downfall and Adrian's revenge, but she was determined to mask her own role in the affair. If she felt any compunction for leading Nicola into a trap, she banished it immediately. Nicola deserved a set down.

Paxton, crossing the hall, was struck by Julia's smug expression. Although he would never presume to criticize or question the actions of any guest except to his confidant, Mrs. Edgars, the cook, Paxton found Julia a sore trial. The underservants despised her and Paxton often wondered why Mrs. Wynstan insisted on these yearly visits. Obviously Miss Nicola had little in common with her cousin and Julia certainly felt no affection in return. Although he would not lower his dignity to listen at doors, he had heard a bit of the Marquis's and Roger Forrest's conference with the General before they had all hurried off to find Miss Nicola. And Paxton had not been unaware of Julia sidling off on mysterious errands every morning for the past week. She was involved somehow and he didn't like what that portended. His voice was sharper than usual when he informed Julia that Mrs. Wynstan was asking for her.

"Yes, I know, Paxton. I will attend her presently." Julia spoke brusquely. She sensed Paxton's disapproval and had never learned how to mollify him.

Nicola and George, the groom, set off on a brisk canter down the back drive and across paths separating the various fields where crops were just beginning to respond to the warm June sunshine. The General took a deep interest in his inherited acres and with the help of Arnold, his factor, managed them successfully. He treated his tenants and laborers well and had, as yet, encountered none of the dissatisfaction that had risen in other parts of the country.

After a half an hour of galloping, during which George was

hard put to keep up with Nicola, the pair turned toward the woods. Always a favorite refuge for Nicola, for some reason, this morning as she entered the heavy stand of trees that bordered her father's land and the Cranbourne acres, she felt a sense of foreboding. George was some distance behind her when they reached the deepest part of the woods where Nicola intended to dismount and pick bluebells. Almost before she realized the danger, a masked man jerked her mare to a stop and another man threw a sack over her head as she struggled. George, coming up on the scene, rushed to her rescue, appalled, but before he could make any attempt he was felled by a heavy blow and toppled to the ground. His horse snorted and plunged off, racing back toward his stable, the reins flapping. The trio of men who had captured Nicola wasted no time in sending her mare in the same direction. Nicola was bundled across the saddle of the third man's horse and the attackers, with their struggling burden, melted away into the depths of the woods.

Nineteen

It was barely twenty minutes later that Georgie, groggy and befuddled, staggered to his feet. He rubbed his head ruefully. Some help he had been, and he would catch it, allowing Miss Nicola to be spirited away by those masked men. Cursing, he began trudging back toward the stables, knowing he would be roundly damned by the General and MacGregor, the head groom, for not preventing the kidnapping. He had hardly gone a hundred yards when he came upon the Marquis and Roger Forrest entering the woods.

"Them varmints has taken Miss Nicola," Georgie blurted out as the two men came to a halt, shocked by his appearance.

"What happened?" the Marquis asked, viewing George with disfavor.

"They came out of nowhere, masked they was, and dragged Miss Nicola off before I could do nothing. And they knocked me out for good measure." Georgie was aggrieved and shame-faced, but Jocelyn cared little for that.

"Did you see in what direction they went?" Jocelyn asked.

"No way, governor. I was out of it and when I came to they was gone, like ghosts they was, all black and masked." Georgie had forgotten his pains in giving his dramatic account of what had transpired. But the Marquis had no time for him.

"Can you manage to walk back to the manor, my man?"

"Guess so, but I hurts a lot." Georgie was not prepared to be dismissed so cursorily, but then he remembered the real danger to Miss Nicola. "You'll catch them, won't you? Wouldn't want any harm to come to Miss Nicola."

"Yes, yes, but we can't waste any more time here. Come, Forrest, let's be on our way." The Marquis spoke calmly but his heart was racing and his fear barely contained. The two men set off leaving Georgie to his own devices.

The Marquis and Roger came upon the cleared glade in the woods where Jocelyn had first met Nicola. He remembered that meeting with a rueful grimace. How could he have known what she would come to mean in his life? Beneath his horse's feet he could see the bluebells she fancied, but more important he could see signs where horses' hooves trampled.

"See, sir, this must have been the spot where they waylaid Nicola," Roger said, roused by the evidence to an unusual excitement. Roger Forrest was not a man who normally displayed his feelings, but the thought of Nicola in the hands of ruffians stirred him to anger.

"Yes, Forrest, you are right, and the trail appears to lead off here to the left. We must not delay." The Marquis spurred his horse, and Roger rode after him eagerly. Broken twigs and more signs that several horsemen had crashed through the woods continued for several yards, but then the woods thinned and soon the two were out upon the road which led to the village. Surely, the horsemen would not have chanced discovery with their burden by riding through the village. They must have crossed the road to the fallow ground beyond, but Jocelyn and Roger could see no further signs of the kidnappers. They could have gone south along the road and then veered off to either the left or right some miles away. For a long time the pair rode desperately around looking for traces of the villains but at last had to admit defeat.

"We are not accomplishing anything, Forrest. They could be miles away by now and we are merely wasting time in trying to discover their direction. We must return and tell the General of what we have found. Perhaps his better knowledge of the neighborhood would reveal some hidden cottage where they might have taken Nicola." The Marquis hated the lowering feeling of defeat and concern about Nicola's welfare that overwhelmed him for the moment, but he was not a man to lie down under adversity.

"I want to question that sly, devious Overton woman. She knows something and I will have it out of her if I have to beat her," he promised with a look that boded ill for Julia. Roger could only agree. He had a great deal of faith in the Marquis's power to solve the mystery of Nicola's disappearance, but he was equally worried about what she must be suffering at the hands of her kidnappers.

"Do you think Pettifer is behind all this, sir?" he asked.

"Undoubtedly, and he will pay a steep price for his effrontery," Jocelyn vowed.

As the two men galloped back to the manor, Jocelyn showed little of his fear and anger but Roger sensed he was brooding about Nicola's fate and Roger was not deceived by his stern silence. Obviously the Marquis cared for Nicola and would wreak a terrible vengeance if she came to grief. Certainly Pettifer would be no match for the Marquis. As they neared the manor they met the General in the stable yard where he was questioning a sobered and frightened Georgie.

"The lad here claims he was overpowered by ruffians, hit on the head, and left unconscious. He has no idea what happened to Nicky," the General informed Jocelyn and Roger. "Have you discovered any trace of the rogues?"

"We followed their trail through the woods onto the road, but then there were no further indications as to their direction. We were just too late. They could be miles away by now," the Marquis told the General tersely.

"I have sent a party of men out to search, but I waited for your report." The General was behaving as if the disposition of his troops must result in a forlorn mission. He was deeply disturbed, filled with guilt and despair. He had placed such hope in the Marquis.

"That Overton female knows something, and I will drag it

out of her. Forrest here tells me she has been meeting Pettifer in secret at the church. We must question her immediately. She must have some idea of where Pettifer is staying."

The three men hurried into the house where Paxton informed them that Julia had retired to her room with a headache.

"She'll have more than a headache when I have finished with her," growled the General. "Tell her I await her in the library, Paxton, and if she refuses to come tell her I will come up and drag her down." The General's habitual courtesy and kindness had vanished and Roger saw, for the first time, what a formidable officer he must have been on the battlefield.

"I hope Mrs. Wynstan has not been told of this business, Paxton. Miss Overton is involved somehow in Miss Nicola's disappearance, but I don't want my wife worried."

"The mistress has gone to the village to visit Nanny. She believes Miss Nicola has gone on her usual ride and only asked if Georgie accompanied her." Paxton's demeanor now showed his own concern. He suspected that some dreadful fate had overtaken his young mistress.

"Hurry on, man. Get Miss Overton down here." The General barked and walked toward the library with Roger and Jocelyn on his heels. In the library he poured both men a tot of brandy and took a generous glass himself.

"This is a wretched business, Cranbourne," the General muttered, obviously upset.

"I know, General, but we will find her." He did not mention his own fear that Nicola could be suffering horrid indignities and worse at Pettifer's hands. "You know the neighborhood better than I do. Is there any outlying cottage or hovel in which these villains could be hiding?"

"Not that I know of. Arnold, my factor, might have some idea."

Jocelyn turned to Roger. "Why don't you find Arnold, Forrest, and bring him here. We cannot keep the household in ignorance. The affair is too serious. He may have some ideas."

"Yes, Roger. Find Arnold. He might be in the estate office or out in the fields. Hurry, won't you?"

"At once, sir." Eager to take some action, Roger rushed from the room, in the hall passing Julia whom he looked at with contempt.

Julia, thoroughly frightened, had tried to withstand Paxton's command that she appear in the library by pleading illness, but the butler would stand no nonsense. "You had best obey the General's summons, miss, or he said he would come and drag you out himself, his very words." Paxton, now as alarmed as his master and the Marquis, was prepared to accost Julia in her bedroom himself if she proved stubborn, but Julia had decided to obey and consented to be escorted downstairs by the disapproving butler.

"What can the General want with me, Paxton? Do you have any idea?"

"Yes, miss, I do, and if you will take my advice you will answer his questions honestly. He is quite angry."

Julia was now in some doubt if she would be able to brazen out the General's suspicions. How could he know she had been meeting Adrian? Even if he did, he could not guess she was involved in Adrian's plot to kidnap Nicola. One look at the General's stern face was enough to sink her into submission. At her appearance in the library she was surprised to see the Marquis looking equally grim. The men did not ask her to sit down and she stood before them, her eyes downcast, a look of assumed innocence on her face, hoping to disarm them.

"Julia, we understand from Roger Forrest that you have been meeting Adrian Pettifer in the church. How could you betray our trust in such an outrageous manner?"

"I believe Mr. Pettifer was treated unfairly by you all, and I see no harm in my meeting with him. He cares for me and soon I will be his promised wife," she countered boldly.

"You little fool. He doesn't care a farthing for you. He was just using you to seek some fancied revenge on us." The General scowled at the trembling girl in a ferocious manner.

"That's not true, sir. Since Nicola had refused him why should he not look elsewhere for a loving wife?" Julia clung desperately to her delusion that she was the choice of Adrian's for his life's partner.

"Where is Pettifer?" The Marquis asked abruptly, impatient with these fantasies of a stupid female.

"I don't know." Julia stepped back, awed by the Marquis's fierce expression.

"Don't lie to us, girl. You must have some idea of where he is and what he intended. If you don't tell us immediately what you know it will go very hard for you. As it is, our hospitality to you is ended. You will be sent home on the next coach and your mother will be told of your heinous conduct." The General had no pity for the pathetic creature before him. She was a traitor of the worst sort and with her connivance that villainous Pettifer had brought danger to his daughter.

"You are all against me. You have always treated me with contempt, as beneath your notice. If Adrian sought revenge against you it is only what you deserve." Now that she realized there was no hope of lying her way out of this imbroglio, all Julia's venom and envy rose to the surface.

"We are not interested in your spiteful accusations, Miss Overton. We want information. When were you to meet Pettifer again?" The Marquis's dark look boded ill for her if she failed to satisfy him. Julia was far more cowed by the Marquis than by the General.

"I have nothing to tell you. I do not know where Adrian is, and if I did I would not reveal it. We made no plans to meet until he has finished his business with Nicola. And when he's finished with her you will not want her, my lord," she sneered.

The Marquis had none of the General's innate chivalry. He crossed to her and gave her a resounding slap across the face, indifferent to her cry of pain and outrage. "I'll give you much worse if you do not reveal everything you know now. My patience is exhausted." Julia had only put into words what he feared for Nicola.

"You are a brute. Will you stand by and see me abused in this callous fashion, General?" Julia cried, tears of pain and humiliation swamping her.

"Expect no help from me, Julia. You are a sly, mischievous, nasty piece of work. And you have repaid us badly for all we have done for you. Tell the Marquis what you know." The General, if shocked by Jocelyn's brutality, did not evidence it.

Julia sank down onto the sofa and burst into a torrent of sobs. The Marquis towered over her unmoved by her condition. She looked up and realized there was no recourse but to admit her part in the plot.

"Adrian was very angry at how he was treated by Nicola and all of you. Justifiably so, I think. He has kidnapped Nicola, but really intends no harm, just to pay her back a bit for the way she scorned him. And he is furious, too, that the Marquis assaulted him. He will release her eventually after teaching her a lesson. I have no idea where he has taken her. I only know he has been staying in some secret place in the neighborhood, an easy ride from the village. That's all I know and I will say no more no matter how you punish me. You are an arrogant unfeeling family who have treated me hatefully and if I never see any of you again that will be too soon." Julia burnt her bridges soundly, for she realized whatever claim she had on the Wynstans' charity had now been exhausted.

"Go to your room and pack. A stage is leaving at four o'clock and you will be on it. Goodbye, Julia. We will not meet again." The General crossed the room and threw open the door, indicating there was no appeal from his decision.

He called to Paxton, who appeared immediately. "Escort Miss Julia to her room and lock her in, Paxton. She will be busy packing and will leave on the next stage. She is not to leave her room until that time."

Paxton nodded in acquiescence and Julia had no recourse

but to trail after him toward the stairs. Her brief moment of rebellion and spite had sputtered into miserable failure. She was just beginning to realize that she had probably lost Adrian, too, and the years ahead looked bleak. As she mounted the stairs she looked back and saw Roger crossing the hall in company with Arnold. He did not acknowledge her.

Twenty

Nicola, stunned and shocked by the sudden attack, had struggled within the firm grasp of the horseman who had thrown her across his saddle and ridden away. But her struggles had availed her little. More frightening than the sudden assault was the silence of her captor, but she sensed he meant danger. Silence was part of his tactic. She gave a passing thought to Georgie and wondered if he were safe, but as the ride continued, her first fear was swamped by anger. Who were these brigands, for she realized there was more than one, and what did they intend? She remembered the man who accosted her in the woods and from whom the Marquis had rescued her. Could this be some of the same band? Whoever they were their effrontery in seizing her so close to the manor was startling. Her position was alarming but she had faith that Georgie, if he were able, would alert her father and help would be sent. Still, she must try to escape her captors, not rely on rescue soon.

After about a half an hour's ride, the horses drew to a halt and she was manhandled to the ground, still shrouded in the suffocating sack that enveloped her. One of the men grasped her arm and pulled her forward and into what she sensed was some kind of dwelling. Inside, the sack was removed. Her captors, too, took off their masks and she found herself facing Adrian Pettifer. For some reason his appearance did not surprise her.

"What is the meaning of this outrage, Adrian?" she asked, ignoring the menacing gathering of his three cohorts.

"It is my revenge for the scurvy treatment you and your family and that high and mighty lord subjected me to," Adrian replied, leering at her in a manner she found quite offensive.

"You must be mad. What do you hope to gain by this despicable ploy?" Nicola tried to restrain the onset of hysteria. Her only hope was to remain calm and show nothing but scorn for his action.

"A tidy ransom and some repayment for your mean behavior. You had no business to lead me on to a proposal and then laugh at me."

"As I recall I did not laugh, and surely you agree a girl has a perfect right to refuse a proposal." Nicola wondered if Adrian had lost his senses. A man did not kidnap a girl, hold her to ransom, just because she would not become his wife. But it seemed Adrian did.

"Enough of this chatter. Take her upstairs, Bart, and tie her up. She'll soon learn her hoity-toity ways will gain her little here. If you behave," he warned, turning to Nicola, "we will not harm you, but if you try to escape it will be the worse for you."

"You're a fool, Adrian, and will pay dearly for this escapade." She turned away, only hoping her bravado would not be just idle words.

Bart, shaking his head, drew her roughly up the rickety steps toward the upper floor. Looking at Adrian's henchman she thought he was not enjoying his role in the proceedings. Would it be possible to lure him from his allegiance to Adrian?

As he pushed her into a room and prepared to tie her up as ordered, she tried to remonstrate with him.

"You are making a big mistake, Bart. My father will find me and it will go very hard on you and your friends. You could end up on a transport ship."

Since this was an outcome Bart greatly feared, the suggestion only raised his temper. "Shut your gab or I'll gag you, and you wouldn't want that. You can scream all you want here. No one will hear you."

Then he proceeded to tie her hands and feet roping her to a filthy bed that stood in the corner of the dark room. She could see little out of the grimy window but guessed she was deep in some woods. He wasted little time and his task completed, left her to her own devices. She tugged at the ropes, but they were too securely fastened, and did not respond to her increasingly frantic efforts.

Finally she stopped, repressing a sob of frustration. Her predicament was a sorry one and for a moment she gave into despair, but Nicola was not a girl to surrender tamely. She would not give in to her fears. Somehow she would escape from this den and thwart Adrian, whose conduct she neither understood nor excused. How could she have been so mistaken in her judgment of him? Well, she was paying dearly for her gullibility.

For a moment she wondered if ransom was all Adrian intended. What if he meant to harm her, rape or even murder? She shivered. Well, she would not submit supinely to such a horrible fate. Somehow she would resist and escape. But her spirits sank as she realized her precarious situation. And her thoughts turned to the Marquis. Would he learn of her plight and turn his formidable talents to finding her before it was too late? Despite her best efforts she felt her courage flagging.

Nicola might have been comforted if she could have seen Jocelyn repressing his fear and fury as he questioned the General's factor, Arnold. She would have been in little doubt that she mattered more than a little to him then.

"So you have no ideas about any hiding place to which this band of ruffians could have taken Miss Wynstan?" he asked, barely containing his impatience to ride out again. But he knew aimless scouring of the countryside would not help. He must have some concrete knowledge.

"No, sir. There is no such place on our lands. And I am sure you have surveyed your own possessions. Except for the woods which border your land and the General's there is little land where these kidnappers could be hiding."

"Come, man. There must be some spot." The General intervened, less able than Jocelyn to contain his fears.

"Some place within an hour's ride. They cannot have gone much farther, I think," Jocelyn added. "Whose land abuts mine in the south?" Every minute they delayed here trying to resolve the problem meant added danger to Nicola, a situation that would not be eased by railing and ranting, Jocelyn thought, although he was nearly as distraught as the General, even if he had more control over his reactions.

"The Mumfords, my lord."

"Of course. I should have remembered."

"My men have combed my property and yours, Cranbourne. I think we must now alert the Mumfords." The General now attempted to take charge, but Jocelyn could see that he was not in a condition to direct events.

"There is one area that might hide the villains," Arnold suggested. A plain, middle-aged man whose weather-beaten face showed the effects of his outdoor life, he rarely lost his temper or gave into his emotions. He had served the General well for many years and was a trusted and loyal employee. He had watched Nicola grow up and was fond of her, but like Jocelyn, he saw no use in expressing his fears for her safety. His energy must be expended in finding her.

"Well, where is that?" Jocelyn barked in his impatience.

"There is a fallow heavily brushwooded swamp along the edge of the Mumfords' land. Some years ago an old gamekeeper had a cottage there but it has fallen into ruin, uninhabitable. They might have taken Miss Nicola there but it is in terrible condition. No one could live there even for a short time."

"We must try every avenue," the General insisted, his face scored with a scowl.

"Yes, lead us to it, Arnold. How long a ride is it?"

"At least an hour, my lord."

"General, you stay here in case any news comes in while we are away." Jocelyn was not aware how domineering he sounded, but the General agreed with amazing docility.

As he and Arnold prepared to leave Paxton burst into the room with none of his usual proper polite demeanor. "General, a young ragamuffin, Jed Collins, just delivered this note. I tried to hold on to him, but he scooted off up the drive as if the devil was after him." He held out a folded paper to the General, who tore it open.

"These bold miserable curs. Listen to this, Cranbourne: *Dear Sir, If you wish to see your daughter Nicola alive again place two thousand guineas in the large oak tree in the woods where she was apprehended. Any attempt to restrain the man who collects the money will result in you never seeing Nicola again. The money should be placed in the tree just after dark. Do not try any tricks or she will suffer, I promise. A well wisher.*

"Well wisher, indeed, a scurvy knave. And where can I find 2,000 guineas by tonight?" the General scoffed.

"I can help there, sir, but perhaps that will not be necessary." Jocelyn took the note from the General's hand and scanned it briefly.

"Thank you, Cranbourne. But I can't take any chances. I must get Nicola back and quickly. How can I wait until tonight? And I haven't told her mother about this deplorable mess." The General was rapidly losing his composure under the threat to his daughter.

Jocelyn could see the man needed a task to distract him from his consuming worry. "We are going to discover this old gamekeeper's hut now and while we are gone, you try to find that Collins boy and learn who gave him the note. I suspect Pettifer, and if that's true he will pay dearly for his insolence.

"We'll be off then. Try not to worry, sir, and comfort your wife. She will need your support." Jocelyn felt he had done what he could for the General, but Nicola was his first concern and he yearned to be off on the chase. He feared that Pettifer had lost whatever sense of reason he had possessed and Nicola's fate at the hands of that madman could not be imagined.

Nicola had been aware that one or more of her captors had ridden off soon after she was led to her prison. She had heard their horses hooves gradually fading away. What did that mean? Could they have left her alone in this hovel, thinking she was secure under the restraint they had imposed? If ever she was to escape it must be now while the odds against her had lessened. She tugged at her bonds but with little success. Both her legs were tied to the posts and her hands tied in front of her. Surely it would have been safer to have tied them behind her, a foolish mistake on Bart's part. She sensed that the man had not liked his task, and had been distracted by her warnings that if apprehended he would end up on a convict ship to the Antipodes.

Somehow she must persuade him that his only chance of leniency was to let her go. But if he did not reappear, even that slim possibility was remote. If she could get free she might be able to reason with him, bribe him, or threaten him. Adrian was the inhibiting factor. He seemed to be in a grip of some madness, consumed by his desire to seek revenge on her and her family. She would never trust her judgment again.

First she had been wrong about Jocelyn and even more grievously about Adrian. Well, fretting about her lack of common sense would not help her now. She tugged uselessly on her bonds yet again, then remembering what she had once read in one of Mrs. Radcliff's novels, she brought her strong teeth down on the ropes and worried at the strands. Slowly she felt some fraying, and breathing hard, continued to gnaw away. She thought she heard a step on the stairs and stopped for the moment, perspiration breaking out on her forehead, but no, she was mistaken. All was quiet. At last the rope gave way. It must have been rotten, for it had been easier than she suspected. Within moments of freeing her hands she fumbled with the ropes binding her ankles. She stood weakly to her feet, trying not to make any noise that would alert her guardians below the stairs. Now she felt some hope that she could extricate herself from this horrible plight.

She tiptoed to the window, and peered out, rubbing her hand to clear the grimed glass. If she tried to break the window surely the noise would alert her watchers below stairs. And she had no idea how many of them had ridden away. Surely they would not all have gone, and if they had, they could be returning at any minute, thwarting her escape efforts. She almost gave way to despair, but rallied her courage. Moaning would avail her nothing. Then she had an idea. She removed her riding boots with some struggle. Usually Betsy was on hand to help her with the unwieldy task. Then, taking a deep breath, she swung the heel of one boot against the glass in the window. It shattered with a noise like a gunshot. Backing away from the window she positioned herself behind the door, and true to her expectations heard the sound of heavy steps on the stairs. One of the men was coming to investigate, as she hoped. She waited as he opened the door, looked at the empty bed and broken window with an oath. Before he could make a further move she hit him as hard as she could with the heel of the boot. He crumpled to the floor, for the moment unconscious, but she had no time to waste. She crept down the stairs, boots in hand, ready as a weapon for any onslaught.

But on reaching the main room of the hut, she could see no one. Obviously Adrian had left only one of his men to guard her, but she must escape before the man upstairs came to his senses. Not waiting to put on her boots she ran in her stocking feet out the door and down the rutted path, her heart in her throat, expecting any minute to hear the sounds of pursuit and a heavy hand on her shoulder. She had proceeded painfully a few hundred yards when she heard the rapid clop of horses coming toward her. It must be Adrian and his henchmen returning. She staggered off the path and concealed herself behind a scraggly bush, its thorns scratching her hands and pulling her hair. Her breath came in gasps and she tried to calm her fears. She glimpsed the dark head of the leading horse, a black stallion, and then recognized the rider. It was Jocelyn. Crying out his name, she struggled from her hiding place.

"Jocelyn, thank God. Here I am."

Frightened by the sudden apparition that loomed before him, Jocelyn's stallion reared, almost unseating his rider, but Jocelyn quickly brought him under control, and threw himself from the saddle, catching Nicola up in his arms.

"Nicky, Nicky, are you all right?" He held her in a tight grip and despite the presence of Arnold and Roger behind him, covered her face with frantic kisses.

"You little fool. What have you done? Where is Pettifer?"

Recovering under his passionate caresses, but delighted at this evidence of his concern for her, she laughed weakly, biting back hysteria.

"Really, Jocelyn, are you going to berate me for trying to escape my captors? How typical! But I forgive you since you happened along most opportunely. I suspect one of the brigands that took me will soon be on my path. I hit him soundly but perhaps not hard enough."

"You'll be the death of me, girl. But at least you are safe now." Jocelyn laughed in relief. He might have known she would not lie down under any attempt to coerce her. And he surely had committed himself, kissing her with such abandon before Forrest and Arnold, who stood patiently by, the latter smiling at the happy outcome of what could have been a tragic situation.

"I think we should wait here for those villains to return," Forrest suggested, a little embarrassed by these passionate embraces. He did not quite approve of the lighthearted way that Cranbourne and Nicola dismissed her past danger nor her enthusiastic response to the Marquis's kisses. A nice-minded female would be succumbing to the vapors.

Seeing that the pair had no eyes or ears except for each other, he recalled them to the impropriety of their standing in this dismal wood kissing and exchanging nonsensical remarks.

"I think I hear someone coming."

"Probably the man I hit to escape," Nicola agreed happily, not making any effort to remove herself from Jocelyn's comforting arms. He put her aside reluctantly.

"Here, Forrest, help Nicky on with her boots. She looks a pitiful sight. I'll manage this brigand."

Just as he uttered the words Bart burst on the scene and taking one look at the company, groaned and turned to run back to the safety of the hut where he had left his gun, but Jocelyn was too quick for him. Drawing his own pistol, he grasped Bart's arm and raised the gun to his head.

"No, you don't my man. You aren't going anywhere. How dare you treat Miss Wynstan in this violent manner, exposing her to these indignities?"

"Not my idea, governor. I was under orders. I was agin it from the start. Knew no good would come of it." Bart spoke with patient resignation. From the beginning he had feared just such an outcome to Adrian's stupid plot. Now, he would be for it, and where were his confederates? If he went down they would go with him, of that he was determined. He made no effort to escape Jocelyn's restraining arm. "No need to threaten me, governor, with that pistol. I'll come quietly."

By this time Roger had succeeded in pushing Nicola's boots onto her aching feet and helped her to stand. Not content to leave the disposal of Bart to Jocelyn she interceded.

"He's quite right, Jocelyn. He was against the plan, poor man, but I suspect Adrian is holding the money so he could not help himself."

"Mighty kind of you, ma'am," Bart agreed cheerfully.

"I think we had better remove Miss Nicola, my lord. The rest of these brigands will be returning and might put up a fight." Roger put the practical problems tersely. He felt some apprehension about their next move.

"Don't be stupid, Roger. We must wait here for them, and ambush them," Nicky said, having recovered her usual spirits now that she had the reassuring presence of Jocelyn beside her, and the knowledge that whatever he might say later, he had proved that he cared for her. She was all for finishing the matter, capturing the rogues who had been terrorizing the countryside, and seeing to it that Adrian got his just desserts.

"I commend your sentiments, Nicky, but Roger is right, you know." Then, turning to the subdued Bart he asked, "How many in your little band?"

Realizing the game was up, Bart was not about to shield his co-conspirators, "Just Pettifer and my two chums," he admitted guiltily.

"Where have they gone?"

"To deliver the ransom note. Never thought we needed more than one bloke to guard this little madam here. Couldn't have been more wrong, could we?" Bart grinned as if applauding Nicola's bravery and she gave him an answering grin. She found she could not really despise Bart and only hoped he would not suffer too much for his obedience to Adrian's wicked designs.

"Then they will be returning shortly. Did you acquaint the men searching for Miss Nicola about our direction, Arnold?" The Marquis, having recovered his aplomb, was all business.

"Yes, my lord. They should be following us, and I think I hear some horsemen in the distance."

Arnold was correct. But were the horsemen friendly or hostile? Throwing Nicola up on his waiting stallion, Jocelyn mounted behind her, his pistol still holding the quiescent Bart in its sights.

"If it's Pettifer, he won't be expecting us. Let's just wait here to see."

Bart, content to await events, made no demur, standing

helplessly by while he heard the horsemen near. If he had any notion of trying to warn his confederates he thought better of it under the Marquis's minatory eye. But the quartet of horsemen who burst on the scene were indeed the men from the manor, Georgie among them. He would not be denied his part in Miss Nicola's rescue.

"Good, men. You've arrived just in time. Miss Nicola is safe and here is one of her captors. Tie him up and one of you men can ride him in to the village. If you are up to it, Nicky, we will wait for Pettifer and the other two."

"Of course. I wouldn't miss it for the world." Nicola was beginning to enjoy herself, now that the worst part of her adventure was past. She wanted to see Adrian apprehended. But she was denied that pleasure. Although they rode back to the hut after dispatching Bart and two of his captors to whatever justice awaited him in the village, the other members of the band did not appear. Could they have been warned? Before he left Bart reminded them that the loot from the various raids was hidden somewhere in the vicinity of the hut. Adrian had not divulged the whereabouts of the cache, and Bart suspected he might decamp without giving them their share.

After waiting about an hour, the Marquis decided they must return to the manor, for the General would be worrying, and despite Nicky's insouciant claim to feeling fine, Jocelyn thought she looked pale and exhausted. Overriding her protests he gathered his forces, sending Roger ahead to tell the General the good news and rode his argumentative fiancée home. And during the ride he made it quite clear that from now on she was under his protection and had better behave accordingly. For once she did not argue.

As they neared the entrance to the manor, the door flew open and the General, his wife and Paxton all appeared on the steps.

"Thank God, Cranbourne, you have rescued her." The General was overcome at the sight of his disheveled but safe daughter. Her mother stood by crying helplessly, unable to utter a word. Paxton, restored to his normal composed demeanor, allowed himself a broad smile. He, for one, had never doubted that Miss Nicola would be restored to them.

Helping Nicola down, Jocelyn said wryly, "Well, I can't claim much credit, sir. Nicky had managed to release her bonds, knock her gaoler over the head and was hiding behind a bush when we arrived on the scene."

"Don't be silly, Jocelyn. If you hadn't appeared that poor Bart would have found me, and I would have been chivvied back to that horrid hut."

"For some reason, sir, Nicky seems to have a strange sympathy for this Bart, who, as Forrest must have told you, is now in custody in the village. Unfortunately Pettifer and two of his allies are still at large. Much as I want to join you in this happy reunion I think I must try to discover their whereabouts. They are dangerous."

Nicola looked up from her mother's embrace and warned Jocelyn. "You will be careful."

"Of course. I suggest you have a soothing bath. You look a bit the worse for your ordeal." He laughed at her disappointment. He suspected she would like to join in the hunt, his irrepressible darling.

"Don't despair, Nicky. We will soon resume our interesting endeavors in the woods," he promised with a wicked grin.

If the General and his wife wondered to what the Marquis referred they were too concerned with restoring Nicola to pay much attention. But Nicola understood and agreed that this was not the time or the place to confess their attachment, much as it would delight her mother.

"I'll be back as soon as possible." Jocelyn wheeled his horse without more ado and galloped off down the drive, leaving Nicola to hug her secret and answer her parents' anxious questions as to her welfare. She limped painfully into the house eager to seek that bath and satisfy her sudden hunger.

It seemed ages since she had eaten. Her father shook his head, and her mother was equally dumbfounded. After such an experience Nicky had no right to be so cheerful.

Twenty-one

Adrian, confident that his captive was guarded and that within hours he would be in possession of enough money to satisfy his demands, was making a circuitous ride back to the hut. He had watched as Jed Collins, having delivered the ransom note, scurried away from the manor. All was proceeding according to his plan, he told himself smugly. He had never considered failure, and paid little attention to the muttering of his companions as they rode toward the hut. Joe and Reg did not share his conviction. Although Adrian had proved infallible so far, they were beginning to distrust him. They wanted their money and this latest caper would arouse the neighborhood and both the villagers and the army would be on their trail. Just because their leader had a dirty taste for revenge on some female who had scorned him, they could all end up at the end of a rope or on some convict ship and the idea made them less than enthusiastic.

"We wants our share, squire," Reg said riding beside Adrian. That was one reason they had accompanied him to the village. They would not give him the chance to escape with their part of the proceeds.

"You'll get it, my good man. All in good time. Tonight the General will place the guineas in the oak tree and we will retrieve it and put this cursed place behind us forever."

"But what about that female?" Reg persisted.

"Not your concern. I have plans for her." Adrian's evil grin boded no pleasant outcome for Nicola, and Reg protested.

"You ain't goin' to do her in?"

"Not at all, although I warrant before I'm through she will wish I had."

Not reassured by Adrian's expression or his baleful words, Reg shook his head. "I don't bargain for no murder, squire."

"Hold your tongue, man. I have managed very well so far. Why would you doubt me now?" Adrian was not prepared for any rebellion from his cohorts, and not for one moment did he contemplate they would oppose him as long as he held their money. He had dominated his companions in thievery by their awe of his planning and the successful outcome of the raids they had made in the past, but this latest caper, a personal vendetta in which they saw little advantage to them, raised their doubts. They were afraid Adrian's luck had run out and they would suffer with him. So far they had managed to elude capture but they realized the longer they stayed in the neighborhood the more likely it was they would be discovered. Some old codger would remember this hut and then retribution would fall. Superstitious, uneducated, credulous and greedy, they had a certain measure of common sense and they felt the odds had lengthened against them with this kidnapping. And they did not like the threats Adrian uttered against their prisoner.

As they neared the hut, Reg, in the lead, looked up and saw the shattered window which roused his fears.

"See, squire, that window where Bart put the mort is broken. Mayhap she tried to escape."

"Nonsense, and if she tried it Bart would easily have overpowered her." Adrian, in the grip of his obsession, would admit no possibility that his plans could go awry.

The men dismounted and tethered their horses to a nearby tree. Entering the hut they were confronted not with Bart but Lord Cranbourne, who rose from one of the chairs by the fireplace. In his hand was a business-like pistol.

"Come in, gentlemen, I have been waiting for you. And if

you have any ideas that three to one are good odds I must warn you that a party of angry men are just behind you."

Adrian whirled and saw to his surprise that the doorway was blocked by several men holding shotguns. They looked like they would enjoy using them.

"Where's Bart?" Reg asked, recognizing that his worst fears had been realized.

"In custody where you will join him shortly."

"How dare you threaten us?" Adrian blustered, unwilling to admit defeat.

"I would enjoy doing a great deal more than threaten you, Pettifer, after the attempt you made on Miss Wynstan, so don't tempt me. The game is up, so you would be wise to surrender peaceably, and we want to know where the proceeds of your robberies are hidden. Your colleague, Bart, has confessed to your part in the highway raids and there is little doubt you will be convicted and hung for your treachery. Turning over the loot might cause a judge to grant some leniency."

Adrian, lost to all reason, drew his gun, prepared to shoot Jocelyn in the grip of rage and disappointment. How could his clever plans have failed? He cocked the pistol but before he could get off a shot, Jocelyn had fired, hitting him in the arm that held the pistol and Adrian dropped the gun and watched in shock as the blood poured from his wound.

"You tried to kill me."

"No, if I had tried I would have succeeded. It's only a flesh wound. Bind it up and tell us where the valuables are hidden."

"You'd better do what he says, squire. He's an ugly customer, might shoot us all and say we were trying to escape," Reg urged, recognizing there was no way they would escape retribution.

Adrian, cursing and groaning, confused by the debacle of his plan, finally led them to his cache. Besides a healthy pile of gold there were some significant jewels, mementos of the several raids they had conducted for the past months. The

Marquis bundled up the proceeds in an old sack, ordered his men to secure the villains, and ignored Adrian's blusterings.

"You will be kept overnight in the constable's room in the village and then sent to Chichester where you will be tried. I feel sorry for these poor men you persuaded to join you in your wicked crimes, but for you, hanging is too good, and I will see you pay the full penalty for your sins." The Marquis looked at Adrian with loathing.

"Unlike these men here you have had the advantages of a respectable upbringing and a good education. Greed and conceit has brought you to this pass, and your effrontery in kidnapping Miss Wynstan denies you any clemency." The Marquis's disgust made no impression on Adrian, sunk in his despair, but even then, trying to find some way out of his dilemma. Reg and Joe appeared resigned to their unenviable fate but he cared nothing for them. Tuning his back on Adrian Jocelyn directed the men with him to escort the trio of villains to their temporary prison. Much as he would have liked to save the government the trouble of a trial and dispatch Adrian himself, he restrained his violent emotions toward this charlatan who had abused Nicola and her family, unleashed a wave of terror on the countryside, and all to satisfy his avarice and conceit. The man deserved all he would get.

Much restored by a bath, a hearty meal and a few hours of sleep, Nicola faced her family in high spirits that evening. Dinner had been put back to a late hour to accommodate her and the Marquis who had sent a message accepting the General's invitation to dinner. He had promised to tell them about the arrest of Adrian and his band when he joined them. He also intended to speak of more pleasant matters to the General before dinner. When Nicola arrived in the drawing room dressed in a demure white muslin gown trimmed with eyelet lace, her curls carefully dressed and looking the picture of a proper lady, she found them gathered in anticipation of her story.

Elizabeth Shillingford greeted her friend with indignation. "You certainly do not look the worse for your adventure, Nicky. And Ned and I missed all the excitement. Too bad of you not to include me. I would have loved to have been kidnapped and imprisoned."

"I doubt it, Elizabeth. That hut was really moldy and grim. Wasn't I clever to chew off my bonds, though? I am quite proud of myself."

"Don't get above yourself, my girl," Jocelyn warned although he was grinning at the sight of her looking none the worse for her ordeal.

"Too true, if you hadn't appeared in such a timely fashion I suspect Bart would have recaptured me and I would have been tied up again to await whatever horrid fate Adrian intended."

"How can you mock what happened, Nicky?" Mrs. Wynstan protested for she had heard an edited version of her daughter's plight from her husband and it had sent her into a fit of vapors. The General had not yet the opportunity to tell her some news that would banish all thoughts of Nicky's recent ordeal and send her into alts.

"Well, better to ridicule than moan. Jocelyn arrived on the scene before any real harm was done. However, I do feel sorry for that man Bart. I suspect he tied my hands in front rather than behind my back so that I could make an attempt to escape. It's just a good thing I have strong teeth." Nicola realized that it would be far better to treat the frightening episode lightly to spare her mother's feelings. And she felt some guilt for inflicting Adrian on her family in the first place.

"What will happen to Adrian?" Elizabeth asked.

"Highwaymen are usually hung. And there is also the fact that his raids have disturbed the populace and called out the army." Ned was always conscious of his professional responsibilities.

Nicola, in all the excitement of the day, had overlooked the absence of Julia. After the company were seated for the first course in the dining room, she asked where her cousin was.

"She has been sent home in disgrace. That wretched girl conspired with Pettifer. We would never have known a thing about her part in the plot if Roger, here, had not had his suspicions about her frequent absences and followed her to the church where she met the knave."

"Good for you, Roger. I am in your debt." Nicola rewarded him with an approving smile, which raised a blush to that modest young man's cheek.

"She was behaving in a very puzzling way. I never trusted her, and she was filled with bitterness and envy."

"I can't understand Julia. We had always been so kind to her, and to repay us with such scurvy treachery!" Mrs. Wynstan would never forgive Julia for betraying them all, after their hospitality.

"A thoroughly nasty female, Mother, as I have suggested many a time. You really strained our patience with your invitations to her," Ned remembered with a shudder Julia's mincing attempts to lure him into matrimony.

"Well, you won't be bothered with her again, Ned, and if it took my abduction to force her banishment, I would say it was probably worth it, although I had no idea she was so foolish to believe any lie Adrian might have told her."

"As I remember, Nicky, you appeared to find the young man credible about the tunnel and rather forced him on your family." Jocelyn was not about to let Nicola escape some blame for the disaster that had almost cost her life and perhaps an equally reprehensible fate. He believed that Adrian had not intended to return her to her family and had also planned to force himself on her in a manner which would have caused her lasting sorrow. That was a prospect he did not intend to discuss with either Nicola or her parents.

Usually quick to resent any criticism of her actions, this time Nicola realized his strictures were only too justified, and she was honest enough to admit it. They continued to discuss Adrian's villainy over dinner but the General finally put an end to it.

"Now that the fellow is in custody and destined for the hangman's noose we can forget about it. The last hours are not ones I want to relive again."

He looked at his daughter fondly, but a bit sternly. From now on the responsibility for her tempestuous actions would be in other hands. He only hoped she had the sense to realize her good fortune, but with Nicky one never knew. She was perfectly capable of rebuffing the Prince Regent if it suited her.

The ladies adjourned to the drawing room, leaving the men to their port. There Elizabeth continued to quiz Nicola about her ordeal, agog to learn all the details, but she had hardly been satisfied when the gentlemen joined them. The Marquis crossed to Nicola's side and stood over her in what she thought was almost a threatening fashion.

"Your father has allowed me to talk to you alone, Nicky. I am sure Elizabeth will excuse you."

"Yes, of course, my lord." Elizabeth, wide-eyed, looked at Jocelyn with a knowing glance. She had a very good idea what the Marquis wanted to talk to her friend about.

For once docile, Nicky rose and allowed Jocelyn to escort her from the room, leaving behind an interested company who had little doubt as to the result of the coming interview. Ned crossed to Elizabeth's side and joined her on the settee.

"It looks like it is all up with Nicky. She'd be a fool to turn him down," he confided.

"Oh, she won't. I think she's madly in love with him. At last Nicky has found a man she can neither cajole or deny. I think she's most fortunate. The Marquis is both exciting and eligible. I quite fancied him myself."

"Oh, you did, my girl? Well, you can forget him and concentrate on a more humble admirer." Ned had made up his mind, too, and was not about to allow the delectable Elizabeth to slip from his grasp.

In the morning room, where Jocelyn had led Nicky, he ushered her in, closed the door carefully, and without more ado took Nicola in his arms and resumed the passionate kisses which he had bestowed after her rescue. She responded enthusiastically. When she finally emerged from his embrace, flushed and delighted, he placed her in a chair and stood over her with a glint in his dark eyes that promised a resumption of those drugging kisses if he heard any argument.

"Your father has consented to our marriage, and by the warmth of your response, I take it you would not be averse to the idea, but a female should always have the chance to say no." He waited but she continued to regard him with a bemused expression, and a slight shadow of alarm crossed his mind. Could she just have been playing with him, grateful for his rescue, enjoying their lovemaking but unwilling to surrender?

"Well, Nicky, what do you say? You must know I love you damnably and want you for my wife."

Reassured now that he really was worried about her answer Nicky gave in gracefully. "I just wanted to hear you admit you loved me. You must know I feel the same way, Jocelyn. From the beginning, at our first meeting, I felt you meant trouble and how right I was." But she laughed and did not protest when he pulled her up and into his arms again. After some very satisfactory exchange of kisses she finally pulled away and he let her go with a rueful smile.

"You are a minx and a load of trouble, but I cannot resist you. I should warn you that any further adventures with discreditable young men or even admirable ones will not be allowed. You are for it, my love. I suspect we will have a tempestuous time of it, but I am looking forward to it with the keenest enjoyment."

"I fear I will not be a conformable wife, sir. The future looks exciting. Now, kiss me again and then we must inform the family of our news."

"Shocking and scandalous. No well-brought-up young woman should be so eager for the mysteries of the marriage bed. But, as a gentleman I must oblige."

It was some time before Jocelyn and Nicola joined the expectant family in the drawing room. They were unaware of the Wynstans' impatience, being more profitably occupied.